CALDERA-
A MAN ON FIRE

DAN BALDWIN

Caldera-A Man on Fire

A Four Knights Press publication

Credits

Cover photo by Dan Baldwin

Editing by Harvey Stanbrough

ISBN-13: 978-1475230086

ISBN-10: 1475230087

Dedication

Bob and Dottie Ferrington
"There's nothing ill can dwell in such a temple."

Acknowledgements

Harvey Stanbrough, my editor who stomped the extra mile behind the computer and through the Arizona desert to take Caldera off the page and into the mind.

Doctor Helene LaBonte and Dr. Bashir Aqel for the in-depth research that made certain this book would be in your hands today.

Jane Foreman, Rusty Galle and Gus Wales, friends and inspirations from the little one room ad school who were there at the beginning of a long journey.

Prologue

His name, so to speak, was Robert Quiller, a newspaper and magazine columnist on a personal and professional quest for an obscure Wild West character named Caldera. The subject of his quest was born a happy-go-lucky kid who became a Confederate scout, mad man, cold-blooded killer, hero and enigma. Quiller's only reliable connection with Caldera was a 117 year old Pima Indian called Prospect, Caldera's surrogate father who called him his "sometimes son." While Hitler's army marched through Europe, the Empire of Japan conquered the Pacific, and FDR promised to keep the U.S. out of foreign wars, Quiller squatted on an Indian reservation south of Phoenix. Prospect guided him back to the era of mountain men and explorers in the high country, miners and ranchers in the hills and valleys, bandits and murderers in the towns and on the roads, and Geronimo and the Apaches—everywhere.

Caldera's story begins with his father, Bull McKenzie, a drunken mountain man who followed Gayle McCracken and a group of outlaws and adventurers on a raid into Mexico. Most of the men were killed or captured by a detail of the Mexican army led by an officer named Malon. Bull, McCracken and a few others escaped. McCracken sacrificed his men to throw off the vengeful villagers. Bull struck out to make his own way through the desert.

A young Pima named Keli'hi rescued Bull and brought him to his village near Arizona's Gila River. A grateful Bull said that the young man had changed his prospects for the better and began calling him Prospect. While Bull was recuperating, the age-old enemy of the Pima, the Apaches, attacked the village and killed Prospect's family. Bull tried to join the battle, but he was too weak from his wounds and his ordeal in the desert. He passed out to be awakened later by legendary mountain man Pauline Weaver. He was told a wild story of a fortune in gold mined by the Mexicans and lost in the nearby Superstition Mountains.

Later Bull wanted to thank Prospect before leaving the village, but the young man had left to seek vengeance. Bull was relieved. He did not like people, nor the attachments they brought.

Weaver took Bull north to Punkin, a nearby camp on the Salt River. The chief resident, "No Brains" Monaghan provided a grubstake and Bull headed into the Superstitions where he discovered some of Weaver's lost Mexican gold. Bull began a long and dangerous search through a rugged no man's land. He found more gold. He often saw Apache raiding parties, but he never intervened even when women were raped, men tortured or children killed. Pushed to his limits, he eventually staggered back to Punkin.

Years later a wealthy and powerful Bull McKenzie returned to a small-but-growing settlement on the edge of the Superstitions. It was named for one of its most popular establishments: Privy.

He became the bank's largest depositor and a silent partner with its owner, Chandler. He also bought into the Armageddon Saloon. Following the negotiations, his new partner suggested they boost their profits with a bath. He packed a box with bottles of cheap booze and glasses. A confused Bull followed him out the door.

The bath is a public one taken by Belle Delcour, proprietor of the town's only brothel. She was a large and attractive but aging woman. She taunted and teased the crowed of lonely men until they provided enough gold or silver for her to reveal all and slide into the water. Belle further enticed the crowd with Memphis Minnie, a sad, barely conscious alcoholic wreck, and a young, attractive woman named Alice Chacon.

When Alice took her bath the cheers aroused Belle's jealousy. Bull, wanting a better look at Belle, placed a large number of silver coins on the scale and Belle's moment in the sun arrived. She was assisted by two midgets named Short and Round who had a well-earned reputation for thievery, dishonesty and cruelty and were collectively known and ShortRound. As Belle bathed she never took her eyes off Bull McKenzie. He said it was the best bath he'd ever taken.

Bull and Belle became lovers and business partners, with Belle solidifying the relationship through sex, profits and new ideas for making more profits. But her jealousy grew and at one point she nearly beat Alice Chacon to death.

Alice became pregnant and when the child was born his resemblance to Bull McKenzie was unmistakable. The boy was named Caldera. Bull sent Alice to California where she would be safe from Belle's revenge. Because she was too weak to care for their son, he was forced to keep Caldera in Privy. Prospect became a surrogate father who taught his sometimes son the Pima ways of war, peace and life. Bull had as little to do with his son as possible.

The Pima warriors planned an attack on the Apaches. Circling Hawk, elected leader the war party, wondered when his close friend would appear. The friend, Prospect, lived in the world of vengeance. He had become a one-man war party, supporting Pima attacks, but also carrying out his own vendetta.

After the Pima victory, he followed a wounded Apache into the desert. He won a savage battle, but was severely wounded. As he crawled to his village he believed he heard the voice of a spirit. "Well, I'll be a son of a bitch," it said. Bull, his rescuer, took him to Privy. To rid himself of his debt to the young Indian he arranged a marriage to a mute Pima woman named Tatoo. She had a sister named T'othern, verbal shorthand for "the other one."

Bull threw the biggest "shebang" in Privy's short history: the wedding and the celebration that followed. The community held the dance at the Armageddon, and McCracken and his gang crashed the party. Bull rescued Alice from McCracken's advances and the wedding festivities continued. As her whores fussed over the new bride, Belle's dark eyes remained fixed on Alice.

Belle expanded her operation by sending whores out to the miners who had to stay on the job while the others went into town, a trade Bull called "whores on wheels."

Alice returned and worked as a maid at Belle's whorehouse, but according to Bull's orders she wasn't permitted to whore. Ignoring his command, Belle sent her to the mines. She and the "whores on wheels" driver were killed. Indians were blamed, but Prospect knew Malon and his gang were the culprits. He also knew that Belle set up the situation and that she was ultimately responsible.

Caldera and T'othern grew close, married and were expecting a child.

Belle's hatred for her step-son remained unchecked. When T'othern became ill, she was taken to the cleanest facility in Privy: Belle's whorehouse.

Sometime later Caldera got drunk at the Armageddon. Belle encouraged T'othern to get her husband and helped the ailing woman into the shadows at the rear of the saloon. Then Belle brought out Caldera, shouted "Apache!" and pointed at T'othern. Caldera drew his pistol, but dropped it. Belle shot T'othern, then ran into the saloon and blamed the murder on Caldera.

He was chained under guard to the town "jail," a tree stump in the middle of the main street. Belle told him that he had killed his wife and unborn son.

Prospect arranged an escape and his sometimes son rode into the Superstitions.

He met an older Apache whose eyes reflected a shared sorrow. Each had lost a family. Instead of killing each other, they formed a bond. Asked his name, the Indian replied in Spanish, "Jerome." They parted company without violence. A day later he encountered an army patrol who had captured and were torturing Jerome. He helped the Apache escape.

Caldera wanted nothing more than death. He realized that if he was to die he would have to perform the act himself. He remembered the story of Christ's crucifixion. Driven crazy by guilt, he tied himself to a tall Saguaro cactus and endured two days of extreme, self-induced torture. He hallucinated, seeing weeping women, Roman soldiers, and a centurion approaching with a sword to end his life and his suffering.

Prospect found his sometimes son and healed him in a hidden cave. The "Romans" were Apaches who now respected Caldera for enduring such suffering. He sent the young man on a vengeance trail, the only way to burn out the madness that was destroying him. He mission was to kill the men who murdered his birth mother. Prospect gave him a chain to wear as a constant reminder of his crime, part of the chain that held him to the Privy jail.

He rode off weak, half-blind and driven mad by a desire for vengeance and atonement.

Prospect told Bull what has happened. If the young man survived, he would kill his sometimes son. Caldera would have to pay for the murder of T'othern and the child. Bull said he would not allow that, and a decades old friendship was broken.

Although for years the mail occasionally brought a link or two from Caldera's chain, the young man never returned to Privy. Prospect looked at Quiller one day. "The greatest sadness in my life was my inability to set things right with Caldera."

Prospect was ill and near death. Desperate for more information the writer asked, "What happened next?"

Chapter One

Caldera shouted from the darkness. "Hello, the camp!" The glow from a bright flame nearby broke up against the shapes of a wagon, horses, and three people. The two women tried to back into their own shadows. The man, squatting on the ground, didn't move.

"I'm comin' in. Don't shoot me." He led the horse to the edge of the light from the campfire and let the pilgrims get a good look at him. Sitting around a campfire swapping yarns with pilgrims was the last thing he wanted to do, but he needed information; he needed people. Caldera steeled himself to be decent. "Mind if I share your fire a while?"

"Come on in, Mister," said the man. His voice was heavy with drink.

Caldera hobbled his horse quickly and joined the group. He had to pause a few seconds to remember a proper greeting. "Thank you for your hospitality."

The man offered a bottle. "Name's Isaac... Lee Isaac.

Caldera shook his head. "Caldera."

"Funny sounding name. No offense, Mister."

Caldera started to say something, but was cut off.

"Don't matter. These are my wives, Margaret and Sallie. Come on out of the dark. If he was trouble we'd already be dead."

"No, we wouldn't." The women stepped forward. "I'm Margaret." She held a rifle on him.

The other eased into the light. "I'm Sallie." She held what appeared to be a Bible.

"You can lower the gun, Ma'am. I'm just a traveler. Like you folks."

Margaret spoke first. "Our resources are limited, Mr. Caldera, but may I offer you some stew and bread?"

"Thank you, Ma'am."

Isaac did the serving, clumsily. Margaret lowered the rifle. Caldera accepted the tin plate and fork with genuine gratitude. He had eaten very little in the past couple of days.

"What brings you to these parts, Mr. Caldera?" asked Margaret.

"Just Caldera. There ain't no mister."

If he thought he had dodged the question he was wrong.

"And your business?"

Isaac looked up and smiled. "It's a woman's privilege to be nosey."

Sallie glared at him. "And it's a man's duty to remain sober, Lee Isaac. The Lord may soon forgive you, but I shall not. 'They that be drunken are drunken in the night, but let us, who are of the day, be sober,'" Sallie said. She hugged her bible and eased farther back into the darkness.

"Quiet, woman. We have guests. Squat down, Caldera. I know that word. Means a volcano that burns so hot it collapses in on itself, don't it? What are you burning for?" Isaac seemed to forget the question the moment he said it. He took big swallow from his bottle.

This was the first time Caldera had heard the meaning of his name. A year earlier he would have been curious. He decided to make conversation about other matters. "Dangerous country hereabouts."

"We have the protection of the Lord," said Sallie.

"And Mr. Sharps," added Margaret. She held the carbine as if she had some experience in its use.

Isaac laughed. "Now don't I have a pair of wives? Praise the Lord, but hand me a rifle!"

"Are you reluctant to share your business, Caldera?" said Margaret.

"No, Ma'am. Begging your pardon, I was just sizing you folks up."

Sallie didn't even look up from her book. "We are a God fearing folk, Mr. Caldera."

"Fear of God is a healthy thing in these parts, Ma'am." He looked to Margaret. "So is fear of Apaches. Truth be told, I'm looking for some bad men, killers... and worse."

Sallie shuddered slightly. Margaret clutched her rifle a little tighter. No one needed to describe "worse."

"You know that such men are about?" Isaac asked.

"Such men are always about, Mr. Isaac."

"Lee."

"Where are you folks from?" Caldera hated the talk, but he needed to keep the conversation going.

"Utah Territory," said Margaret.

With pride in her voice, Sallie said, "St. George."

"The kingdom of Utah and long live the king," Isaac said bitterly.

"Mr. Isaac." Margaret's voice was calm, but forceful.

Isaac said, "Fetch Caldera a cup, Sallie."

"I will not."

"He is a guest and will be treated with courtesy."

Sallie produced a tin cup from the wagon. Caldera accepted it and the whiskey that followed. Sallie climbed into the wagon.

"Go on, Margaret. The men need to—" He took a swig from the bottle. "Commit philosophy."

"Good night, Mr. Isaac. Mister Caldera."

"Good night, Ma'am. I'm a light sleeper and will be on guard tonight."

"As will I." She nodded good night and climbed into the wagon.

Isaac placed a couple of small logs on the fire. The men sat with little movement, sharing the night, the crackle of burning wood, the whiskey and their own personal demons. Time allowed for a closer look at the older man, who turned out to be not so old as Caldera had first thought. His thin frame and pure white hair gave him the appearance of someone in his sixties. The hallowed and haunted look in his eyes added even more years, but by his skin and the tone of his voice he couldn't have been more than 45 or 50.

"You'll pardon me for inquiring, Caldera, but you seem to be a man on a mission."

Caldera thought for a moment. *I need this man to talk, so I also must talk.* "Yes, Sir, I am."

"A mission of vengeance I guess. If you don't mind the inquiry."

9

Caldera didn't know what an inquiry was, but he figured answering the man's questions was the best way to keep him talking. "Something like that."

Isaac poked at the fire with a stick he'd been using to keep coals from spreading out. "Be blunt, Sir. Are you a Danite?"

The term gave Caldera pause. *Dan Knight....* He knew of no such person. *Some of the educated whores tell tales of a king over in England. He has knights. He sends them off on missions to slay dragons and demons.* "Well, Mr. Isaac, I am on a mission if that's what you mean."

Mumbling began inside the tent. Sallie was saying something about "forgive us" and "Lord have mercy" and such. Margaret was silent, but he knew she wasn't sleeping.

"You are a destroying angel, then," said Isaac.

"Nobody ever called me an angel, but I come this way to destroy. That's a fact."

Isaac sank into himself like a leather water sack shot with a high-caliber rifle. He was full and then all of a sudden empty. He struggled to get up. "I must urinate." He staggered to the far side of the wagon, paused a minute, and then stumbled into the darkness.

"What the hell?" Caldera grabbed the bottle and poured a couple of shots into his cup.

It was awful stuff. He used Isaac's stick to shove the small logs around the fire so they'd burn slower and kick up less flame. He finished the whiskey in his cup with a grimace. *I think this has some rattlesnake in it.*

Caldera turned to see Margaret at the edge of the wagon, the Sharps back in her hands. "Are you here to kill us, Mr. Caldera?"

He stood up and faced her.

"We're not gentlefolk. There's no need for formalities," she said.

He'd only meant to put himself in a more defensible position, but he allowed her to think it courtesy.

"Looks like I won't be killing anybody for the moment, Ma'am."

"We've suffered enough for the past. Mr. Caldera."

"Ma'am, I don't rightly—"

"Have you been sent to kill us?"

"No, Ma'am."

"I heard you and Mr. Isaac speaking. Are you a destroying angel?" She raised the rifle and pointed it at his chest.

"Ma'am, unless you folks belong to a gang led by Malon—"

Margaret took half a step back. Her face twisted, ever so briefly, in fear, and she whispered, "Malon!"

"If I'm to do any avenging, Ma'am, he'll be the one who gets it. Him and his gang."

"But you said you were a destroying angel!"

She was interrupted by the appearance of her husband. He'd ripped his shirt open and he held a skinning knife in his right hand. His lack of forward movement, and Margaret's aim with the Sharps, kept Caldera motionless.

Isaac took a step forward, cocked his head to the side, and offered the knife to Caldera. "Here! Take your blood atonement! Kill me and be damned!"

Sallie's "all the saints in heaven" and "Father save us in our hour of need" and other mumblings continued at a much higher volume and at greater speed.

Margaret turned to her husband. "Lee! No!"

Caldera used the moment. He drew his pistol from his belt. "Drop the knife. Drop the gun. Now!"

"Sweet Jesus in our hour of need—"

"Sallie, shut up!" Margaret set the rifle against the wagon. Isaac dropped the knife. Sallie shut up.

"Now, somebody tell me what in the hell you people are talking about!"

Margaret looked at her husband and then at Caldera. "Then, Mr. Caldera, you swear you're not a Danite."

"Like I said, Ma'am, I don't even know what you folks is talking about."

Margaret walked to the fire, leaving the rifle against the wagon. She poured some whiskey into the cup and swallowed it all. "Sit, Mr. Isaac," she said. "This man is no enemy. At least he is not our enemy." Isaac shuffled to the fire and sat down. She passed the bottle to him. Caldera stared for a moment and then sat down with them. The bottle began making the rounds. The tension had built up and then released so fast that the trio was in a form of shock.

Some moments later Margaret broke the silence. "You may continue, Sallie."

The mumbling from the wagon commenced.

Some considerable time passed before anyone spoke. Caldera was too confused by the whole scene and too embarrassed for his hosts to ask questions.

"You bring out the wicked in people, Mr. Caldera." Margaret stood up, walked to the wagon and returned with another bottle of whiskey and a third cup. "It's better than that poison Mr. Isaac bought at Tubac."

Caldera accepted the bottle and poured a round. At last, the conversation had touched on subject of his interest. He was learning a valuable lesson, too. The man who speaks very little hears a lot.

"I was the biggest flatbacker in Arkansas," she said.

"Margaret, that life is in the past."

"Like the Mountain Meadows?"

Her question stirred something in Caldera's memory. Years earlier he'd heard rumors of a wagon train trapped up in Utah being wiped out by a pack of Utes. But there were other rumors. The Utes weren't alone in the killing, nor in the sharing of the spoils. White men were responsible. But that was back when he was a kid. Nobody talked about it any more.

Margaret continued. "I was surely on my way to the cribs. You know about cribs, Mr. Caldera?"

He nodded. He surely did.

"Then Mr. Isaac and the faith saved me. And here we are. Moving and settling. Moving and settling. And moving again."

"Sorry, Ma'am." Caldera was getting lots of information, but none so far that would help him find Malon or members of the gang.

She smiled. "It's a better life than the other."

"Well, what are you folks doin' wandering out here all these years?"

"We preach to the Lamanites," said Isaac. He spoke as if everyone should know his meaning. Caldera's confused look said otherwise. "Indians, Caldera. The Indians of America are descendants of the lost tribes of Israel. It's in the book. We try to bring them back into the fold, so to speak."

"That explains a lot," said Caldera.

"I don't understand," said Margaret.

"How you folks have lived so long out here. The Apaches don't come near crazy folk."

No one laughed.

Time passed, as did the bottle of whiskey. Eventually Sallie's murmurings faded. The stars moved ever so slowly and the confessions began flowing. Margaret dropped her head when Isaac began speaking.

"They told us the pilgrims were invaders. They boasted of killing our prophet and of other things. Some said they poisoned a water hole and killed some Indians. And we were getting ready for war, too. The U.S. Army was moving on Utah Territory. It was a time of insanity."

Isaac was trying to justify something terrible. Caldera had an idea of what would come next. He felt trapped and he didn't want to hear any stories. He wanted to saddle up and ride. He'd had enough of people for a while.

"Mr. Isaac hasn't spoken of this in years," Margaret said. Her head was still down.

Caldera realized he was in the middle of a ritual cleansing, something like the sweat baths Indians sometimes used to purify mind, body and spirit. *Hell, I'm in for a long night.* He grabbed the bottle.

Isaac mumbled on, lost in a trance and seeing a frightful past play out in the bright red, flickering coals. "They said we were rescuing the pilgrims from the Utes, but that wasn't what our glorious leaders had in mind at all. I couldn't believe what they told us to do. *Told us*, mind you." He paused, knowing his next words were a lie.

"We had no choice. They talked those folks into surrendering. Promised protection and an escort, they did. Well, they escorted the women folk and the children over the hill. They escorted the wounded into the wagons. And they... we... I... escorted the menfolk down the road a bit. Not a one of them had a gun by then. Why they gave 'em up I'll never know."

"Mr. Isaac, you don't have to tell me this."

"I think he does, Mr. Caldera," Margaret said.

"I ain't no priest, Ma'am."

"I heard you say you're on a cleansing mission. That surely is the work of God."

"Truth be told, Ma'am, I work for the other fella', the one from the fiery pits and all."

She was far too concerned with her husband's confession to pay much attention to the meaning of his words.

Isaac's voice became a drone, almost a mantra. "We marched with them side by side. Every pilgrim had his escort. When the order to fire came, I shot, but I fired over the head of my man. That didn't matter. The Utes took care of the few we left. I could hear the screams of the women and children from over the hill." Isaac tried to continue, but his voice gave way. "It didn't stop for nearly half an hour."

Caldera struggled for the right words to say and failed.

"The Apaches, Caldera... they are perhaps the worst of the Lamanites. And we're worse than them. We good folk killed 120 Christian men, women and children. God have mercy."

Margaret stood up, a bit wobbly, and walked to the wagon. She returned with a couple of blankets, draping one over Isaac's shoulders and handing the other to Caldera. "He's about through for the night, Mr. Caldera. Thank you for your patience."

Again, Caldera was at a loss for words. "Ma'am."

She crawled into the wagon. Isaac continued mumbling for a while and eventually fell over. Caldera tucked the blanket around his shoulders. He spent the rest of the night drinking the whiskey, poking at the dwindling fire, and pondering the minds and hearts of his fellow man. The night was long, and for the first time he realized that others shared the darkness.

He saddled up and rode out at false dawn, his mind focused. The evening had not been a total waste after all. They'd purchased the Taos Lightning they'd been drinking from a hole in the wall saloon between Tubac and Tumacacori mission: Bannister's. If there was information about Malon or his men, he would hear it at such a place. As he reached the crest of a low hill he turned to look back at the camp. Margaret was standing beside her husband, the Sharps in her hand. Caldera waved, but she must not have seen him. She remained immobile as he rode over the hill.

Chapter Two

Caldera rode south, trying to put the strange events of the previous evening out of his mind. It wasn't much of a challenge. He'd finished off the last of Lee Isaac's whiskey before stumbling into sleep. The muffled thumping produce by the blood flowing through his head sounded like war drums. A few arrows in the back would have brought merciful relief.

Bannister's, he thought. Margaret did not think much of the saloon or the proprietor. "Mr. Leon Bannister is a killer. I recognize the type." Her husband had dropped his head, thinking she was referring to the shame in his past. He was standing behind her at the time and only Caldera noticed. "No telling what other sort of evils he is involved in... or with whom."

Sounds like just the man I'm looking for, especially the "or who" part. He could be Malon.

All thoughts of Isaac and his family were soon just more dust in Caldera's trail, forgotten. Men were in need of killing, and if he was to be an avenging angel he would be a willing one. He had earned an ignoble death, also, but these men would have to die before he did. That was his mission. He would cleanse his own sin by ridding the world of these rapists and murders. Then he would be free to finish the task he'd begun in the Superstitions. He owed that to T'othern and their unborn child.

Caldera wasn't a religious man, but he thought if there was a heaven and hell they would surely never meet. She and the child would be above while he suffered in the fires below.

He reached Bannister's place mid-afternoon, his head buzzing from the alcohol and the brutal sun reflecting off the white rock trail. An erratic breeze from the east carried a faint odor of rotting meat.

Must not bury their leavings. A natural cave had formed in the rocky hill above the wash. A wall of rubble about three feet high held a door just wide enough for a man to walk into a space about the size of a of Bang Ong's restaurant back in Privy. A man stood watch in the shadows. He was dressed poorly, wore a wide straw sombrero, and held a Spencer .44 caliber carbine. The man, a mix-blood Indian and Negro, reminded Caldera of a small falcon. He was a bird of prey always on the hunt, yet fully aware that he could easily fall victim to larger birds. He lived for and feared the hunt. The only movement when the lone rider approached was in his eyes.

Play possum all you want. I see you. "Hello! Is this Bannister's place?"

Discovered, the guard became animated. "Si, amigo. Come. Get drunk. We got a woman. Get lucky." The man had become an advertising sign and about as honest as the *Good Spirits* sign in the Armageddon. Caldera smiled and waved. The thought of a hair of the dog that bit him the previous night was overpowering. He tied his horse beneath the meager shade of a Palo Verde tree. The horse dipped his head to a half-barrel of stinking water.

"I watch your horse, Amigo. Apaches don't steal. You got money?"

"Touch my horse and I'll kill you."

"No touch, Amigo. You go up. Spend money. Have fun. I watch."

The base of the cave was about ten feet above the wash. As he ascended the rough steps hacked out of the stone he peered deeper inside. The cavity was at least 20 feet deep, perhaps a bit more. A couple of old quilts hung high in the rear, probably to create Bannister's sleeping space. If there was a woman about, the wall probably did double duty to make a crib. The bar was an old door laid across a couple of whiskey barrels. Rough shelves behind it held dusty bottles of cheap whiskey and mescal.

"What'll it be, Pilgrim?"

"Whiskey. You Bannister?"

"I am." He poured a shot. Caldera killed it in one gulp. The arrival of the fire down his gullet was like the homecoming of an old friend. Once again he forced himself into a friendly attitude to acquire information. "Make it two, Mr. Bannister." Another round was followed by another gulp. "Oh, *that's* what I needed."

Bannister didn't wait for a command to pour and Caldera took his time with the third shot.

Bannister was a big man gone to seed. Two decades earlier he might have been a lean mountain man, but his muscle had long since turned to fat. He was nearly bald and the sun had been cruel to his skin. He carried an old .36 Navy revolver stuck in his britches.

The barrel had worn a hole in the cloth. Caldera noticed the barrel had been cut down for easier use close in and for concealment. A less-hungover Caldera would have given that fact more thought.

The two chatted, neither saying much of substance. Caldera hated the talk, but Bannister would probably be the only source for the kind of information he needed.

"Another, Mister?"

"Why not? I got no place to go."

"Why you in these parts? If you don't mind me asking." Bannister was as polite as he was fat. He, too was playing a verbal game.

"Looking for work. Anybody hiring 'round here?"

Bannister laughed. "Sorry, Mister. 'Cept for Pete Kitchens and Bull McKenzie there ain't a single job in all of Arizona Territory."

"I figured."

"Well, now." He moved from behind the bar. "Let's sit down while I think on it a spell. Wouldn't hurt me none to have another customer around here." He pulled two home-made chairs to a table in the back of the room. "Here, have one on me." He sat down.

Caldera followed and accepted the free drink. His back was to the curtain, so he had a clear view of the cave's opening. It was a position anyone wise to the ways of the West would have taken. He felt secure until he realized Bannister had maneuvered him into that very position for a purpose. Caldera heard the slight "whoosh" from behind the quilt and was already in motion to stand when he was knocked unconscious.

"Nothing in the saddlebags, Señor Bannister."

"Well, we got the horse and saddle. That's something."

"Him?"

"His gun. Some coins." Bannister laughed. "And he's got a chain doubled around his gut."

"Es loco."

Caldera fought his way to consciousness, but he kept his eyes closed. He'd figured it out, but a second too late. Someone was hiding behind the quilts, someone with a club. *No telling how many times Bannister's pulled that stunt. What next?*

"When he wakes up, you walk him to the pit and put a bullet in his head."

"Si." There was an awkwardness in the man's voice. He cleared his throat. "I kill a man, I get a reward."

"Yeah. Sure. You can make her grunt tonight. You got work to do now."

A soft whimpering came from near the bar. Caldera cracked open his eyes to see a young woman cowering against the rock wall. He closed his eyes quickly, but the image remained. At one time she had been attractive and well dressed, probably an Apache captive traded for whiskey or guns. She would be used, traded, and used again until she was no longer worth the trouble of keeping her alive. The hollowness in her eyes held no details, but told the entire story. She was a young woman who in going "out West" had gone to hell. But that wasn't his problem.

"Kill him first. Go ahead and do it now."

"Si."

Caldera spoke. "I got something to trade for my life."

The guard pulled his pistol and cocked the hammer.

Bannister said, "Don't splatter his guts in here, you ignorant son of a bitch~" He walked over to Caldera. "What you got to trade, Mister?"

"Gold."

"Aracha, take this bastard out of here and kill him."

"McKenzie's gold."

That brought things to a halt. Aracha eased the hammer back down on his pistol, but he kept it pointing at his prisoner's gut. Bannister squatted down. "You got some of that bastard's gold? Where?"

"I know where he found it. There's more."

Greed replaced the practicality of destroying the evidence of their thievery. Bannister was intrigued. "And how the hell do you know that?"

"He's my pa."

Quick as a rattlesnake, Bannister struck Caldera across the face, then stood up and stared at his captive. "I hear he's got lots of bastards."

"I'm the bastard who knows where he found the gold." Caldera knew he was gaining the upper hand. He played another card. "You stupid son of a bitch."

Bannister grabbed his gun.

"Señor Bannister!"

"I ain't gonna' kill him here."

"If there's gold, Malon should decide."

The terrified woman suddenly sucked in her breath. The act fleshed out her story. Bannister's place was a sanctuary for Malon and his rape gang. Caldera's work would begin here.

"Put him on the hook," Bannister said.

Aracha motioned with his pistol. "Over by the wall, Señor Caldera."

Someone had poked an iron hook into a crack in the wall about ten feet off the floor. Brown marks stained the wall beneath the hook. It seemed to be crying blood. Aracha tied Caldera's wrists together with a strip of narrow leather, looped a rope through his arms, tossed it over the hook, and pulled Caldera up against the wall. Aracha jerked hard, grinning, hoping to pop his prisoner's shoulders out of their sockets. He failed, but he kept on grinning. He squatted down to tie his prisoner's feet.

"Keep his legs wide apart. I might have to kick his bullets some. Just hobble him,'" Bannister said.

"Si." Aracha tied a long leather thong around each of Caldera's ankles, leaving enough of a strand to permit easy walking when they were finished with him. He stood up. "This Caldera, he belongs to Malon now."

"He belongs to me," Bannister said. "Malon just gets to say when he dies."

"Si. Malon."

"Now you get back out there and stand guard."

"The woman?"

Bannister sighed. "Si."

Aracha practically skipped out of the cave. Bannister looked at the woman. "Deanna!"

She must have said "Yes, Sir," but Caldera only heard a terrified squeak. "Bring another bottle. I'm going to work me up a thirst." He turned to Caldera and put on a pair of work gloves.

During the latter stages of the beating Caldera passed out. When a painful consciousness returned he awoke to the smell of cheap tobacco and the sound of a fat man in rut. He knew his entire body must be in pain, but the agony in his shoulders was overwhelming all other sensations. His blood-drained arms were numb and useless. He cracked an eye. Aracha sat near a fire pit in the floor. He stirred the coals and added a small log to build up a bed of cooking coals. His eyes continually darted to the quilts separating the dirty little man from paradise.

Bannister, red faced and sweating, stepped out. "Make it quick," he said.

Aracha practically jumped across the room.

"None of your games, Aracha." Bannister began tending the fire. When a series of joyful curses, intermixed with grunts and shouts, bounced off the walls, a sick grin came across his face. The girl, Deanna, never made a sound, or at least one that the prisoner could hear. Coldly and carefully, Caldera eyed his surroundings, looking for a weapon, an edge. He could see only one.

Deanna stumbled quickly through the opening in the quilts and hit the cave floor. She had been shoved. Aracha stepped through. He started building a cigarette.

"You didn't hurt her none, you son of a bitch?"

"Nah. I just showed her who's boss."

"Malon's gonna' want top dollar for that little bitch. He don't want to sell no damaged merchandise."

"She ain't damaged. On the outside." Both men laughed. "And he won't be back in these parts for months."

"And ain't that just too bad." Bannister picked up a small stone from the floor and flipped it against Deanna's head. "Start cooking!"

She cringed, but began working. Deanna moved automatically to prepare their meal. She said nothing, made no sound, but her every move was a frightful, cowering one. Caldera wondered whether he could use her to his advantage. *Would she help, or would she side with the two-against-one odds?*

After their meal the men began to get drunk. They killed a bottle of Taos Lightning, the same they'd sold to Lee Isaac. Aracha opened a second and the drunks began forcing Deanna to drink. Caldera watched intently. Like the one rattler out of ten that never rattles, he was coiled and ready to strike without warning at any opportunity. Drunken captors, if they didn't get busy with gun or knife, could mean an opportunity.

Deanna drank the whiskey, but she managed to spill more than she consumed. As the evening wore on she even began taking large swallows, but spitting out most of the liquor when the men weren't looking. Once she even threw up, apparently on purpose. Bannister and Aracha nearly choked with laughter.

Sometime during the second half of the second bottle Aracha passed out. "Little pissant," said Bannister. He kicked the half-breed, but the little man didn't move.

Caldera's blood was up. Few people would have looked at the situation his way, but his odds had just improved. Bannister grabbed Deanna around her shoulders and put the bottle to her lips. "Drink, Darlin'." He bloodied her upper lip when he jabbed the bottle to her face. She drank, spilling most of the liquid from the sides of her mouth. Bannister took a huge swallow. He farted loudly, then laughed. "Hah! I'm feeling frisky again, Deanna."

The frail woman shuddered and seemed to fold herself within herself.

Caldera's voice was low, sounding far weaker than he felt. "What about the gold?"

"Gold?" Bannister shook his head to clear the haze from his eyes. "What gold?"

"McKenzie's gold. Remember?"

"Yeah."

The prisoner fell silent, having planted the seed in fertile ground. The man was a pig and he would act as a pig acts. He pushed Deanna away and stumbled across the room.

Caldera continued to play the role of weakness. "Just lying on the ground. You don't even have to dig." His voice was low, barely audible.

The fat man stepped closer. He stumbled forward and fell against Caldera. The pain was searing. Bannister backed up, but Caldera continued to lure him back. "Spanish gold... sacks of it."

Bannister leaned his head forward as if to get a closer look at his prisoner. He was already spending the newfound wealth when

Caldera snapped his legs up, the right higher than the left, and encircled the man's fat neck with the leather strip loosely tied around his feet. He jerked down with all the force he could muster. Bannister went down, his own weight adding to the choking force of Caldera's powerful legs. The big man was on his knees, gagging, slapping for his gun, but too drunk and shocked to grasp it.

Deanna, no longer pretending to be drunk, looked on with wide eyes and crept toward the wall. Bannister's face was bright red. His eyes were wide. He looked into Caldera's face. Pain and stress and effort were reflected there, but the younger man's eyes were cold. Bannister had known fear in his life, but this was the first time he had faced outright terror and the certain knowledge that he was about to die. He kicked and struggled. He even vomited, but there was no outlet for his bile.

Inevitably the leather around Caldera's feet choked the life from Bannister's body. Caldera hung on long after he felt the man's death rattle just to make sure. When he finally unwound the thong from the man's neck and let the body fall, he was exhausted. The struggle and the weight had nearly pulled his arms from their sockets. But he couldn't rest. He placed his feet up under his butt and against the wall, pushed hard and upward, raising his arms as he moved, and clearing the hook. He landed on top of the man he'd just killed. The stench was awful. The fat man's last act on Earth had been to foul his britches, a fitting death knell.

Caldera rolled away, too worn out to do anything else.

Aracha's words were slow and slurred. "What the hell's going on, Boss?" His eyes were closed, but flickering open. He squinted, trying to make sense of the multiple images that danced in front of his face.

Startled, Deanna backed closer to the wall.

Caldera, weak and still bound, looked her in the eyes. "Well, Deanna, you gonna' help me or do you want another night with Aracha?"

She stood up, back still to the wall. She was torn by her fear of the known and the unknown. The unknown proved the lesser of two evils. Deanna stumbled and staggered with small steps to Bannister's body and grabbed his knife.

"Hurry, Deanna."

She dashed to Caldera and cut the thong binding his hands. "Get me his gun. Quick."

Aracha wiped his hands across his eyes. When he opened them he had just enough time to realize he was a dead man. Caldera put a shot through the center of his face.

Deanna winced from the effect of such a blast in a confined space, but a hint, just a tiny hint of a smile curled her lips. "Bannister... is he really dead?"

Caldera was stunned. Her voice was lovely, melodic. He thought she sounded like an angel who had been through hell. He stood up, cocked the pistol and put a bullet through the back of the fat man's head. "Yes."

He stuck the pistol in the waist of his pants, then sat down and began loosening the leather bindings from his feet. Finished, he paused to take a deep breath. The air was foul, but it brought relief to his mind, body and spirit. Candle light glinting off the metal chains around his waist caught her eye. As with Deanna a few moments before, a tiny hint of a smile curled his lips. "These were Malon's men?"

"Yes, Sir."

"It's Caldera." He fingered the last two links in the chain.

Deanna began backing away. She kept her eyes on her rescuer, wondering whether she had exchanged one devil for another. She had, but this devil had no designs on her flesh. He didn't have time. "What is to become of me?"

"I don't rightly care." He stood up, stretched his arms, tossed a length of chain on each man, and walked out of the cave and into the darkness.

Chapter Three

My wife nearly dropped her glass. "He just left her there, Robert?"

I nodded. "I can replace the Coke from the ice chest. If you want more rum I have to go back out there." *There* at that moment meant the 105 degree heat of a desert summer. The Arizona sun blasting the streets, parking lots, and sidewalks added another 15 to 20 degrees of misery. I'd faced it for my book and I'd face it again if my wife so desired. With me investing most of my time interviewing Prospect or burying myself in the backwaters of local libraries, this wasn't much of a vacation for Annette.

"I want," she said.

"I will."

"You said that once before."

"And I meant it. Still do."

"Seriously, we're running out of a few things. I made a list."

"I'll run down to the store after sundown." I took a sip of her drink. "Is there any more?"

"Enough for one each."

"Do it."

She mixed the drinks, tossing the empty Coke bottles into the trash but placing the empty rum bottle into the ice chest. Our drinking was nobody else's business, she thought. Annette drank to excess four or five times a year at most: New Year's Eve, birthdays sometimes, and on vacations. Still, she didn't want to be thought ill of by strangers. "So your—" She stopped to search for the appropriate word. "*Subject*... he rescues this poor woman and then leaves her for the rest of the rapists and murderers? Do I have it about right?"

"As usual, no."

"Well, did he... you know?"

"You've been reading too many western paperbacks." I sat down on the bed and enjoyed the cold burn of iced cola laced with rum.

"I've been listening to history. Straight from the horse's... uh, mouth."

"Steady."

"I just call 'em as I see 'em."

"Malon and his rape gang, and some of the thugs who rode with men like McCracken, were an aberration, an exception to the rule."

"What rule?"

"For the most part, and I mean overwhelmingly so, women were respected in the West."

"Like Alice Chacon?"

"She was paid the going rate for her work."

"Right."

"And when she was killed, a *woman* arranged it."

She stuck her little finger in her drink and flicked a few drops my way. I pretended to catch them in the air with my tongue. "Thanks."

"Swine."

"Anyway, that's why Malon was so hated and feared. His gang was far out of the norm, even for hardened criminals."

"I don't believe it."

"Read your history."

"I'd rather read *your* history."

I shook my head. "Wish I knew how it ended."

"He's going to tell you isn't he?"

"I think he wants to. I think this is the only thing keeping him alive. He doesn't have much time."

"Then neither do you."

"He's in the driver's seat."

Annette sat up. "That's not what I mean."

I finished my drink and stood up. "I'll run down to the store. Anything not on the list?"

"You have to tell him, Robert. He's earned it."

I took a deep breath and only then made my final decision. Of course, she was right. "I'll tell him."

"When?" The mother hen in her was taking over.

"When the time is right."

"Time. Robert, that's the one thing Prospect doesn't have."

I stepped through the door and into the blast furnace of downtown Phoenix. Making a tough decision is supposed to create a sense of freedom or at least release. Hell, Davy Crockett's decision to stick it out at the Alamo didn't bring freedom, but at least he knew his fate. He and every man there knew exactly what was coming over the walls and the precise consequences of their actions. There had to have been a certain sense of release in that. No more unknowns.

But what of Prospect? I had respected the man long before I'd met him. I'd grown to like him immensely. And he'd made a connection to the past that I could never have made on my own. I owed him more than he could possibly know. I owed him the truth. What would he feel? Joy? Relief? Would he feel anything at all? Would he feel betrayal? I felt a bit like old Davy Crockett myself. Something big was about to come over the walls. Unlike the former congressman from Tennessee, I hadn't a clue as to how the showdown would play out.

I made my way across the parking lot to our car. As I drove to the store, those unknowns, especially the big one, were becoming oppressive.

A saloon selling package liquor was on the way, so I turned in. "I think I'll get the big bottle."

Chapter Four

Bull McKenzie fired a single shot from his Colt .44-40 and blew the head off a pelican. He shot three more birds, the last as it was taking wing. It fell into the edge of the sea and washed ashore. "Go collect our supper."

Rob Blakey stared at the beach, afraid to look Bull in the eyes. "That ain't no turkey." He was so slow and dim-witted that folks called him Blankee. That he was on this quest was a sad comment on the dregs of the States that were drifting into Arizona. Hell, even the Apaches had a sense of purpose and were good at their job: robbing and killing white men and Mexicans. The Pimas were such good farmers he wouldn't be surprised to see them growing corn out of solid rock. And the early pioneers, Bull among them, had withstood hardships that would have broken most men. *But this lot...*

Blankee shuffled off toward the pelicans at a pace that an injured sand crab could outrun. "So slow it looks like he's got dead lice fallin' off him," Bull said. He thought about firing a shot into the sand behind the man, but dropped the idea. Blankee had only one speed: as slow as he could get away with.

He turned to survey the rest of his party. *My mama raised a fool.* Ford—fat and balding Ford—pretended to an education he never had. His eyelids were always half-closed, but beneath them were eyes in constant search for opportunity—legal or otherwise. He often used words without having a clue as to their meaning, but his lack of education and experience never prevented him from pontificating on a given subject. He often began one of his lectures with, "Before I digress." Ford had left a wife and three children back in Michigan and seemed proud of the act. "Bitch don't own me."

Johnson was a big man from south Texas who believed in his right to lead by virtue of his size and his ability to shout. He wasn't very smart, but he was a careful and crafty man. He would be useless in a fight. In a serious brawl Bull would have him down and out by fists, knife or gun within seconds. Looking for treasure with this crew was like swimming with lead weights.

He shot another pelican no more than ten feet from Blankee. The man didn't even flinch. "Damn!" Bull wondered how a man could function when he was apparently unconscious.

Three months earlier, the banker Chandler had approached him with an offer for increasing his wealth and, more important to Bull, for seeing new country. The banker had struck at the perfect moment. Bull McKenzie was bored.

"Bull, I'm not saying that this is a 100 percent guaranteed venture, but you know I have a knack for earning the almighty dollar."

Bull had looked around the bank. The first time he'd met Chandler, the bank was a canvas-covered wood structure. The teller's cage and storage shelves were boards hung by ropes from the ceiling. The floor had been pounded dirt. As Privy prospered, Chandler had moved into an adobe building with a wooden floor and even a wooden sidewalk in front. He had installed a legitimate teller's cage, which was actually a bar he had purchased up in Prescott. Real tables and chairs had replaced the old planks and boxes of the early days. Chandler had done well, but his success was almost irrelevant at that moment. Bull wanted to see new country. He drummed his fingers on his chair. "Well?"

"Spanish treasure, Bull... a fortune in pearls."

Most Arizonans would have laughed and walked away, but Bull's empire was founded on Spanish gold he'd discovered decades earlier in the Superstition Mountains. He leaned forward, knowing a pretense of disinterest was not necessary with Chandler. They'd been partners in too many enterprises for such a ruse.

"And gold I suppose?"

"The beauty of a pearl can only be truly appreciated when reflected in a golden setting. There must be. I have acquired a map."

Bull sat back. "Hell, man, do you know how many hornswoggling sons a' bitches have taken a run at me to stake 'em for a treasure hunt? Every damn one o' them bastards had a map."

"I've had people who know about such things examine the document. The parchment is several hundred years old. The ink appears to be of the same age. A captain who has sailed those waters says the terrain represented is accurate."

Bull remained silent.

Chandler continued. "Every damn treasure map in Arizona leads to gold or silver. Always. This map refers to pearls. That alone makes it, shall we say, more intriguing."

"I suppose there's some kinda' legend."

"Not that I know of. That too is intriguing. You manage the expedition and we'll split the profits right down the middle." Chandler threw in his trump card. "And it will get you out of the confines of Privy for a while."

"Where?"

"West to Yuma, south to the sea, and a hard trek along the eastern shore."

Bull shrugged. "Why the hell not?"

Chandler accompanied him as far as Yuma where one of his many contacts had outfitted the expedition, including Johnson, Ford and Blankee. Bull pushed them on immediately and soon they were in Mexico. Except for the vast body of water to his right, the country was remarkably like much of southern Arizona. Had he been alone Bull would have felt right at home. They traveled several days without incident and although they had to ration their water, there was plenty of game. They ate well thanks to Bull's hunting skills. He always followed up the rear of the little caravan. It wasn't that he feared being shot in the back, only that one of the absentminded and clumsy trio would do something stupid to put an end to the expedition.

"I think it's Sunday," Blankee said. "We ought to rest."

"You'll rest when we camp," Bull said.

"But we should hold some services."

"The only thing you want to service is your lazy ass." He held his palm at arm's length just beneath the sun and then moved it down to the horizon—four palm lengths. "We got two hours of daylight. You ride ahead and find us a half-ass decent campsite. And collect plenty of driftwood for a fire."

"But—"

"Git!"

Blankee headed south. The small party came upon him about an hour later. He was on his knees at the water's edge, his britches

29

soaked waist high by the tide. His chin and the front of his shirt were brown with vomit. His eyes were wide and vacant.

Bull dismounted.

"I seen something." Blankee swallowed his sentence.

"What! What the hell have you seen?"

"I seen—" He bent over, dry heaved and pointed inland.

Bull mounted up. He looked to Johnson. "There's some cinnamon in the medicine pouch. Give him a bit to settle his innerds. And don't touch nothing else." One of the medicines was the Western cure-all—a bottle of whiskey—and he didn't want it to disappear their fourth day on the trail. He rode inland to see what all the heaving was about.

Blankee had good reason to toss his guts. About a quarter-mile from the shore the remains of a man lay face down next to the remnants of a fire—not a body, remains. He was old, probably a lone prospector. The flesh had been scraped off his arms and legs. Bits of charred flesh decorated the ashes. The fire was cold and at least a couple of days old, a fact confirmed by the bloating of the old man's torso and the hundreds of marks left by the seashore's meat eaters. Faint tracks of bare footprints circled the scene and led back into the interior.

Blankee appeared to be better when Bull returned, but he was doe-eyed and rattled. "We gotta' move now," Bull said.

"What was it?" Ford said.

"Dead man."

"He's seen dead men 'afore."

"Not like this one. Mount up."

Ford helped Blankee on his horse and mounted his own.

Johnson didn't move. "What's special about that dead man?"

"He was somebody's supper."

Johnson blanched and wasted no time getting on his horse. Bull pushed them well past dark. The Indians were probably long gone, but he was taking no chances. Chandler had warned him that the natives of the region had a reputation for cannibalism and he did not intend to have his fat dripping into a communal fire. They made camp around midnight. Bull, Johnson and Ford took turns at watch. Blankee slept, whimpering till sunrise.

Bull could just see the bottom of a water can tipping up behind the head of one of their pack mules. He cocked his pistol and took aim. "I'll blow your brains out and use 'em for fish bait."

Ford quickly stepped out in the open. "I was just gettin' some water," he said.

Bull holstered his pistol and took the can. It was almost empty. He took a swallow and passed it to Johnson, who handed it to Blankee.

"What about me?" said Ford.

Bull grinned. "Thieves drink last. If at all."

Blankee left a couple of swallows for the thief.

"That's it," said Johnson.

"What we gonna' do, Mr. Bull?" Blankee was still doe-eyed and he had a bad case of the shakes.

Bull wasted no time. "Load all the water cans on that mule. If I can't find water in the desert it ain't there to be found." Within minutes he was riding toward the rugged mountains just to the east. He wasn't concerned. Chandler's map was crude but detailed and, so far, accurate. It showed a spring about a mile inland. He hoped it would prove to be just as accurate about the shipwreck and the treasure.

He found the location of the spring, but no water. The nearby vegetation was dead or dying. The sand was easy to dig, but as far as two feet down it was as dry as the surface. The spring was dead. There were no other water sources between their present location and the hoped-for wrecked treasure ship. He had to find water now or face defeat and head back north. He kicked the mule and headed further inland.

Hours later he came across the sign he was seeking, a narrow wash leading up into the mountains. He followed it for more than half a mile before it curved to the north. He looked carefully but, seeing no greening of the vegetation, he kept going. Sparse grass and a few small bushes dotted a spot on the low side of the next bend. He took a small spade and dug into the sandy soil. He found nothing other than more dry dirt, not even a hint of moisture. His poor luck followed him through the next three bends in the wash.

He found human tracks crossing a wide, sandy area. One of the men wore boots. The boot tracks were probably made by a partner of the old prospector they'd found. The impressions indicated that the man had been running. Two other sets of tracks were made by men running barefoot. The number of bug tracks across them indicated that they were at least a day and probably two days old. *Some sumbitch is already some other sumbitch's lunch.* Bull moved on.

He paused, turned back and followed the faint trail of footprints out of the wash. Decades earlier he would have left the scene without giving the man a single thought. But decades earlier a wounded and near-death Bull McKenzie had been saved from death in the desert by a young Pima named Keli'hi, the boy who became the man known as Prospect. *Damn me for a fool.*

He moved carefully through the rocky pass. Tracking was unnecessary. The jagged rocks towering a hundred feet or so above him permitted only one narrow passage. When he emerged into a flat slope, a sudden wind sweeping through the rocks blew his hat to the ground. When he picked it up he noticed two birds flying beneath a mesquite tree. They were flying in an impossible pattern—back and forth as if on a swing. He mounted up and moved closer. As the wind died down the birds appeared to hang in the air.

They weren't birds. They were a man's hands tied to strings— Anglo hands. He stared for a moment and then turned back to the wash and his search for water.

A couple of hours before sundown he came to another bend. This one featured a cluster of leafy green shrubs. He found moist sand less than six inches below the surface. About a foot down the sand was dark and wet. He expanded the hole, then sat back and watched as water seeped in. The movement was slow but constant and within half an hour several inches of muddy water covered the bottom. He soaked it up with a rag and squeezed the liquid into his mouth. It was dirty and foul tasting, but he enjoyed every drop.

He prepared for a long night. The process that would save their lives was simple and tedious. Soak the rag. Squeeze the water into one of the cans. When the can was full pour it into another can. Another rag tied to the top of the second can filtered the dirt. When he headed back down the wash before sunrise he left with a full supply of water.

He came across one of their mules as he neared camp. It was wandering slowly toward the mountains. It brayed on seeing him and ran south over the rocky ground. Bull had a hell of a time catching the frightened animal. *This can't be good... can't be good at all.*

Chapter Five

Johnson rode up as Bull approached the camp. "You got water?"

"What the hell happened to the mules?"

"It was Blankee. He wasn't watching 'em like he should. It ain't my fault."

"Go get that mule."

"How about that water?"

"You get water when you get the mule." He rode on to camp as Johnson charged after the mule. Blankee was on his knees in the surf. "What's he done now?"

Ford was sitting in the foul-smelling, but cooler shade of a mule. "He done drank sea water. I think it made him sick." The sound of heaving at the edge of the sea punctuated his report. Blankee's stomach was long past empty. A wave washed ashore, he heaved, and the retreating water carried little flecks of blood out to sea.

Damn fool. Bull began unloading the water cans. "Go get some sticks and build a fire. We're gonna' need some charcoal." Bull allowed him a drink of water before he left. "It ain't fit for hogs, but it'll do for the likes of us."

Ford shook his head in confusion, but he got up and ambled toward some nearby driftwood, returning to start the fire. "What are we cooking, Mr. McKenzie?"

"Wood."

"You can't eat wood."

"That idjit will... or he'll die on us. Pile on some more driftwood and let it burn down to nothin' but charcoal."

"Okay, but it don't make no sense."

"What the hell would you know about sense? Do it!"

Johnson returned with the mule. He and Ford reached for the water can at the same time. Bull stepped in and grabbed the can. He pulled a cup from one of the packs, poured it about half-full and handed it to Johnson. "We're on half rations till we get to the next spring... if there *is* a next spring."

When the fire burned down Bull went to Blankee. The man was semi-delirious and covered with vomit. He used a couple of sticks to pull some charcoal from the fire and used the butt end of his knife to crush it to a fine black powder in one of the drinking cups. He mixed this with water and handed it to Blankee. "Drink it."

"I ain't done nothin' wrong."

"It ain't punishment. It's medicine. Drink it."

"Uh-uh." Blankee dropped to his knees, bent over and dry heaved.

"You done dried out your innerds. This will settle your stomach and then we'll get you some real water."

"I ain't." He dry heaved again.

Bull looked at the other two men. "Hold him down."

Johnson and Ford grabbed their partner and pinned him to the shore. Ford giggled as Bull held Blankee's nose and force fed him the brackish mixture. Once he had swallowed it all, Bull clamped his hand over the man's mouth until he was sure Blankee wouldn't spill his guts again.

"Get that son of a bitch on his horse," Bull said.

Ford was still giggling as he shoved Blankee on his mount. "You enjoying your many happy returns, Boy?"

This time Bull led the way, but he rode leading the mule carrying their water.

Blankee was half delirious, mumbling, "I seen... I seen... I seen..."

Bull looked back. The man was wobbling in his saddle and still doe-eyed. *Dead weight... and we need to make time.* Chandler's map indicated one more spring before the wreck and the hoped-for treasure. After his desperate search for their last water source he had little hope.

He had other worries. They were eating well. He'd shot deer, rabbit and pelican, but everything was lean meat. They had no vegetables. Scurvy was a real possibility. When he caught sight of a Palo Verde tree on the edge of the rocky hills he rode over and filled a sack with its dry bean pods. They contained enough vitamin C to stave off the disease. Bull didn't know, understand or care why they worked. He just knew they were good medicine. Prospect had told him all about it and other medicinal plants in the desert. The others refused to eat.

"I ain't eating no tree," Johnson said.

Bull took a bite. "Well, let me know when your gums start bleedin' so I can prepare some words to say at your burial."

"Ain't gonna' happen, Mr. Bull McKenzie."

Bull moved on without a word. This country offered a man many ways to die and these men seemed bound and determined to find at least one each. He began to calculate how many pearls a lone man and a couple of mules could carry.

Bull allowed each man only a quarter-cup of water morning, midday and evening. They bellyached about it, especially Ford, but they couldn't argue with his logic—or his .44-40. They chewed cactus much of the time. The pulpy mass kept their mouths from drying out, but did nothing to slake their thirst.

As with the men, the mules ate well, but had nothing to drink. One crumpled to its knees and fell over. It could go no further. They transferred as much of its packs as they thought the other two could handle. Bull, concerned about Indian danger, didn't waste a bullet and quickly slit the animal's throat.

"You gonna' eat it?" Blankee's words were slurred and his eyes were wider than ever.

"I ain't that hungry," Johnson said.

"Cut the meat offn' its legs and eat it. That's what they do to men in this country. It's good enough for a mule," Blankee said.

"It's a *mule*, Blankee!" Johnson kicked the dead animal. Blood spurted from its neck.

"I want me some of that." Blankee staggered to the mule and tried to drink blood.

Bull shook his head. "Get that idjit mounted." He couldn't make up his mind as to which was the greater problem: lack of water or the three wretches hired to help him.

Ford and Johnson pulled the man up, but he broke away and ran into the sea. By the time they dragged him away he had consumed several hands full of sea water.

"He's done gone loco on us," Johnson said.

"Hell, he's useless," Ford said. "Shoot him and be done with it."

"I said get him mounted. Tie him down if you have too, but I ain't leaving a man behind," Bull said. *Hell, I wanted to see new country, but I didn't sign on for this.* He thought of Prospect, a capable man on any trip and once a damn good friend.

Blankee's retching brought him back to reality. "Let's move." Chandler's map indicated a spring about five miles south. The wreck and the treasure should be about five miles beyond that. At their slow pace and with the necessary rest stops, that meant two more days instead of one. As much as the land itself or the Indians, time had become an enemy.

Blankee's babbling became louder and more incoherent with each mile. "Cut off my legs... that's what you want to do... cut off my legs and build a fire... I know... I seen...." Bull knew the man would never finish the expedition. With his mind gone, the body was sure to follow.

They pushed on well after sundown, hoping to make the spring. The map was accurate and the location easy to find even in the darkness. But the spring was dry. They took turns digging, feverishly, but found nothing but more dry sand. After giving up they made camp, building a fire more out of habit than need. They ate as much food as their parched throats and a quarter cup of water allowed. Blankee refused to eat. He just stared west, out to the sea.

Ford looked too. "All that water...." He dropped his head between his knees.

Johnson threw a piece of driftwood on the fire. It kicked up golden sparks that floated on the air and quickly died. "What do we do now, Mr. Almighty Bull McKenzie?"

"We push on."

"You're gonna' kill us."

"Not if we push on. If we leave before sunup we'll get to the wreck some time after sun down. Rest up. Tomorrow we make time." He scooped out depressions in the sand for his hips and shoulders, tossed down his blanket and was soon asleep. Ford and Johnson did the same. Blankee sat against the rocks, shaking and mumbling nonsense.

Some time later Blankee's shouting awoke the camp. "Water! I found water!"

Bull's eyes opened instantly. Squinting to clear them he could see the Big Dipper, the most reliable clock in the world. The time was about three a.m. Blankee was at the water's edge. He was butt naked and grinning like a fool. He pointed to the sea. "There's good water out there. The farther you go, the better it gets."

"Loco en la cabeza," Ford said.

Johnson stood up and scratched his privates. "What?"

"Crazy in the head."

"Johnson, get that son of a bitch back in camp," Bull said.

Johnson stretched and started walking toward the shore line. Blankee saw him coming and slowly backed into the water.

Ford cupped his hands to his mouth and shouted. "He's nekid, Johnson, watch out he don't try no back door work." His giggling had a sick and silly inflection.

Blankee kept backing up. "Swim out there and dive down about ten feet and you come to clean water, Johnson." He kept backing up till the water was chest high. A wave caught him, he tumbled and then began swimming out to sea.

Ford rushed down to join Johnson. "What the hell is that boy doing?"

"Looks like a suicide, but I don't think he knows it."

Bull stood up and shook the sand from his blanket. The three men watched till Blankee became little more than an indistinct, bobbing form in the water. When he dove again, the last thing they saw was a pair of legs. He didn't resurface.

"Well, we're up. Let's move on." Bull was already saddling his mule. Ford and Johnson followed. They reached the wreck late the following evening. Exhausted, they fell asleep within minutes of making camp.

Sunrise would bring triumph and treasure or despair and possibly death.

Chapter Six

Normally Bull woke up well before sunrise, but his state of thirst and exhaustion had shattered his internal clock. His eyes opened to a glint on the horizon of the sea. A beam of light was shining through a crevice in the mountains to the east. It was a single golden spot, darting about the shallow waves. He thought of Blankee floating somewhere under that vast body of water, his eyes still wide with madness and his mouth open as if still drinking the water that killed him. *That's the only marker that stupid son of a bitch will ever get.* The sun rose and went behind the mountains and the marker faded away.

He looked around. They had camped on a small peninsula. The jagged rocks just beneath the surface would surely crush the hell out of any craft striking them. A small island glistened in the distance, too submerged too much of the time to grow anything more than slime. Although he wasn't a sailor, Bull could tell this was a dangerous place for sailing craft. Perhaps Chandler's faith in the map would pay off.

The sea washed into a small cove that led to a small canyon littered with wood. Driftwood was piled high, but he noticed handmade planks among the rubble.

"Wake up, you bastards! Get the cricks out o' your getalongs. We got work to do." He allowed them a quarter cup each of water from the last can. The hollow sound when he put the lid back on reminded him of a drum at a funeral. It was half-empty. They were in serious trouble. *To hell with it.* Bull led the way into the narrow canyon.

Several driftwood logs lodged in the rocks 30 or so feet above them proved the power of the sea. A treasure ship might, just might wash ashore in such a place.

"There!" Johnson was the first to spot the busted prow of a ship. He rushed up to it and began a furious search. After seeing nothing on the surface, he grabbed a short plank and began scratching in the dirt. "We got it, Mr. McKenzie! We got it!" Ford jumped in with another plank.

Bull walked up and shook his head. *Idiots.* "Look at it, you dumb bastards. It's too damn small."

"But the map!" Ford held the plank as if holding on to a life preserver.

"It's some kinda' row boat or something. It ain't no Spanish treasure ship. We're moving up the canyon. Ford slammed the plank against the fragile remains of the tiny craft. The rotten hull cracked with the muffled thump of rotten wood.

Bull pointed to the sides of the canyon. "Spread out. And look for anything big: planks, beams, anything." They walked on, staggering from thirst and fatigue. They came across hand-hewn wood of all sorts, some of it small, some of it rather large. None of it was hundreds of years old. Bull guessed that they were walking among the graveyard of fishing boats and nothing more. He pushed his crew of good-for-nothings on with faint hope winning over certain knowledge.

They found a small, broken mast, half a rudder, rotten fishing nets and the detritus of fishing craft. Finally they found the end of the canyon, piled high with wood, worn and gray like bones in the desert.

"It's got to be there," Ford said. He started running toward the pile. Johnson followed, more out of desperation than hope. Bull walked slowly and steadily toward their last chance. Within a few steps his hunter's eyes, trained to see the smallest movement or shape from great distances, saw the futility of walking any farther. The treasure ship wasn't there. The rock protruding from the earth showed that it couldn't be buried beneath the sand—too shallow. He sat down and began softly laughing. *New country.* Well, he'd seen it. Now all he had to do was to survive long enough to get back to the old. "I'm gonna' kill Chandler." He didn't mean it, but the banker would surely be paying for several months of evenings in the Armageddon Saloon, evenings with just "the good stuff," the finest Cuban cigars and thick steaks from Bang On's restaurant. He would hit Chandler where it hurt the most: in his money belt.

First they had to find water and then get back to a settlement, any settlement, up north. He sat back and let Ford and Johnson rummage around the ruined ships and ruined dreams for several hours. When they gave up he announced his plan. "The map shows a ranch some 20 miles in. Help might be there. Surely there's water for stock. It's our only chance."

"When do we go?" Ford's voice was as desperate as the look on his face.

"*We* don't. Only one of our mules might make it. One man with all our water cans goes. The other two wait here, probably eatin' mule."

Ford stepped forward. "I'll go!"

"Johnson goes," Bull said.

"Why me?"

"You're tougher'n Ford. You got a chance."

"What's wrong with me?" Ford said. His tone was belligerent and defensive. Bull also noticed a hint of greedy despair.

"Because I don't trust you, Ford. I don't trust you with our one mule. I don't trust you with our supplies. And I damn sure don't trust you with our lives."

Ford placed his hand on his pistol.

Bull had his Colt out, cocked and pointed right between Ford's eyes before the man drew another breath. "Two drink less than three."

Ford lifted both hands, palms up. "Didn't mean nothin.'"

"I did."

Without conversation they loaded the one good mule with all their water cans, splitting the last half can between the traveler and the two who would remain at camp. Nervous ticks in his face and shaking hands showed Johnson's fear of the task ahead.

Bull showed him the map and pointed to a narrow slot just north of the area they had been searching. "Take that canyon through the mountains. They run north and south so it shouldn't take you more'n a day or two. Then you hit open country. The ranch is supposed to be about 20 miles due east. Just follow the sun."

"It moves."

Damnation! "When the sun comes up, pick out some rock or something that way and go to it. And keep going till you come to water."

"What if I don't find any water?"

"Well, it's a lonely way to die, but there's one little bloom on the rose."

"What's that?"

"At least you won't have to die with Ford. Now, git!"

He rode off and was soon in the canyon and out of sight. He had a quarter-can of water to get him through. Bull and Ford had the same amount.

"You didn't have to say that," Ford said.

"Let's make us a camp. We got a lot of waiting to do."

They staked out the mule and began setting up a campsite. They collected more firewood than necessary for the night, but each felt a need to keep busy, to focus on survival. They soaked jerky in salt water for their supper. It was salty and added to their thirst, but it was soft and moist enough for dry mouths and parched throats. Bull augmented his meal with Palo Verde beans. He slept with the water can nearby and his pistol loose in its holster.

The first day passed slowly and without incident. Ford had more faith in Chandler's map than he did his own eyes. He searched the canyon and wasted precious energy on digging out the mast of a tiny sailing ship. But he never found gold or pearls or any indication of an old Spanish galleon. Bull knew from the previous day's exploration that none of the boats was more than 50 or so years old. They had searched for pearls and found a lie.

Ford, worn out and dry, returned to camp. "Nothing!" He shouted to the canyon. He picked up a piece of driftwood and threw it as hard as he could toward the pile of refuse that had been his dream. It fell far short. He slowly pulled out his pistol and was raising it to shoot when Bull spoke. "Just how many Indians do you want to bring down on us, Ford?"

The man holstered his pistol and fell to the ground. "We're dead, ain't we?"

"Speak for yourself." Sunset was a couple of hours away, so Bull gathered some sea water and began soaking more jerky. Ford kept eyeing the water can, but he knew better than to reach for it or even ask for a drink. Bull demanded that they drink once a day and only in the evening after eating. That way they would experience at least a tiny bit of comfort before bedding down. This restriction did practically nothing to stave off dehydration, but it did provide some psychological relief.

"Where do you think he is?" Ford asked.

"He'd better be halfway there."

"Or?"

"Don't think about it. You ain't equipped to handle them kind of thoughts."

Another day passed without incident. A dead fish washed ashore and they squeezed a mouthful each of water from it. They also ate it for supper, forgoing the jerky. Ford was bleeding slightly at the gums, but he still refused to eat any Palo Verde beans. Bull didn't force the issue. It was beginning to look like Blankee wouldn't be the only suicide on the trip. Ford and Johnson had become useless baggage—too heavy to carry and without value.

They napped most of the next day, too tired to do anything other than watch the waves roll in and out and hope for another supper to wash up. They were lucky. An eagle snatched a large fish. Its grip was off or perhaps a gust of wind hit it just right, but the fish dropped to the shore. Ford was up and had it in hand before the eagle could circle back. They got another meal and a couple of swallows of water squeezed from the catch. They ate and crawled into their blankets.

Ford awoke to find Bull tossing bits of driftwood into a small fire. He had a determined look on his face. "Pack the mule with our water cans. Leave everything else here."

"We goin' back? What about Johnson?

"We'll follow his trail. I figure when he finds that ranch he'll send riders out for us. We'll meet 'em halfway."

"Think we can find him?"

"That idjit will leave a trail a city boy could follow. Let's get to it."

They packed all their supplies and gear against the cliff and braced it all with rocks. The only thing packed on the mule was a sack of jerky and their nearly empty water can. He seemed overly burdened even under that light load.

As the sun rose they moved out. They had no need for tracking during the first part of the journey. The canyon allowed only one passage through. Once on the other side Johnson's tracks were easy to pick up in the hard-packed sand.

"Well, at least the fool is headed in the right direction," Bull said.

"What are our chances, you think?"

"I'd say hoverin' mighty close to none at all."

Something seemed to break inside Ford. His drooping shoulders drooped even more and his sigh was a lament. He staggered on behind Bull. Ford's trail zig-zagged, but stayed on course. They traveled well into the night before stopping for a sip of water and a night's fitful sleep. They had chewed cactus pulp all day. It kept their mouths moist and offered a false sense of security.

They pushed on before sunrise. Bull had to kick Ford awake. The man didn't even grumble. *He's a goner... I'm on my own now.* Around midday Johnson's trail began to veer slightly off to the northwest. Bull could see no landmark or feature to cause such a deviation. Johnson must have been getting delirious from the heat or, just as likely, he was being stupid.

They followed the tracks, which sometimes turned in tight circles, for a couple of hours. About midday they found his body face-up under the meager shade of a mesquite tree. His mouth, shirt and hands were covered in dry blood. He'd been dead about a day and was already bloating. The sickly sweet odor gave Ford the dry heaves. The mule, also dead, was nearby. Its throat had been cut. Very little blood had spilled on the land.

Ford fell to the ground next to the animal. "He drank blood. Mule blood."

"A lot of good it did him, the damn fool." He stared at the man, pondering their next move.

Ford made the decision for him. "Maybe that ain't such a bad idea."

Bull turned around. Ford had his large knife in a shaky hand. His eyes were wild as he licked his cracked lips. Had there been any water in his system he would have been drooling. The blade wobbled in the air as if he was holding a great weight at arm's length. "You're a mighty big man, Mr. Bull McKenzie." The implication was clear.

"This is a hell of a place to die, Ford."

"You're gonna' find out." He looked down and reached for his pistol. He was slow and his fingers fumbled on the handle. As he looked back up a bullet from Bull's Colt ripped through his chest.

Johnson dropped his knife and fell to his knees. He cupped some of the blood from his wound in his hand, raised it to his lips and fell forward.

Bull lacked the strength to bury the two men, and the shot might have attracted Indians. He didn't even have time to drag them to a wash and kick dirt over the bodies. He loaded the water cans on the one remaining mule and considered his options. The ranch, if it existed, was at least 15 miles to the east and a big gamble. It would be all over but the rotting if it were not there. He would never make it back to the coast where there were proven springs somewhere to the north. Bull played the odds and started marching back to camp. He only had to travel a short distance, but it would be a long journey.

Chapter Seven

Bull staggered through their camp and fell into the sea. He crawled far enough out to immerse himself up to his neck, remaining in the water until his body temperature cooled down. For the first time since Blankee's strange death he understood the almost overwhelming drive to drink sea water. He washed his face, the salt stinging his eyes and cracked lips, but he refused to drink. Maybe Blankee had been right and out there and ten feet down the water was clean and pure, but he wasn't about to take on such an expedition. He walked back to camp, fell into the sand and slept the rest of the day and all night.

He woke up well after sunrise and chewed more cactus while soaking jerky. His gums were beginning to ache. There being no Palo Verde trees or cactus fruit within sight, scurvy was becoming a serious concern. The discomfort was most likely a false alarm, but it added an extra touch of urgency to his mission."I gotta' get the hell out of here. And now."

But he could barely move. A short walk to cool off in the sea drained him of all energy. He could barely swallow the softened jerky. He rested all day and slept till the sunlight stung his face the next morning.

He would never make it to the next spring without water and lots of it. He had a vision of the future, his body face down in the wet sand being devoured by crabs and coyotes and maybe even other men.

"No way in hell," he croaked.

Bull wasn't a thinker, never had been, but sometimes events force us into unfamiliar territory. He was staring at a small fire when he entered that territory. The rising smoke reminded him of steam and the water that steam often leaves on a metal surface—pure, clean and drinkable water. "Christ almighty! I can make me a still!"

He began collecting rocks to make a fire ring. The effort was exhausting and he had to stop for a rest every minute or so, but he kept at it and soon had completed the ring and stacked up a pile of driftwood. He took a nap.

Half an hour or so later he woke up and continued building his salvation. He sacrificed a water can, punching a hole in the lid. He scrambled through the jumble of their remaining supplies and found the essential element for his still. He thanked whatever god there may be for Chandler's contact in Yuma who had outfitted the expedition. He had included a number of items for which Johnson, Ford and Blankee could see no need. He thanked that god again that the three fools hadn't discarded those elements. One was a length of three-eighths-inch copper tubing.

"That man knew a long horse from a mustang." Bull owed his life to a man he didn't know and had never seen. "If I find that feller, he'll be set for life. That I swear."

He built a fire, placed one of the water cans on it and poured it full of seawater—about a gallon. He placed the lid on and weighted it down with rocks. As the water began to heat he placed the copper tubing just inside the hole in the top and ran it over to another water can. Within about half an hour he had nearly a cup full of water. He drank slowly, allowing the liquid to sooth his agonized mouth and throat. Later, as more pure water formed, he drank faster. He continued drinking all day as it condensed, cup after cup. At one point he felt such joy that he was actually drunk. The mule, too, enjoyed the respite.

That evening he cut up some jerky and cooked it in clean water, pretending he was eating stew. Bull was still worn down to near death. He drank and ate for two days before he felt up to the task of trekking north. *Desert, sea and Indians be damned; I'm going home.*

Back on his reliable internal clock, he was up before sunrise. He packed the filled water cans, the sack of jerky, the makings of his still and his rifle and ammunition on the mule, then set his sights north and moved out at a slow and steady pace. He did not mark the days. Counting the time would be irrelevant in his current physical condition. He would arrive at safety whenever he arrived. He was "thinking Indian," like Prospect. A job takes as long as it takes and this one was going to take a while.

He had the makings of water and his rifle assured him of food along the way. He was confident, tired of the fruitless pursuit and more than ready for a long afternoon and evening at the Armageddon. He shot a jackrabbit just before sundown and ate well. He slept even better, but awakened to a nightmare. His mule was dead.

Day One. Bull had to make hard decisions. The smart move was to rest and sleep by day and travel by night. The sea shore provided a perfect compass pointing all the way north. But a good part of the journey was through rough country, including swamps, where he would have to judge the placement of every step. He had suffered deadly heat and a brutal sun before and once the decision was made, he gave the challenge no more thought.

Bull could carry only a fraction of the mule's load. He fashioned a crude backpack for the still, the jerky and his ammunition. He converted rope and leather thongs into carrying loops for the water cans, then inserted a strong driftwood limb into the loops and hoisted the cans on his back. He looked like a man on a weighted cross. The limb partially rested on the back pack, which helped ease the discomfort. He carried his rifle in his hand. Everything else was left to rust and rot on the beach.

He shot another rabbit at midday, but he didn't stop to eat. He gutted the animal and added it to his driftwood cross. Late in the afternoon he realized the rifle and its ammunition were too heavy to carry any farther. The weight was just too much. With much regret he placed them against the rocks. He moved on and gave the matter no more thought. *What the hell... I'll eat dirt if I have to.*

He traveled slowly, taking long and frequent stops. Still, the days would pass and he would make his way to safety.

Day Two. Indian sign. The beach was littered with footprints. He couldn't tell how many, but there were enough hunters to kill a worn-out and wasted treasure seeker. A crack in the rocks led to a wider path into the low mountain. He scrambled up, always keeping a boulder, a tree or shrub between himself and the beach. No Indians were visible from the crest, but he pushed on as cautious as ever. The hard choice of traveling by day had just saved his life.

After bushwhacking through the rocky terrain for a couple of hours he began a slow and dangerous descent. Fortunately, the grade wasn't steep. Even though he had to slide down some sections, he reached the beach without accident or injury. He made camp, distilled some more water and rested all the next day.

Day Four. He walked along the beach till early afternoon. A small cave caught his attention, really little more than a fracture in the rocks smoothed by wind and tide. Rest and sleep came easily.

Day Five. The beach was wide, flat and easy to follow for several miles. He killed a turtle near the shoreline and, in retrieving it, discovered where it had laid its eggs. He dug into the sand and found nearly two dozen. He ate them on the spot and saved the parent for his evening meal.

With plenty of food and water and no sign of Indians, he rested the next day. Small boils appeared on his upper legs. *Stings? Bites? Scurvy?* The pain was negligible compared to the possible danger. Even a small infection could put him under.

Day Seven. A brief glint of sunshine in the rocks led to a flowing spring and clean water. He filled his empty cans and moved on, keeping the equipment for his still. He moved out quickly. The Indians would know of the spring and might come for water at any time.

Day Eight. Swampland. They had passed this way, and on horseback the mile or so of mud wasn't even an inconvenience. Now it was an obstacle and a threat to life. The muck stretched inland for miles. He would have to slog his way straight on through.

He crossed the mile-wide stretch in several hours. The mud was knee deep in some places and at least ankle deep everywhere else. Each step required careful balance and agonizing movements. Rest was impossible. The best he could do was to stop and bend over, placing his hands on his knees, to catch his breath. He couldn't even take off his cross and risk his supplies and equipment getting stuck in the mud.

A small cluster of trees near some rocks on the other side of the swamp provided shelter. Bull collapsed in the shade. He slept most of the afternoon, went hunting before sundown and used his pistol to bag a couple of pelicans. He distilled more water while cooking the meal and then went back to sleep. He remained at the shelter two days. The boils on his legs became more and more painful, but there were no Palo Verde or fruit bearing plants to be found.

Day Eleven. He came upon an area as beautiful as the swamp had been ugly. It was a peaceful lagoon ringed with weeds and full of wildlife. Nearby was a forest of tall cactus which promised more game and possibly edible fruit. The wind was a problem, blowing constantly at ten miles an hour or so. Here he would rest and recuperate. Before making camp, he scouted the entire lagoon looking for Indian sign, but found nothing. *Good. I need a vacation.*

He planted a number of large cactus spines in the sand. They were about a half-inch each in diameter and made perfect poles for the tarp he made from one of his thin blankets. He secured them as best as possible with long, driftwood logs on each side of the base. He scooped out sand for his shoulder and hip comfort and used the other blanket as a ground cloth. A ring of rocks surrounding a large depression dug into the sand created a fire ring for cooking and warmth. Bull settled in, using a large driftwood log as a back support.

Days Twelve Through Fourteen. Bull just rested. Pelicans weren't very tasty, but they were plentiful and provided breakfast, lunch and dinner. He ate them with a side dish of sand, which blew onto everything in camp. He found some nuts, something like acorns, in the cactus forest. They were edible and after cooking in boiling water proved tasty.

Day Fifteen. Bull thought he saw a sail bobbing up and down on the horizon. He couldn't be sure, but he waved and shouted like a madman. Perhaps it was just an illusion brought on by desperation, fatigue and hope. No rescue sailed toward the shore and he wished he had not seen it. Hope dashed is more deadly in a desperate situation than Indians, killer beasts or poisonous reptiles. Yet he would not allow himself to sink into despair. *Chandler owes me and I will collect... in hide and in damn good whiskey.* It was time to push on.

Day Sixteen. Bull came across an abandoned mine dug into the hill, an excellent place to spend the night. He placed his supplies just inside the entrance and started looking for food. Sundown was less than an hour away.

He came to what appeared to be a large cluster of small brown and yellow rocks about the size of large pecans. They were snails, which he collected and cooked for his supper. He cracked them open with a rock and enjoyed the meat. Boiled weeds augmented the meal. They weren't very tasty, but would probably help stave off or at least slow down the scurvy he feared was coming on. Some blood was beginning to seep from his gums. He was full and satisfied when he dozed off for the evening.

Bull examined the mine at sunrise. He and his group of miscreants had passed it during a night ride on their way in. The bits and pieces of metal were badly rusted and almost dust in some places. The beams were weathered, broken and battered by the elements. The diggings had to be a couple of hundred years old or older—a Spanish treasure mine! A cursory examination showed that the small vein had played out and that the claim was worthless.

Spanish treasure at last. Bull started laughing, and he didn't stop for nearly a quarter of an hour.

Day Seventeen. Nothing. Nothing but trudging one painful step at a time. He made very little progress. Even the strongest man has his limits and Bull McKenzie was concerned that he was about to discover his. The sun was merciless in its heat and worse in its light, which reflected off the water and bright sand. He cut a two-inch wide strip of leather from one of the storage pouches and cut two slits, eye holes, in the center. He tied the mask to his face. He might develop a funny sun tan, but at least he wouldn't go blind.

That afternoon, after nearly fainting, he made camp in another one of the numerous caves that lined the rocky seashore. He finished off his water, but was too exhausted to begin to distil more or to hunt for food. He slept.

Day Eighteen. The first thing the next morning he built a fire and began distilling water. The process took all day and a good part of the evening to get enough water for all the cans. He hunted, but was again limited to a diet of pelican. A sail appeared on the horizon and disappeared behind a wave. Or was it just another illusion? Bull didn't care anymore. If he had to walk all the way to Privy, so be it.

He rested another full day before heading out.

Day Twenty. A long day. He kept pushing himself all day. His hunter's sixth sense signaled hope. *This just might be the day.* A few hours later he looked up and saw a camp about half a mile away. Several tarps were up and rough wooden tables had been constructed beneath them. Bull stretched, dropped his cross and walked till he entered the shade of a canvas tarp. No one was present, but the camp was a work station. He would not be alone for long.

The tables were made for drying fish and there must have been a thousand or more. The smell was overwhelming, but delightful. It meant food, water and salvation. The camp was loaded with supplies. He drank water, rested and then fried bacon and made flapjacks. He drank more water and sat in the shade to wait for the fishermen to return.

Their sail appeared about an hour before sunset. They were Mexicans and Mexican/Indians. They didn't see him until beaching their crude boat. One of the men grabbed a machete and approached. The two men stared at each other, but neither showed fear or anger.

"Habla ingles?" Bull asked.

"Un poquito, Señor."

"I'm Bull McKenzie."

The Mexican simply stared, uncomprehending and unimpressed. *Made one hell of an impression, I did.* "Can you help... ayuda... me? Ayuda, por favor."

"Si. Si." He jammed the machete into the sand and motioned for the others to join them. They did, but slowly. Bull kept his pistol on, but made no moves or gestures toward it.

The leader pointed to his own chest. "Tomas."

Bull copied the gesture. "Bull McKenzie. Bull."

"Si! Un café, Amigo?"

"Yes. That would be great."

"Que... uh... what?"

"Bueno. Muchas gracias, Tomas."

The arrival of a stranger who appeared to be no threat was cause for something of a minor celebration. They ate well, there was a bit of singing and they even brought out a small jar of wine. Between his meager Spanish and their equally meager English Bull was able to pretty well tell his story. They marveled at such a tale of survival. Another jar of wine appeared and the singing went on into the night.

The men fished for another three days. Bull stayed in camp and recuperated. The fishermen were pleased that a powerful man was guarding their catch and supplies. They had been robbed of everything several times in the past few years. Through concealment, patience and an animal that moved in too close, Bull brought down a small deer with his pistol. He dressed it and had a fine meal cooking when the Mexicans returned.

The next day they took him to a small town several miles to the north. Bull left them all that he could: his pistol and small pouch of ammunition, the water cans, and directions to his rifle and ammunition down the coast. They could easily find the weapon if the Indians hadn't gotten to it first. His rescuers were singing as they sailed away.

He had seen telegraph wires and was already preparing an amazingly short, amazingly blistering message to Chandler as he walked into the small village. A shadow cast by a soaring bird flickered over him. He looked up to see a lone eagle on the hunt and flying into the unknown. He had a sudden and unexpected thought: "Caldera."

Chapter Eight

Caldera dragged the bodies from the cave after removing their gun belts and knives. He could handle Aracha with one arm, but Bannister's stinking bulk required all his strength. Two trips were required to dump the bodies into a narrow ravine several hundred yards from the cave. "Coyotes gotta' eat." *And bugs and worms.* Bannister had mentioned a pit, but Caldera didn't have a lot of time and he didn't intend to waste it looking for a hole full of rotting flesh somewhere out in the desert.

He checked on the horses and they were well tended. He watered and fed both animals before bringing them back to the mouth of the cave. With no posted guard, horses left alone in the night would most likely become Apache property before dawn. He and the woman would have to take turns keeping watch. They had no other choice. Caldera didn't like the situation, but his options were limited. His battered body needed food, water and a day or so of rest. He also needed information and that brought his mind back to the woman.

He'd given her no real thought after leaving the cave and was prepared to leave her to her fate and move on. Some miner, rancher, outlaw or Indian would find her soon enough—her or her body. The coldness that men and women of late had seen in his eyes had flushed throughout his mind, body and what was left of his spirit. He was a man on a vengeance trail, death and self-destruction. He was focused, without emotion, and he was quite mad.

When he returned the woman was kicking dust over the blood stains on the floor. "Deanna?"

"Yes."

"Can you fix up some beans and bacon or something?"

"What are your intentions toward me?"

"I intend to eat. Cook for two if you want."

He tended his wounds as best he could. Cheap whiskey makes for a powerful, yet painful antiseptic. Strips of cloth from the blankets hanging across the room were sufficient for bandages. Deanna soon brought a plate of beans, bacon and even some tortillas. She offered to make coffee, but he chose a bottle of tequila from one of the shelves. She ate standing up with the bar between them.

"Again, Sir. What are your intentions?"

"I ain't gonna' ravage you, if that's what you're talkin' about." She nodded, but remained tense. She ate heartily, but in tiny bites like a rabbit. He couldn't tell whether she was well-bread or just scared out of her mind. A little bit of both, probably.

"Why'd you hit me in the head?" he said.

"Bannister." She actually shuddered when she spoke his name. Memories foul and frightening registered on her face.

Caldera didn't really give a damn, but he needed information. He had to keep her talking and establish some trust or at least reduce her level of fear. "Did you use that frying pan to bang me on the head?" He forced a weak smile to show he bore no ill will.

"You and others. Where shall I go?"

"Good question. You know anybody in these parts?"

"I'm from California. Sir, if you have any decency within you, you cannot leave me here."

The battle for survival, the food, and most of all the tequila were taking hold of Caldera. He took a large swallow of the thick liquor and then wanted nothing more than a bit of rest. He stood up and walked to the blankets that formed Bannister's sleeping area. Deanna backed against the wall. Her eyes showed a desire for the stone to wrap itself around her, envelop and protect her.

"You keep watch for a couple of hours. Come get me if you hear anything out there. And be quiet about it."

She nodded. Her arms were close to her sides, defensively held as if she were expecting to be grabbed or beaten. Instead Caldera grabbed Aracha's gun belt and handed it to her. "This works a lot better'n a fry pan."

She took the weapon from its holster. He could tell she'd never held one before. "If anybody comes through that door point the barrel, pull back the hammer and pull the trigger."

"Hammer?"

Caldera let out a breath of air. He was really tired. "Just scream and throw the damn thing."

Again she nodded, holding the pistol butt up as if it were a hammer.

"And you be thinking about Malon. Help me find him and I'll get you out of here." He stepped through the blanket wall and in less than a minute he was sacked out on the rough wooden box that passed for Bannister's bed. Some of the dirty blankets were spotted with blood. He soon closed his eyes and fell into a deep sleep.

The events of the past months had transformed Deanna Corley. In California and during her many trips to the civilized parts of the nation she had been haughty, spoiled, and reckless with her own life as well as the lives of those around her. Brought up by a widowed father who molded her into an empty vessel, men in later years would have labeled her a "rich bitch." She lived the part well. Many men had enjoyed her company, none of them her body, her respect or her long-term interest. Lives were shattered in her honor and a duel had been fought over her on an island off Galveston Bay. One man died. The other survived, but with his once-handsome face shattered. Deanna never bothered herself with a hospital visit.

A letter from San Francisco shattered her world as surely as her indifference had ruined that young man's face and future. Her father's business had undergone a number of severe reversals. Loans had been called. Contracts had been lost and in the midst of the crisis the old man had collapsed. An accompanying letter from her father's legal firm spelled out the tragic details. The business as well as her father's mind was shattered. The old aunt with whom she had been traveling, a poor and distant relation dragged in to act as chaperone, refused to travel west. Deanna, boldly and with complete disdain for the increasing severity of the warnings along the line, continued her solo trip to whatever remained of her home and life.

A telegram delivered in West Texas brought news of her father's death. All of his remaining assets had been seized to pay for the burial. She continued on. The practical and fearful side of her knew that regardless of the depth of her grief she'd soon need someone to take her father's place in her life. San Francisco was a rich town full of rich, handsome men and she could build a new life. Someone would take care of her.

She arranged passage to California with a small band of immigrants looking for the promised land, but all her plans turned to prairie dust when a group of men from Malon's gang raided the party. The haughty young woman had since been robbed of what little funds and jewelry she'd been carrying. She had been kidnapped, raped and forced into slavery in a hellhole of a cave in Arizona.

For a moment she considered using Aracha's pistol on herself, but that act required a level of courage or fear she did not possess. When a snore or a grunt from behind the blankets caused her to jump, things changed. The young man, Caldera, could survive the hellhole. He must have strength and courage. He had killed two killers at a moment when the killers had every advantage. He was smart and resourceful. More than that, and unlike any of the few men she'd encountered in the past month, he hadn't given her orders, beat or taken her.

And then there was the gold. He had mentioned gold. Caldera was rich, or could be. She needn't travel to San Francisco after all. She allowed him to sleep throughout the night and when he awoke she fixed him a hearty breakfast.

Caldera rested there for three days. Deanna nursed him and was at his side virtually every moment. Her presence annoyed him, but like a dependent pet she was always there. She generally spoke only when spoken to and was mindful of his every need. Eventually he turned her attentions to his advantage. She had seen several of Malon's gang and could provide accurate physical descriptions. She knew their habits, manner of speaking and, sadly, details of a more intimate nature. Caldera, caring only for his mission, dragged out the information. Bit by painful bit he drained her of knowledge. Often she broke down and began weeping, but he kept probing until he knew all that she knew. Because of his knowledge of the desert and the men who lived there, he actually knew much more.

Always Deanna turned the conversation back to the same subject. "What is to become of me?" The answer had become Caldera's problem. She begged to come with him, an impossibility. "I'll cook for you, tend the horses, take care of you when you're hurt."

"Stop."

"If you want you can—"

"I said stop."

"You can't leave me to these people!" She broke down again and buried her head in her hands. When she looked back up he recognized something in her eyes. It was the same desperate, hollow look he'd seen in the eyes of Alice Chacon. She too was a woman who had seen a vision of her fate. Fear and even panic was there, but worse was the look of sad resolution.

"I'll take you to someone who will care for you," he said.

"You—"

"No to whatever the hell you're gonna' say."

He stood up and began packing his saddlebags. "Grab your things."

She had nothing other than the tattered clothing on her back, so she rolled up a couple of blankets and threw some food into a sack and she was ready.

"Bannister! Ho!"

The ragged voice was followed by the sound of footsteps moving toward the cave's entrance. "Open me a bottle, you old son of a bitch!"

Deanna cringed and stepped behind Caldera. She knew the voice.

"Bannister! You in there?"

Caldera whispered, "One of Malon's men?"

Her voice was a weak gasp. "Shaw."

"Come on in!" he shouted.

The footsteps halted. "Who the hell's that?"

"The man with the whiskey. The girl's still here, too. C'mon up."

They heard a faint laugh and the footsteps continued. The man entering the cave was small and he walked with the swagger that sometimes accompanies small men. He was well-armed. He was also careless. "Don't know which I want first."

Caldera pulled his pistol and fired a shot into the man's chest. Shaw flew backwards. Another shell struck him in the stomach as he hit the ground. Caldera put one more through his skull just to make certain. He holstered his pistol and fingered the chain around his waist. "You sure he's one of Malon's men?"

She clutched at his back, keeping him between her and the dead man. That was all the answer Caldera needed. He shook her off, crossed the room and began to pull off the man's clothes. Deanna backed up farther, not knowing what kind of sickness she'd now be forced to endure.

"These ought to fit you."

"I can't."

"You can't ride through the desert in a dress is what you can't. Put 'em on." He tossed the pants, shirt, vest and boots at her feet. She stepped behind the blankets. A moment later he heard the sound of ripping cloth. When she stepped out she wore everything except the shirt which had been replaced with the top of her dress. "The blood... it—"

"Let's move."

Moments later they were on the trail and headed north.

Chapter Nine

They traveled carefully and but directly. He took no chances, but he also knew they would find more safety in speed than in too hefty a reliance on stealth. Luck was the best defense against the Apache. Beside, he needed to dump the woman.

"Where are we going?" she asked.

"Settlement." He waited for the inevitable question.

"And what is to happen to me?"

"There'll be folks there I can leave you with."

Anger. "No!"

"There or here. Your choice."

Fear. "You can't."

He turned back, his face blank and his eyes an open portal into the madness within. She recoiled, perhaps from the sudden movement, perhaps from the glimpse into his soul. She shut up and they continued in silence.

They were two days into the journey and he was considering just riding off and leaving the pest to whatever fate had in store for her. She had attached herself to him like a human tick that just wouldn't let go, but his obsession with Malon left no time for babysitting.

"Smoke," she said.

Damn it. The woman's made me careless. Smoke was coming from just over the next rise. *Hell, I should have smelled it earlier. Damn her.*

The Apaches, perhaps the world's greatest masters of concealment, appeared to arise right out of the earth. It was if the blowing sand had gathered itself and formed human beings—angry human beings.

Caldera had heard of such things. Years earlier a captured Apache named Bylas bet an Army colonel that he could enter a field surrounded by U.S. troopers and make his escape, and he would do it in broad daylight. The colonel, some buffoon from New Jersey who might have been a brilliant tactician in the swamps, got a painful lesson in desert humility that day. The colonel selected a large expanse of flat desert south of Privy. He posted armed troopers every ten yards around a large perimeter. A sergeant with some experience in the territory practically begged his colonel not to allow the escape of a valuable chief. The colonel laughed. He then sat down in a comfortable folding chair, lit a cigar and prepared to enjoy the show. Bylas walked calmly into the center of the human enclosure and disappeared.

The colonel dropped his cigar. He shouted orders for his troopers to close in on the center of the field, arms at the ready. Many of the soldiers in that field would meet Bylas later, but no one saw him again that day. The soldiers were ordered to form a search party. As they scattered the colonel muttered, "Magic."

His sergeant replied, "Apache."

The Indians facing Caldera and Deanna Corley weren't there to perform magic shows. Banker Chandler would say, "They have arrived to conduct the most serious of all business."

Deanna issued a terrified screech. "Shoot me!"

Within the first seconds of the Indians' appearance Caldera had calculated the odds, figured his options, and come up with a plan. He was outgunned ten to one. His options were to die with a fire built on his gutted belly or some worse torture—or he could die in a fight. Deanna could be raped, tortured, and enslaved or he could blow her brains out. His pistol was already in his hand and the hammer pulled back when the first blow struck his head. Many other blows followed before he surrendered to the darkness. *What the hell*, he thought. *It's like going home.*

He looked at one of his killers and slurred out a curse, the Pima word for dung. "Biht!" His last sight was of a warclub raised above his head. His last sensation was a hand on his shoulder.

Darkness gave way to a dark awareness. He was alive. Caldera held his breath, pretending to be dead. Grim chuckles nearby proved the folly of his effort. They were watching, but at least they weren't killing. He took stock of the situation. He wasn't being tortured, a plus unless they were just saving him for later. Before he attempted to look around he used his other senses. A fire crackled and the smell of cooked meat floated on the air. There was another, vaguely familiar smell. A nose caked with dried blood blocked any further identification. The nearby whimpering proved Deanna was at least alive and not being used by their captors, at least for the moment. Even in the most desperate situations the unexpected reality of life after one has given oneself over to death is a shock. It breeds hope.

Caldera opened his eyes. Pain. His face was swollen, bruised and bloodied. A swift series of subtle movements throughout his body revealed soreness, but no broken bones. The images he could make out were blurry, like looking at distortions through a poorly made piece of glass. Deanna appeared unhurt. Her face wasn't cut or scratched. She wasn't bound and her clothing was dusty, but intact. It hadn't been ripped from her body. *Curious....*

An animated conversation was taking place. He had no doubt that the subject was when, where, and how slowly to rip the prisoners to pieces. Apaches were believers in true democracy. Leaders led, but any man with courage, some leadership ability, maybe a record of thievery, and a good idea could become a leader. They debated in the Apache way. They spoke in quiet tones as if they didn't even want the grasses or scrub brush to carry their words. A man had his say without interruption. Every man spoke. The argument could take some time, and time was what he needed. Somehow there must be an escape. Perhaps he could take a few seconds to slit Deanna's throat or grab a gun and fire a shot into her heart before he fled into the darkness. She was a pest, but considering her likely fate, it was the best he could do for her.

The talking stopped. A figure approached and squatted down beside him. The Indian took a bite off something and chewed on it a moment. That's when he recognized the other familiar smell: tobacco. A moment later the Indian started filling the cuts on Caldera's face and head with the smelly stuff.

"White med-cine," said the man.

Caldera looked up. The Apache was close enough to identify. The square face, the angular knife slash of a mouth, and the eyes reflecting an inner darkness matched by his own could belong to only one man. "Hello, Jerome."

"Buenas noches, Caldera." He stood up and walked away.

The young Anglo closed his eyes. At least for the night he could sleep.

They remained with the Apache party another day and a night. Caldera studied what he could of this incredible and deadly race for he suspected he'd face them again.

Jerome, never smiling, seemed to be the agreed-upon leader, at least of this group for this time. Clearly he was the reason for their lives being spared. Life must be repayment for Caldera's rescue of the man back in the Superstitions. Jerome checked his ward carefully several times a day and seemed pleased with the recovery. Caldera still hurt like hell, but he agreed with Jerome's occasional nods of satisfaction. He would mend quickly.

Deanna joined him the moment she saw he was conscious. The tick was back. "Thank Providence you are unharmed, Caldera."

"I been through worse."

"Savages!"

"I wouldn't provoke 'em." He wanted to nourish the seed of rescue. "We're a long way from getting you to safety."

"How can we make our escape? What must I do?"

"You 'must do' nothing. If we get out of here alive it'll be 'cause they say so."

"The dower one seems to have some affection for you," she said.

He didn't know what dower meant, but he understood her message. "Saved his life once."

"An Apache?"

Several of the braves recognized the word and looked up. They were not pleased with the tone of her voice. Jerome shook his head ever so slightly and the group went back to its gambling.

Caldera seethed. "That man is the only reason you ain't butt nekid and staked to the ground with your privates burnt off!"

She turned white. Her voice was a choked whisper. "Will they let us go?"

"Maybe, but there ain't no guarantees, so you mind your damn manners 'round these boys."

"I will, but—"

He shook his head. "*Shut... up.*"

She bowed her head and remained silent. A number of the Apaches grinned, apparently with approval of his command over the woman. Caldera studied them as best he could without staring. Clearly they loved gambling. Several pieces of clothing, some ornaments, and even a gold watch, for which they had absolutely no use, changed hands several times. Tempers exploded periodically, but not for long and no one seemed to mind losing. Upon reflection that made a strange sort of sense. They lived in small bands. What a man lost today would always be available in his neighbor's wickiup and could be won back tomorrow. The last hand dealt in Privy's gambling rooms was often holding a gun or knife. He was surprised that they played cards. Somehow he had never featured Indians, any Indians, playing a game so identified with white culture.

Another fact of Apache life that surprised him was their love of swimming. They came to a small river with muddy, running water. A couple of scouts were sent out to survey the landscape while the rest made a day camp. When they returned and the braves were certain no enemies were about, they all stripped and jumped in. The sight of tough, experienced warriors playing like young children in the water was astounding.

Deanna turned her head and refused to look upon their male nakedness, but she stayed close to Caldera. She always stayed close to Caldera.

Whatever mission these men were on had been interrupted by the arrival of Caldera and Deanna Corley. Caldera guessed they were a raiding party heading away from some posse or a raggedy ass army patrol. Provided they let him go he really didn't give a damn. He had to be about the Devil's work and he had the feeling Satan was not a forgiving task master. The more he dawdled with the Indians and this woman, the more scattered Malon's gang would become.

The Apaches, all but Jerome, disappeared into the night the moment darkness made seeing difficult. They were silent and serious and headed for deadly work. Some ranch or mining operation or Mexican village would be short a few steady hands when they attacked in the morning.

Jerome came to him one last time. "Caldera," he said patting him on the shoulder. He almost smiled. Caldera wondered whether he had the ability.

"Jefe," Caldera said, the Mexican term for chief.

Jerome looked puzzled and then shook his head. "No." He paused, looking for the right word in three languages. He pointed to himself. "No jefe. Hombre. Med-cine.'"

"Medicine man."

"Si."

"Well I'll be damned." He reached out and took the Indian's hand. The man recognized the gestured and they shook. "Amigo."

Jerome said nothing. He stood up, mounted up and rode away.

Caldera's voice was low and flat. "I don't like the sound'a that."

Deanna, as always nearby, said, "Whatever do you mean?"

"He didn't call me friend back."

"That is significant?"

"Yeah. Next time we meet we might have to kill each other."

"Perhaps you'll never meet."

"It ain't like that out here. Get some rest. We ride before sunup."

He doused the fire. The Apaches were unlikely to attack at night, but they were great thieves in the darkness. Sometime soon the whole area would be up in arms and he didn't want to attract attention from anyone. He checked the horses. Nothing, not even his weapons, had been taken. They had a chance, and with his knowledge of the desert it was a good one.

"Will you leave me?" she asked.

"Not if you shut up."

She was quieter than usual as they headed out into the grey light of early morning. Eventually enough sunlight crept over the ridges for her to see that they were on a trail parallel to the river. The sun was to her right, so they were headed north, away from Mexico. That was good. She'd heard enough on her stage ride west about the generations of hatred between the Mexicans and the Apaches.

The bloodshed was a main topic of nervous conversation. Caldera couldn't be sure about the direction Jerome and his warriors had taken, but he had a good notion. They were across the border and raising hell. Deanna wasn't relieved. The more distance between her, her man and that inevitable bloodshed the better.

Had Caldera known that she thought of him as "her man," he might have blown her head off right there. Considering his state of mind, he might have even staked her out.

Luck was with him. Two days later they came across a small camp. Caldera actually grinned. He was about to lose a burden and Lee Isaac was about to gain another wife.

Chapter Ten

The growing population of Punkin had followed the trend and changed its name to Pumkinville. "No Brains" Monaghan was outraged. "I started this damn 'town' and I damn sure ain't gonna' let you change the name I give it!"

The good folks ignored the old coot, painted up a board, stuck it on a tree and that was that. And image-conscious, proper Pumkinville soon had another name, Phoenix. Monaghan got drunk for a week and then took a job as a guard at one of Bull's silver mines, swearing he'd never return unless it was with dynamite and a lighted fart.

Privy had changed a lot too. A half-dozen pair or so of well-worn overalls hanging from the cottonwood outside of town told the whole story. No doubt about it, Privy was growing up. More than that, the old desert whore was getting downright civilized. The Apache wars would rage nearly another two decades. Cochise, Victorio, Nana, and worst of all, Geronimo, still ruled much of the land outside the small outposts of terrified white encroachment. Gangs such as the Malon bunch or Gayle McCracken's thugs roamed vast areas unchecked. The government was taking its time sending in the army, and the law was afraid, bought and paid for, outgunned and outmanned, or just nonexistent. But the news wasn't all bad. Troopers were filtering back in and some communities were taking the law to the lawless. Forts and camps were being established. Towns were coming back as settlers moved in to take advantage of the significant increase in mining operations, ranches, and the businesses that supplied them. Some soldiers at Fort McDowell were even experimenting with the ancient irrigation canals and were returning barren fields into productive farm land.

New gold and silver discoveries were being made on what seemed to be a daily basis.

Privy even had a town council and a small police force. Bull McKenzie volunteered for the position of sheriff before any other names could be submitted. He was unanimously and, for some, grudgingly elected. The salary was at best moderate, but as an incentive to promote law and order, he established a fee system. Considering the level of drunkenness, meanness, and hostility in and around the small town, a one dollar per arrest fee brought in a considerable monthly income. Bull's first act was to hire on the town's first constable. Backhand Benny knew saloons, cards and con games. He also knew Privy and he had turned out to be a reliable ranch hand. He received a tiny salary, but earned 35 cents of every dollar on arrest fees. Considering that cowboys in the area were earning no better than $20 a month and miners earned about $3 a day, the young man was stepping up in the financial world.

Things were busting out and booming all over, and that was just fine with the new sheriff. Increasing the size and value of his kingdom kept his mind off the annoyances that buzzed like angry bees around his life.

Annoyance number one was Belle. The town no longer shook with laughter at their bellowing, bouncing love making. Like the town that had made her, the old madam took on the trappings of civilization. She didn't give up her brothels. She was far too savvy a businesswoman for that kind of nonsense. Besides, whoring out West, handled properly and provided the appropriate taxes were paid, was still a semi-respectable profession. Belle wanted more than respectability. She wanted to be the queen of heaven.

She built a large, elegant home, grand by Privy standards, and stocked it with the finest of everything. She even brought in an educated Negro named Charlie Jefferson from San Francisco. He was to run the house in a civilized and cultured manner. She told everyone his name was Hephaestus, a proud name befitting her new major domo. She decked him out in a series of military style uniforms, which he wore with dignity and more than a little hidden embarrassment. Naturally, the good people of Privy called him Major Festus. Charlie didn't care what they called him. He had a good job, good pay, three squares, a roof and a boss who'd believe any damn thing he told her. And he told her a lot. She wanted to know everything the cultured people of San Francisco were doing, thinking, saying and buying. Major Festus was more than happy to provide the information. Every moment sitting on his butt making up stories was a moment away from his long list of chores.

Bull was one of the richest men in the state, but he never went in for fancy living. All he cared for was getting what he wanted when he wanted it. He didn't really mind the constant expenses—a lot of the money was hers anyway—but he hated people putting on airs, and Belle was moving right up into the thin stuff way up the mountain.

The overalls on the tree finally caused their split.

"A madam of a whorehouse wants Indians to wear button-up britches?"

Major Festus was in the house, so Belle tried not to let her anger rule. She tried to not be herself. Her response was low and frighteningly controlled. "They come into town butt naked with their peacemakers hanging out."

"Hanging peacemakers is how you make your money."

"They're Indians! Their privates ain't for decent folks to see."

"Decent folks? In Privy?"

"The town's growing up. That's why we hung up them britches. Somebody's got to make 'em wear the damn things."

"That's growing up?"

"The word, Bull McKenzie, is progress."

"The word is cow flop."

She eyed him coldly. *"Bull... flop."*

Belle often compared Bull to the smelly byproduct of the animal for which he was nicknamed. He should have been used to it, but standing in her fancy, gussied up home, which was gaudier by far than most fancy bordellos, he exploded. They argued about putting on airs, about finances and about Major Festus. They fought about each other, and somewhere in the fourth or fifth round they both realized they'd had enough.

"I'm going to San Francisco," announced Belle.

"You've been listening to them fancy stories from your fancy house boy, ain't you?"

"Get out!"

Bull left on one of his great hunting trips, and when he returned a few weeks later Belle was gone. She left without knowing of her final victory. The good people of Privy kept the overalls hanging from the tree.

For Bull, Caldera had become something more than an annoyance. *What the hell could you say about a fun-loving kid who grows up to gun down his wife and unborn child? What could you say?* Bull said nothing and the people of Privy knew better than to bring up the subject. Still, in the early hours Bull wondered how the hell things had gotten so fouled up. All he'd done was spill a little buttermilk into a little whore decades earlier. He'd never wanted a family and never considered he'd ever have one. He'd fallen victim to the "what if" game and there's no way any man wins that contest.

It never occurred to him that his three chief annoyances were the three people closest to him. Perhaps Prospect had become the greatest annoyance of all. He was the only man alive Bull could call brother. They had fought Apaches, bandits, drought, economics, and the West in general, but they had never fought each other. They didn't fight now. They just... didn't. Things went on pretty much as before except they kept contact with each other to a minimum, mostly accidental meetings in Privy. They never spoke. Each knew they'd someday have to kill the other. Bull would kill in the name of property rights to his son's destiny, and Prospect would kill for the right to kill a man he loved like a son. Caldera's penance would be paid someday, and someday his madness would be burnt away. Caldera would return, and more blood would stain a once pristine desert.

Prospect stepped from Bang Ong's restaurant into the dusty street. He'd just dropped of a sack of ripe saguaro fruit. The Pimas had taught Bang how to boil the egg-size pods down to a thick, red, sweet syrup. He and Mary Beth did amazing things with that syrup and some ranch hands and miners had been known to forego the pleasures of whiskey and women for a taste of their desserts. Tattoo, always a hard worker, earned a lot of extra money collecting the pods during the growing season. She and the other women of the village were out now gathering more pods. Prospect's thoughts were interrupted by a shout from down the street.

"Prospect! Prospect, you old sumbitch!"

Backhand Benny jogged across the street, stepping into a large pile of horse manure on the way. He was carrying a small wrapped package. He moved with a purpose that belied his friendly manner.

"Constable Ben."

"Prospect."

"I have heard many people say the law in this community stinks."

"Huh?"

"Till now I have withheld my opinion."

"Huh? Oh." Benny grinned and tried to remove some of the manure from his boots by scraping them in the dust. "I just love to hear you talk, Prospect. Got something for you."

"May I have it?"

"Oh, sure." He handed over the package. It was a small wooden box, wrapped tight for mailing. "I was wondering if maybe it was some word about Caldera."

"I would not know, Ben."

"Well, why don't you open it? Then I'll buy you a drink at the Armageddon."

A smile crossed Prospect's face. Backhand Benny was as obvious as hell, but he was willing to pay the price for being nosy. *What the hell?* Staying in good graces with the law was smart policy for an Indian. Besides, Indians weren't very welcome at the Armageddon anymore. He liked the idea of having a city official buying him a drink there. "Thank you, Ben. I will open it there."

Prospect made a point of walking in first just so he could see the anger rise on the bartender's face. That was almost as good as watching it fall when he recognized the constable. They each got a mug of beer and then moved to a table in the back of the room.

"I wonder why it was sent to the police," said Prospect.

"Oh, it wasn't. Came addressed to you through the bank. Chandler dropped it on me and I'm dropping it on you."

Prospect tore away the wrapping and opened the box. Both men stared at the odd contents before Backhand Benny spoke. "Damnation. Read the letter. Maybe that makes some sense of it all."

The Indian handed the letter to the constable. "I speak them, but I do not read the words."

Benny unfolded the paper. "It's from some fella' named Isaac down Calabesas way. He says a man named Caldera wanted him to mail them things to you." He looked back in the box. "It's from Caldera. Do you think it means he's still alive?"

"Oh, he is alive Ben."

Benny grinned.

Prospect dumped the contents onto the table.

"What the hell's it mean, Prospect?"

"A day—what you call a day of reckoning—is getting closer."

Both men looked at the table. Three links from the chain worn by Caldera formed a triangle.

Prospect touched one of the links.

"You really think he's still out there?" said Benny.

"And living with a vengeance."

Chapter Eleven

And that's how the lost years of Caldera continued, with an unceasing vengeance. These were the years of lurid newspaper stories, small references to mysterious disappearances and strange occurrences, and campfire tales that would become an obscure Western legend. Caldera embraced his madness, and his madness drove him on. His tormented mind clawed and ripped at the awareness of his guilt, and he could find release only in an absolute, unrelenting focus on his dark goal.

Patterns emerged from bits and pieces of conversation in saloons, whorehouses and stables. Trails and pathways too challenging for an Apache scout became turnpikes for Caldera, clearly marked and easy to follow. A word here, a bit of information there, or a casual remark was enough to send him across the territory. North, south, east, and west were just one direction, always pointing to the final moments of some outlaw's miserable life.

For dedicated writers, such as academic historians or even Robert Quiller, the clues to these lost years were parts of a fascinating and never-to-be-complete puzzle. Only a few toiled on, trying to connect the pieces to make a whole. Quiller led the pack. To refocus his mind, he reviewed some of the more important notes and clippings in his notebook. The first one was from The Privy Portal, dated January 16, 1872:

MASS EXECUTION
Four Slavers Slain!
DE YOUNG SISTERS FOUND, RESCUED,
RETURNED TO CIVILIZATION
A Full Account From Our Territorial Correspondent
From Calabesas, Arizona Territory

Through the courtesies of noted rancher and Indian fighter, banker and pioneer Stewart Chandler we have been provided the following information.

Evelyn DeYoung, 18 years, and Laurel De Young, 16, who have been missing and presumed dead for a fortnight were rescued this week by a posse organized and ably led by "Banker Chandler," as he is known.

Capt. Ramsey, late of the Army of the Confederacy and now a respected member of the Calabesas community, in a special correspondence to this newspaper reports that both young women are in excellent health and mental well being. He emphasizes that neither was harmed physically during their terrible ordeal.

This is as remarkable as it is welcome. Often the fate of young women in similar circumstances is to be sent as chattel far into Mexico. We need not dwell on the details of such servitude in these pages as such fates are well documented and greatly lamented.

None of the heroic men in the posse were harmed during the search and, as all of the perpetrators of this heinous act have been accounted for, the posse has been disbanded.

The next clipping was marked *Exclusive News via the Electric Telegraph:*

The Electric Telegraph at Tucson communicates the following important and interesting intelligence about the fate of two sheep feared lost and now so boldly returned to the fold.

Both De Young sisters were found huddled in an abandoned stage stop north of Calabesas. The brave and noble women had been provided with food, water and some semblance of shelter. Precise details and an accurate chronology of their rescue await further correspondence, but the following information is reliably reported.

Malon Strikes Again! Strikes Terror!

That the miscreant Malon and his crew of despoilers were responsible for the kidnapping is no longer a matter of knowing speculation. Four men perpetrated the crime and four have paid a most grievous price. Each was shot through the heart, two with a back-to-front trajectory and two receiving their death slugs while facing their judge, jury and executioner. Names of the deceased are not at this time known, but they were recognized by many in Chandler's posse as members of Malon's gang.

Sadly, Malon was not among those receiving the final summons.

During the grey hours before dawn Sunday someone or some ones unknown crept into the miserable camp where these two poor creatures were being held prisoner. The hero or heroes of the hour rushed the camp and with cool head and cold precision dispatched the evil doers with a minimum investment of time, lead and powder.

Miss Evelyn De Young reports, "I saw only one man. He spoke very little, inquiring only as to our health. He deposited some provisions and disappeared before we could proffer our gratitude."

A strange bit of business is associated with this rescue. Additional correspondence, not yet verified by this publication, provides the intelligence that clutched within the fist of each of the deceased was a single link of chain. The purpose of such a marker, for a marker it surely is, remains unknown.

Whether the mysterious rescuer is a legitimate hero, merely a dissatisfied member of the gang, or an unheralded member of Mr. Chandler's posse remains an open question

Quiller shook his head, then turned a page in the notebook and found an extract from a letter from J.E. Roberson, the general manager of the Bullhide Mine, Mule Mountains, Arizona Territory. The letter was dated March 25, 1875:

Although Paine and George obviously had some experience at this type of work, both performed at a level just proficient enough to maintain employment. They will not be missed.

The bodies were found at the 1200 foot level in shaft 13 (ironic that) just beyond the final turn. As you will remember from my report of June last, that section pinched out at approximately 275 yards in and has been abandoned since. It was assumed that, as with many here, the men had merely left the mine for opportunities elsewhere.

I believe the lateness in discovery of the bodies can be attributed to (1) distance from existing operations and (2) cool temperatures which, for a time, impeded decomposition and the resulting odor which led to the discovery.

Both men had been executed, and I do not use that term lightly, Sir. Their hands were bound behind their backs and their throats had been sliced from ear to ear. On a personal note, I have never seen anyone dispatched in such a brutal fashion.

No perpetrators have been located and it is unlikely that any guilty parties will be found. There were no clues that would aid an investigation, although I am certain that the authorities will eventually get around to that task. They are welcome to it.

One young man, one of our many John Smiths, left shortly after the disappearance of Paine and George and is considered a possible suspect in the killings although I do not personally believe he is involved. His description was given to the proper authorities. He was intense and kept to himself, but he had proven to be very capable and was someone who took to working in the depths better than most.

On a personal note, I believe Paine and George were men in hiding and that we would not have enjoyed their company for much longer a period of time.

Again, Sir, as there will most likely be an investigation, I thought it best to inform you as to my plans.

On the next page he found an excerpt from the diary of DeWayne Lamberton. Quiller could barely make out the faded note next to the man's name: "Died crossing the Colorado River at Yuma in 1875." He read silently.

Monday, October sometime. We this day lef Tuksun in the hope to git to the Pimer villages for water and sum food. We did make slow progress dew to Wilbur Teatea's wagin and the bad wheel to which it is attached to.

Tuesday. Slo goin as to Wilbur's wagin creakin and whining like a babe wth the scatters.

Wednesday. We shud be at the Pimer villages. But we ain't and you can guess the reason. We are brok'd down at the crossin of a big dry wash. Wilbur's wagin can't get over t'other side. I wisht it happened tomorrow cause I wudden feel bad about leavin him behind. I don't feel right about that now as we are on the same side. But as mammy used to say tomorrow is nother a day.

Thursday. We are in the Pimer villages and we are not ded, but I am skert. The dangdest thing happened this morning. We wuz trine to push and shove Wilbur's wagin across the dry wash. But we wuz havin no luck.

A man appered. I mean appered from out o nowhur. They wuz desert and then they wuz him rite in the midst of us. Mr. Hymie, Beaux, Wilbur an me grabbed ar guns but this man he just started in workin on that ol wagin. He dint say nothing at all and just kept on workin and workin til he rigged it up so that we cud get it cross that wash.

He heped us git it over and he still dint say nothing. We dint say much neither cause he had a big gun and the luk of a man who wuz familiar with the workings of it.

That man he spoked only oncet. I offered are thanks and he jus said, "You are on a bad road" and he rided away from us and wuz gone as fast as he showed up.

Well, we weren't morn half a mile over the furst hill when we hear gunfire commencin' like a hail storm on a tin roof. Wilbur wanted us to go back for a looksee, but I wud have non of it. That man was engaged in powerful private business and it weren't non o arn.

I hope he is not killed and I do not think he is. I am jus happy we wuz out of there when he started dealin with some poor folks back ar. We might have been in the middle of it as I do not think he is the type of feller to give thot to things tween him and what he is after.

I am glad we are now gone. He had the darkest eyes I ever seen and I do not wish to make his acquaintance agin.

I hope people is more tolerable in California.

The next page held a fragment of a telegram, perhaps in reference to Caldera, dated 1876:

...alias CALDERA or CALDERON or CALDER... in the disappearance of suspected member of Mal... hold for questioning... armed and dangerous...

Next was a transcript of a radio broadcast interview from Dallas in 1932. The interviewer, a Mr. Weston, was interviewing Evelyn DeYoung, one of the sisters whom Caldera had rescued from four members of Malon's gang:

WESTON: And what were your initial thoughts when Congressman Chandler, then just a successful banker, came riding to your rescue, guns a-blazing, so to speak.

DEYOUNG: Oh, that old goat never came to anyone's rescue. Not even a cat.

WESTON: Miss DeYoung...

DEYOUNG: Yes, I know, young man, the story you know is nothing more than a myth, quite an effective one I might add. Laurel and I were sitting in that old stage stop chewing moldy hard tack when Chandler and his posse made their "gallant rescue."

WESTON: I'm sure this is as startling to our listening audience as it is to me, Miss DeYoung. Why have you never told this story, this *exclusive* story, before?

DEYOUNG: Why bother, young man?

WESTON: History, Miss DeYoung, history.

DEYOUNG: History's what you newspeople make of it... especially back in Arizona.

WESTON: Ma'am, how then did you and your sister escape Malon's clutches?

DEYOUNG: Oh, that bastard Malon wasn't around, just four of his thugs. And I tell you without shame, sir, we were frightened out of our wits.

WESTON: But the rescue—

DEYOUNG: It wasn't much of a rescue. More of a slaughter.

WESTON: I'm sure our listeners would love to hear the details.

DEYOUNG: I would not love to tell them, young man.

WESTON: Uh... did you escape on your own or did you have assistance?

DEYOUNG: (pauses) He was a dark young man, and by dark I do not imply complexion.

WESTON: He rescued you?

DEYOUNG: Truly, I believe not. But we were rescued as a result of his actions.

WESTON: Please explain.

DEYOUNG: As best Laurel and I could put it together afterwards, that man showed up to kill the men who kidnapped us. Don't misunderstand me, young man. I am quite, quite happy that he did. I just don't think he gave us much thought. He was there to kill. Saving us was an afterthought, and one I do not believe he relished.

WESTON: But he'd have been a hero. I mean, Congressman Chandler's entire career was based upon that single incident: territorial legislator, first US congressman from—

DEYOUNG: The old coot needed a cause to get elected. Laurel loved him anyway despite the difference in their ages. In their later years I truly believe he came to love her. I still say he married her just to keep us girls quiet. You know he proposed to me first. Oh—perhaps I shouldn't have said that.

WESTON: We can edit this later, Miss DeYoung.

DEYOUNG: Please do so.

WESTON: I'd like to get back to this mysterious rescuer.

DEYOUNG: I should not. I will forever be grateful to that man, but I should not like to meet him again. Should we meet in the next world I shall not look him in the eye. Once was quite enough.

There followed a pair of brief responses to various requests for information:

Dear Mr. Randolph,

I appreciate your need for information regarding the early days of Arizona Territory and your newspaper's commitment to history. I must decline your offer to allow me to comment. My current business and community interests require my full attention. In addition, those are not times that I choose to remember. Again, thank you for your interest, but I must decline.

Deanna (Corley) Farewell

San Francisco, California

Mr. Mickleson,

In response to your inquiry, I have given a cursory examination of our files and have found eight instances of the type mentioned in your letter. Each victim, and I use that term in its broadest sense, (1) died violently and (2) by gunshot or knife, (3) was a member or suspected member at some time of the Malon organization, and (4) yes, a link of chain was found clutched in each victim's right hand or within immediate proximity to that hand.

People assume that one man is responsible for all these killings, but there is no real evidence to support any conclusion. They are beginning to refer to him as "The Links Killer" and he is perceived as something of a Robin Hood character in some circles.

I will, in the little spare time available, comb through additional records for you and will apprise you if any similar occurrences come to my attention.

B. Mills

Editor, Patagonia Prospector

Following those were a few official and unofficial posters and documents:

ARREST, MURDER

These Circulars are for the use of Officers and Discreet Persons Only

On or about June 6, 1877 one Tesoro Florez was murdered by ambush near Apache Pass, Arizona Territory.

On or about August 14, 1887 one Jim "Mummy" Farago a.k.a. Jim LaFarge was murdered by ambush at the junction of Prospector's Creek and Fronteras Road, Arizona Territory.

On or about November 3, 1887 one "Kansas Patch" Everliegh was murdered by ambush at Monkey Springs, Arizona Territory.

Florez and Everliegh were in possession of a single link of chain held in a death grip of the right hand. No such link was found on or near Farago. It is obvious that "The Links Killer" is involved in the first and third killings and it is believed he is involved in the second.

The individual believed to be responsible may be using the alias CALDERON.

There were no witnesses.

It is believed that the killer resides in wilderness areas and shuns towns, camps and any outpost of civilization.

There is a liberal reward offered by numerous ranchers in the southern parts of the territory as many of the victims were employed as range riders for these enterprises. Inquiries should be made to L.S. Lyndon, Walking L Ranch, Privy, AT.

It can be seen from the above that the individual in question is a desperate character and would likely respond to an arrest with violence. Extreme caution is urged.

If arrested, telegraph the undersigned at Calabesas, Tucson, Phoenix, or Privy, AT.

L.S. Lyndon

Owner, Walking L Ranch

Next was a Vigilance Poster and Statement of Resolution, from a private collection, in obvious response to the L.S. Lyndon poster:

ATTENTION

Whereas, the individual or individuals known as "The Lynx" has never been positively identified, and

Whereas, the individual or individuals known as "The Lynx" has never been charged with any crime of violence against the good people of Arizona Territory, and

Whereas, the individual or individuals known as "The Lynx" has rid said territory of numerous vicious thieves, murderers and worse, and

Whereas The 666 Vigilance Committee wholeheartedly approves of said actions, be it therefore

Resolved that the individual or individuals known as "The Lynx" should be left the hell alone, you ranching sons of bitches!

666

Next came a notice from the August 6, 1883 edition of *The New York Telegraph & Dispatch*:

Arizona Territory, Tucson. *From News Reports.* The much sought after desperado known simply as Malon has been dispatched by a person or persons unknown near the village of Patagonia near the U.S. and Mexico border.

MALON DEAD!

Mysterious End of a Bad Man

Body Found On Sonoita Creek. Bloody Trail. Mystery of the Boots

From Our Correspondent on the Scene: Law-abiding citizens throughout Southern Arizona Territory rejoice at the confirmation of earlier reports on the death of the arch criminal known only as Malon.

Malon led a gang of thieves, murderers and despoilers of virtue on some of the bloodiest and most tragic incidents in this territory's violent history. His body was recovered near Sonoita Creek approximately five miles north of Patagonia.

In intelligence to *The Privy Portal*, special correspondent L.S. Lyndon reports that Malon's body was found sitting upright beneath a cottonwood, his right hand extended outward and apparently reaching for a pair of shiny boots.

"I think he wanted to go to hell with his boots on," says Lyndon. "Why they were off his feet in the first place I do not know. Perhaps someone was denying the killer what he craved most." Malon was noted for the particular attention he paid to his boots, which he kept polished at all times. He is reported to have killed a miner in Bisbee for having the temerity to spit tobacco juice across them.

Responsibility for the noble deed has not been assigned. Speculation runs rampant. Some say, with no authority, that Malon fell victim to a member of his own gang. (This is the least likely scenario in this editor's opinion as all known members of the gang have fallen victim to violence themselves in recent years.) Others surmise that the 666 Vigilance group or some unknown avenger sealed the fate of the killer.

Lyndon adds the significant observation, "The important thing is that I and my posse are bringing in the body of the territory's worst criminal. Justice has and will continue to prevail."

Other correspondents noted a bloody trail leading into the desert from the death scene. These reports at this time have not been confirmed.

Then came a personal letter.

Professor Jacksboro Griffin,

History Dept., Morrill School for Young Men

Congratulations on the arrival of your son. That makes two now, I believe. You see, we do get news even down here.

I am writing concerning the matter of our communication of last year. If you will pardon my feeble attempt at humor, only one more link in your chain has surfaced, yet in a most auspicious situation. I was a member of the posse that found the body referred to in earlier correspondence.

Malon was clasping a link of chain in his right hand when his body was found. Much has been made of the outstretched hand and the boots, etc. It is strange, and strangeness makes for good headlines. Chandler, the least involved in the chase, is of course taking center stage as usual and the matter of the link is losing prominence.

I thought you would appreciate the knowledge. You must come visit me soon and explain the purpose of my investigations.

Ben

Next was a social page from *The Privy Portal* dated February 7, 1880, followed by a brief glossary:

NEWS FROM THE SOUTHERN REALMS:

• Caleb Shahara has acquired 60 turkeys from Mexico and will be selling them at fair prices north of Bisbee on the Benson Road. First come first served.

• The baseball club in Tombstone will host a grand ball two weeks hence on Saturday evening. The sale of ladies notions is noticeably on the upswing in that community.

• The quarter-mile horse races in Patagonia were dominated by White Blaze, which places Langley in the undefeated position for the entire year.

• Bull McKenzie stopped by Tombstone following a successful hunt in the Swishhelms. He was about for fifteen days and dropped a deer for each. It is good to see that the old pioneer still has his keen hunting eye.

• Mrs. H.H. Brakenrige, wife of the prominent San Pedro rancher, lost her life due to fright on account of the Apache depredations in Gila County this past week.

• The old mission at Tumacacori, long abandoned by the good Catholic friars and left to the not so tender mercies of weather, Apaches and cowboy pistol shots, has been reoccupied. This effort at restoration is headed by a small group of Mormon settlers who seem committed more to farming with a roof over their heads than to converting the savages.

• The commanding officer at Ft. Huachuca reports a band of hostiles raiding both sides of the border in the neighborhood of Cedar Springs. The bandit Geronimo is suspected.

Line-up—Round up time on a cattle ranch.

Lining his flue—Eating.

Lynx (The)—A Robin Hood style desperado in Arizona Territory. Perhaps mythical.

Lynx (The Fearless)—A dime novel hero loosely based upon the above.

Linsey Woolsey—A cloth made from the combined fibers of wool and linen.

Lizard—A sled used exclusively for short-hauling duties.

Quiller also had an excerpt from a Dime novel, *Fists of Vengeance, A Saga of the Fearless Lynx* by A. Noye, 1886, Dime Ventures Publishing:

Stood they proudly, unwavering, and as yet unmolested and unblemished, the sisters DeQuincy, Eva and Laura Mae, unbowed before their tormentors. Talon's evil henchmen glowered, lust filling their eyes, at the two helpless doves before the fire.

Whiskey poured, sour and sickly, down the gullets of the gunmen, as all the while brave womanhood prepared to defend its honor, for what has a woman alone in the Wild West save honor? As with that Grand Sacrifice of another day, the guardsmen cast lots for the fate of the sisters.

"I like the look of that fiery little one, Jake," said Farley.

"It matters not who wins who," said Jake.

The bottle of whiskey was getting low. So too was the time before the fate that truly is worse than death met with the innocent sisters of privation.

Bravely Eva faced her masters. "Take not Laura Mae. Spare her and I shall be yours. Move toward her, you curs, and I shall fight you with every fiber of my being!" Such was the nobility and courage of the Old West I once knew.

Such women! Where are they today? Where, indeed?

"I think I shall teach you some manners, young woman," said Farley.

Eva stood, trembling, yet not with fear, but with anticipation of the fight, the struggle and the sure death to come at the hands of villainy. Laura Mae clutched her sister's tattered dress as Farley advanced. His knife, a sword of steel that had tasted much blood, slid from its scabbard as the miscreant advanced snakelike cross the floor.

Suddenly with a crash and a boom the window shattered. A man, a demon, a savior rolled across the floor, righted himself and stood beside the sisters DeQuincy, a .45 Colt in each hand. The cold, dark stare hidden behind a darker mask of black silk cloth known throughout the West identified the man. A shout of identity was not needed.

"We are saved!" breathed Eva.

"Praise Our Lord for he is with us!" whispered Laura Mae.

"We are to meet our doom, Farely!" said Jake.

"That is as it should be," said the demon in black. "For I have vowed to rid the West of your kind."

"Mercy!" Jake and Farley, cowards to the end, begged for what they themselves were never willing to grant. Even so, as they begged they reached for their pistols. Curs indeed!

The glorious demon fired two shots, one from each pistol, and two evil hearts exploded and two souls fell into a darkness from which they would never return.

He swept the women, victims no more, into his arms and out the door to safety, refuge and a life to be lived... yes, to be lived and without shame!

The hero returned to the cabin for one final task, a ritual that struck fear into the hearts of cowardly villains throughout the territory. In the hand of each, a marker and a warning, was placed a

83

single link from a golden chain, priceless not for its metal, but for the justice it represented. He turned, walked through the door. Thus into the darkness, into history, and into glory rode The Lynx.

Chapter Twelve

Fairbank was a well-named town. The small community of less than a hundred people was the center of trade for much of southern Arizona. The town was as well situated as it was named. Its rail line served Benson, Bisbee, Nogales and especially the explosive town of Tombstone just down the road. The town was on the banks of the San Pedro River, a winding path of lush green through the surrounding desert. Fairbank had seen its share of thefts, train robberies and murders. The killing about to occur would mean only one more hole in the ground at the cemetery on a rocky hill just out of town.

Caldera tied his horse on the rail in front of Livingston's Restaurant. A small sign on the door read Irish Need Not Apply. He stepped inside to a most curious sight. Livingston's wasn't luxurious, but it was clean and surprisingly fashionable for such a small town. *They must dress up for the railroad crowd.* What really caught his attention was the silence and lack of movement. At least ten patrons were sitting at tables or standing at the bar. They were all looking toward the rear of the establishment and a table with a commanding view of the entire room. One man was sitting at that table. He was unconscious and his face was buried in a plate of steak and beans. His arms hung at his sides, limp like fresh meat in a smokehouse. A half-empty bottle of whiskey explained the necessity of the nap. Two .38 double-action revolvers with seven and one-half inch barrels had been placed on either side of the dinner plate.

The other patrons were so still that they didn't appear to be breathing. Caldera approached one of them. "Who is he?"

The patron whispered as if not wanting to wake the dead. "Rankin. They call him Mossey. It means outlaw."

"I know what it means and he's the man I'm looking for."

"We would appreciate it if you would kindly do your looking in some other locale, Mr...."

"Caldera." The ice cold stare that was becoming a legend throughout Arizona Territory demanded a response. A few people even knew his name.

"I entreat you to conduct your personal business elsewhere, Mr. Caldera. There is a distinct possibility of someone being hurt... even killed."

"Ain't no possibility at all." He stalked across the room and sat down at Rankin's table, directly across from the man with beans for a beard. The customers, one by one, filed out, almost as if they were walking on tip toes. Caldera turned the pistols on the table so that the barrels were pointing toward rather than away from Rankin. "Ah-*hem*!"

Rankin jerked up and groped for his pistols. As he gripped the barrels his eyes came into focus on a Colt single-action .45 aimed directly between those eyes. He flattened his palms on the table and waited to see just what the hell was going on.

"You Rankin?"

Rankin nodded.

"Then you're a dead man."

In less than half a second Caldera adjusted his aim, fired and blew a hole through Rankin's right shoulder. The man flew back and to the floor as if kicked by a horse. As he struggled to get up, Caldera shattered the other shoulder with another well-placed shot. Neither wound was fatal.

Caldera cocked his pistol. "Jenner. Boggs. Where are they?"

"To hell with you!"

The patrons, at last stirred into action, fled Livingston's like swallows from a burning barn.

Caldera picked up one of the .38 pistols from the table. He looked it over, fired, and blew out Rankin's right knee. "Jenner and Boggs."

Rankin said nothing.

Caldera fired again and blew out Rankin's left knee. The wounded man wanted to scream, but he held it in. Caldera took a steak knife from the table. "All right, we'll do this the slow way."

Rankin tried to squirm away as his torturer squatted beside him. He could barely move.

Caldera played with his victim. He pulled on his hair, flicked his ears, and pulled at his eyelids. He started whittling on one ear and was about halfway through when Rankin began to talk. "Don't know about Boggs."

Caldera sliced off the ear with a single quick cut.

Rankin could no longer hold in his screams. "Jenner! I know about Jenner!"

Caldera placed the sharp edge of his knife against Rankin's remaining ear. "Where!"

"Tubac! He lit out for Tubac! He heard The Lynx was after—" Rankin shrieked, having just realized who was about to kill him.

"What else?"

Rankin squirmed to get away using his elbows, but his shattered shoulders would not support the effort.

Caldera jammed the pistol in his side and fired. The bullet was a purposeful through-and-through—not fatal, but extremely painful. Now more a killing machine than a man, Caldera repeated the act on Rankin's other side. "What else!"

"He done changed his name! Growed a beard and paints his hair I think. He don't look the same. He's got the consumption, too."

"What's he doing in Tubac?"

"Dyin'! Hidin'!" Rankin looked around at the blood soaked wooden planks. "I done told you all I know. You gonna' kill me?" It was a plea.

Caldera stood up, took careful aim and blew a hole through Rankin's head, then walked out of Livingston's. The streets were empty and the homes and businesses were dark. He found the small hotel sheltered by dark cottonwoods. The hotel was run by the man he had spoken to at Livingston's, a Mr. Katzenbach. His expression was mixed. He seemed happy that a dangerous man had been removed from their midst, but clearly he wondered whether someone worse had taken his place.

"I got a few dollars. I'll help clean up the mess in your restaurant," Caldera said.

Katzenbach was visibly relieved. He tuned the guestbook forward and offered a pen. "How long will you be staying, Mr. Caldera?"

"Coupl'a days. Smith."

"I thought you said your name was—" He looked into Caldera's eyes and suddenly saw the world in a different light. "Of course, Mr. Smith. Room three on the right."

Caldera took the key.

Katzenbach put on his best false smile. "You can get breakfast at Livingston's from five a.m. on. Oh! The owner might be a little delayed tomorrow."

Caldera wanted to move on to Tubac immediately, but a wild shot from a card game at the Birdcage Theater in Tombstone had torn a hole through his calf. A ricochet caught him standing at the bar. The wound needed tending and a day or two of rest. Had he not been so close to Rankin's trail he would have held up there for healing. Fairbank would have to provide the short respite. The wound was painful, but not serious. He spent his first day in town washing it and applying medication. He ate two meals at Livingston's where an old area rug had just been installed at a table in the rear. The townspeople were cordial and reserved. They did not initiate conversation, which suited Caldera fine. He was hunting, not touring. He spent a good part of the day trying to imagine Jenner's appearance. He'd only had a meager description, and the man had changed the way he looked. The consumption he suffered would change him even more. He would have to draw the man out. How?

He had finished an early supper on the second day in town when a commotion in the street caught his attention. He went for a look. A medicine man had set up his stand and wagon and had already launched into his presentation.

"Ladies! Gentlemen! Friends, amigos and compadres! Step forward to see and benefit from the medical marvel and miracle of the decade! Yea, of the century!" He had captured a crowd, many of them new arrivals by train. New arrivals meant new money, which explained the timing of the event. The man had drawn the interest of the crowd, but he had not drawn them in.

"I know you are wondering just who in the name of Andy Jackson is this man and what is the nature of the amazing boon to humanity he is offering! Well, friends, I am known, well-known, as Dr. Providence, bringer of health, fitness, well-being and the cure for what ails you! Step up! Step right up and see this miracle of modern science for yourselves!"

The crowed eased forward. A few men shuffled to the forefront as Caldera watched. *Suckers.* One of the men walked with a terrible limp. He used a homemade crutch.

"Why am I, Dr. Providence, here? That, my friends, is an exceptional question and you are wise folk to ask it of me. I have earned wealth beyond most men's dreams. I have fame throughout the States and here in the West. I could retire in comfort to my mansion on the hill, yet I risk life and limb to seek you out, my friends. Why indeed?"

Caldera had seen all of this before. He was always amazed that the more outrageous the pitch, the more likely were people to buy it. Having nothing else to do, he leaned against the wall of the hotel and watched the show.

"My one goal, my friends, is to extend to you the bounty of good health provided by the finest medical minds in the world!" He held up what appeared to be a wide belt. Caldera had seen that too. It was a primitive battery hand-made from strips of copper and zinc separated by blotting paper. When soaked in vinegar the paper and the metal strips created a small and pleasing electrical shock, a mild tingle. The belt, which appeared to be leather, was cheap oilcloth.

A murmur of disbelief waved through his audience. "Ah, I don't blame you for your disbelief. Our precious Lord faced the same doubts even among his own. But, friends, do not believe me. See for yourselves and believe in the miracle of modern medical science." More people edged forward.

"When worn next to your skin this device produces a life-giving, life-restoring and life-enhancing electrical charge. It will cure, among other tragedies of life, colds and flu, rheumatism, cataarh, gout, leading, syphilis, female diseases, consumption...."

Consumption! Caldera took a step forward as the doctor continued.

"Diabetes, ulcers, bleeding gums, asthma, boils, inflammation of the bowels, cholera, grippe, snakebite, scalping and a list of other impediments to health far too long to recite. Health, true health, can be yours and it can be yours beginning today, and for only the paltry sum of 25 cents. I ask you, friends, is 25 cents too much to pay for a lifetime of good, robust health? Is there a sufferer among you?"

The man with the crutch hobbled forward, a look of desperation and despair on his face. "Snakebite," he said and hobbled closer. He pulled up his pants leg to reveal a blood red spot the size of a bowler hat. Two ugly blackened dots were in the center. "I can't work. I can barely walk. Can you help me, Dr. Providence?" The man handed over 25 cents. Providence poured a line of vinegar along the center of the belt, soaking the blotting paper. The sufferer, clearly a shill for the good doctor, accepted the belt and put it on underneath his shirt. "I can feel it, Dr. Providence! I can feel it working!"

He stepped back and looked at the belt, his face beaming amazement and joy. He tossed down the crutch and took a few faltering steps. "This is truly a miracle, Doctor! I must show my wife and my son!" The man walked off. He still walked with a limp, but it was much less pronounced. He followed the road up river and was soon out of sight.

Dr. Providence called to his audience. "Friends, my brothers and sisters who are suffering and in pain, please allow this amazing device to bring you relief, renewed health and vigor, and an end to pain."

The doctor made a good profit that afternoon. After a visit to the saloon he in his wagon and well out of town before sundown.

Caldera checked out of the hotel an hour later.

Chapter Thirteen

Caldera watched Dr. Providence rummage around his camp for half an hour. The man was certainly unused to the wilder parts of the wild West. He built a fire, unnecessarily large for cooking or warmth, and prepared a stew for supper. Frequently he glanced down the road for a man who would never come. Providence cooked and ate in the glow of his fire, often a fatal mistake in Apache country. Caldera had ridden almost into the light before the man noticed him. Providence nearly fell over scrambling backwards. He did manage to hold onto his plate of stew. "I am a poor man, Sir, hardly worth your time in robbery."

"Settle down, tumble turd." Caldera dismounted and tied his horse to the medicine man's wagon. "How 'bout sharing some of that stew?"

"Of course, Sir. I already have a plate set."

Caldera thought, *That would be for the sufferer with the makeshift crutch.* "Your gimp won't be coming along any time soon." He squatted down just outside the glow of the fire.

"I beg your pardon?"

"Your shill."

"I assure you, Sir, that I—"

"Relax. I know the game. Your shill, Morales I believe, has a real broken leg now." Providence blanched as his night visitor continued. "Don't worry. I left him with one of your miracle belts." Providence hesitated and then broke into laughter. Caldera joined in. He hated conversation and the act that had to accompany it, but he needed this man and the cover he could provide.

Providence helped himself to another plate of stew. "I assume you have a proposition."

"You need a shill. I need a job."

"What shall I pay you?"

"Whatever's fair."

"And if I should, perish the thought, prove to be a cheat?"

"You will need a whole mess of them fancy belts of yours."

"Done, Sir. I pray that you are a fast learner."

The following morning they were on the road before dawn. Caldera rode in the wagon, his horse trailing along behind. "Where are you heading, Doctor?"

"Tucson."

"I hear Tubac is coming back."

"I hear that it is nothing more than a pile of rubble. I had not considered it."

"Consider it."

Providence had not avoided tar and feathers, jail or hanging by being foolish. "We'll test your skills in Tubac. Did you observe my dissertation yesterday?"

"Your what?"

"Dissertation. Presentation. My sales pitch."

"Couldn't miss it."

"And what did you see?"

"Man selling some goods to a bunch of suckers."

Providence looked truly mortified. "Young man, you observed the workings of a master creating a masterpiece. That was not selling, Sir. It was art."

"If you say so."

As they rode west Dr. Providence taught Caldera how to create his art. "Everything is scripted, like a great play or a poem. Notice first that I set up on the street. The gulls are forced to stand, and that almost literally forces them to be on their toes. Move inside where they can sit and they get drowsy. Drowsy people do not make purchases."

"Yeah."

"Note also that I use a stage a foot or so off the ground. I am above them so they can easily see, but not so far that I am perceived as being distant. Perception is key in this business."

"You're also closer to their money."

'Yes, well, of course, but—and this is important, my young scholar—people buy *me*, not the product. I have sold patent medicine, land owned by other persons, salted gold mines and now electric healing devices. In every instance the people buy *me*. Whatever item comes with the deal is, for all practical purposes, irrelevant."

"You got a way with words." *Just stop using 'em.*

"Sir, Stephen A. Douglas was a great orator. Great orators could not sell water to a man dying of thirst in the desert. I, on the other hand, could sell that very same man a bucket of sand for his life savings, his farm and his future." He pulled up under the shade of a cottonwood growing next to the river to allow the horses time to rest. Caldera led his horse the short distance to the river. After it had its fill he brought a bucket of water to Providence's animals. The man kept chattering away. "You know why they buy me? Because I do not care a bit what bilge spews forth from my mouth. I just want that magic moment when the suckers hand over their money. Their smile. The hope in their eyes. And my knowledge that I have taken the money from the banker, the mouths of their children, and their future. Ah, to crush another human being and at the same moment have that human being glowing with admiration and gratitude—there is nothing in this world like that moment."

Caldera tied his horse back to the wagon and stepped aboard.

The lesson continued without a break. "Excellent timing is essential. You must know when you have made your joint, the perfect moment to snap shut your trap. You must not strike too early, but it is equally important to avoid striking too late. I tell you, Sir, I have seen fellow businessmen talking a customer out of a sale he has already made. I have seen it, Sir."

The lesson continued until time to set up camp, a chore Caldera did almost single-handedly. Throughout the evening Dr. Providence kept an eye on the road, this time not for his former shill, but for disappointed and angry citizens of Fairgame. Caldera slept away from the campfire, safe in the darkness—and away from the chattering of Dr. Providence.

Chapter Fourteen

The two men rode in together because of a last-minute alteration in the good doctor's presentation. Caldera was a terrible actor. He couldn't deliver his lines. He couldn't *remember* his lines. He couldn't *improvise* lines. The curing of the cripple with the crutch was stricken from the act. Providence desperately struggled to come up with an alternate plan.

"Why don't you tell 'em I already been cured?" Caldera said.

Providence considered the idea. "Yes, yes... there might be something there."

"You could say your little electric belt fixed me up and I hung around out of.... What's that fancy word Prospect uses?"

"Devotion? Yes, you have become my devoted servant!"

"Sure, Doc, that'll work. And I won't have to say anything unless somebody asks me a question." Caldera was desperate, too. He needed the medicine show to bring out Jenner.

"Can you say yes, Caldera?"

"Yes."

"Then say no more. When I ask you a question, just say yes. And say it with conviction."

"Yes."

"Well, work on it."

"Sure."

"What?"

"Oh... yes."

Tubac's location was one of the loveliest in the state. Mountains to the west, east and northeast commanded attention with their beauty and constant changes in light and shadow as the sun moved through the seasons. The Santa Cruz River assured a reliable water source and a pleasant greenbelt through the bleached desert and created a respite from Mexico to Tucson. Desert shrubs and flowers often sent waves of perfumed air to the dusty and weary traveler.

Tubac itself was something far less than spectacular. "It is a pile of rubble," Providence said.

"Tubac means 'burned place' in Pima. There are mines nearby and that means miners and miner's ore. You'll make out here." Prospect had told him it was the oldest white settlement in Arizona Territory. It had been built up by Spanish conquerors and priests, Mexican soldiers and settlers, Mormons and miners. It had been burned out by Pimas, Apaches, Mexicans and Anglos. Somehow something always showed up to give the ruin a new life. Bull called Tubac the town with nine lives.

"One pitch, one pitch only, and then, Sir, we are bound for Tucson."

"Agreed." Caldera did not tell him that the doctor would be leaving for Tucson minus another shill.

"Burnt place" was an accurate description of the town, or more accurately, what was left of the town. Most of the old adobe structures were empty shells half melted by rain into the desert, a building block returning to its source. A few had been reclaimed and had wooden roofs. Others were covered by canvas tarps. Dust, dead grasses, and waste blew through the nearly empty streets.

"What could possibly hold people to such a place?" Providence said.

"From what I hear they do a little farming and a bit of ranching. Some of 'em try to pry a little more ore out of them nearby hills, but the mines played out years ago. I think a lot of folks like this bunch just stick with the devil they know. The one that might be out there is just too scary."

"You are quite eloquent in your own way, Sir."

"Don't mean to be." Caldera didn't know the meaning of the word.

"We shall spend the night and make our dissertation in the morning when the suckers are first out and about. And then we shall be on our way. Quickly, I might add."

Caldera said nothing. He studied the few people walking about, looking for a thin, worn-out man with a bad cough and a new beard.

"Where is the hotel?" Providence said.

"Pick out one you like." Caldera pointed to a collection of ruined adobes. None of them had a roof.

"Godforsaken is far too good a word for this trash heap."

They moved into an adobe facing the main street. Caldera's first action was to kill a rattlesnake coiled in the corner. "That's supper."

Later, Providence accepted the shared bounty, but he ate in small bites and seemed to gag on each one. Bits and pieces of leftover furniture, cabinets, and other wood artifacts provided enough fuel for a half-decent fire. Providence retired early, spending the night fighting fitful dreams about electric belts turning into rattlesnakes.

Caldera went on the hunt. He scoured the town looking for the emaciated form of a bearded consumptive. The townspeople were in such poor health and ragged condition that many of the men he encountered fit the picture. He listened carefully for the unmistakable sound of coughing or of someone spitting up spots of blood. He put on his best "friendly stranger" persona and asked pointed, yet carefully veiled questions. Nothing. He did spread the word everywhere about Dr. Providence and his cure-all electric belt, making sure always to place the words *cure* and *consumption* together. If he couldn't track his prey, he would set bait.

The next morning more dust than people was stirring on the streets of Tubac. Dr. Providence was ready to make his presentation, take in what suckers he could and move on as quickly as possible to the more profitable suckers in Tucson. He began the pitch and within a few moments a surprisingly large crowd of people showed up. They came out of the burnt hovels like spiders from rubbish.

"Ladies. Gentlemen. Friends, please step forward." The spiel rolled off his tongue as if he were saying the words for the first time. Caldera grinned when he lowered the price from 25 to ten cents. "When you can't get top dollar, go for volume," he had said. His "yes man" did his part and some money started coming in. Also coming in was a thin man with a beard and a bad cough. Hair dye streaked just below his beard and hairline. The man came forward, practically staggering, with a face showing desperate hope mixed with fatality. He held a small coin in his hand and his arms were raised almost in supplication.

As the last coin was exchanged for the last hope Caldera leaned forward and whispered the one word guaranteed to fill what was left of the man with terror. "Jenner."

The rapist/killer backed away, his final hope failing. Instinctively he knew he was facing The Links Killer and his immediate death. He stumbled backwards into his adobe hovel. Providence frowned at the distraction and kept springing his traps. Caldera reached back into the wagon for his pistol and belt. As he was strapping it on the consumptive reappeared with a rifle and began shooting. Weakened by disease and fear, he nearly caused a massacre. A miner named Bennett was shot in the shoulder. He twisted around and fell into the dust. A drifter called Roberts shouted, "Stop!" and was hit in the throat. The wound was bloody, but not fatal. He sat on the ground and wrapped his new electric belt around his neck. Providence ducked away from a shot from a .45 that launched his tall hat into the air. Bar owner Johnsen took one in his thigh. None of the shots came close to the intended target.

When he ran out of shells the old man dropped the rifle. He traded glances with Caldera—terror for emptiness. The man they were calling The Links Killer watched coldly as his prey fumbled his way onto a nearby mule and rode into the desert. He swayed back and forth on the animal's bare back.

Caldera saddled his horse and followed at a slow pace. He tracked Jenner farther into the hard rock desert. Several miles out of town the old man fell off the mule. As the animal ran off he crawled to the scattered shade offered by a mesquite tree. The blood he coughed up mixed with the streaks of hair dye and dropped like black tears.

He turned on his back as Caldera rode up. "Water. Anything for water."

"Where is Boggs?"

"I don't know, Mister." In less than a second he was watching the rotation of the cylinder in a single action Colt .45. "Wait. Give me water and I'll tell you all I know."

"Talk. Then water."

"All I know is he got religion. Ran off to Mexico or Montana last I heard." He tried to swallow, but there wasn't enough blood for such a challenge.

"That's it?"

"Ask some of the others when you find 'em."

"Ain't no others."

"You gonna' kill me?"

"Don't have to. You're already a dead man."

"My water."

Caldera spit in the man's face and rode off. *Mexico or Montana! Damn.* He headed back to Tubac hoping that Jenner had been the talkative type. He would find temporary work on ranches, in small town saloons, or near an army post or camp. A clue, one little clue, was all he needed and soon after the vengeance trail would end.

Chapter Fifteen

Annette looked at her husband. "Robert, where are the Cuba clippings?"

"In the other folder."

"Are you going to show them to Prospect or not?"

"Don't know."

"He doesn't have much time, Robert."

"I'm still not sure."

"Then connect the dots. Talk to the old man."

"I have another meeting with him tomorrow."

"You think he has another tomorrow in him?"

"I have to be certain."

"Well, I'm sure as hell certain of one thing."

"What's that?"

"You'd better hurry."

The next morning I helped Prospect out of my car and into the new reservation clinic. He had allowed me to drive him in so we could continue the interview. I realized he knew that his time was short. The clinic was typical of a modern, small-town medical facility. It was clean, shiny, well-designed and busy even on a workday. Farmers chopped off fingers, broke bones, fell and busted their heads. Automobile repairmen got cuts, scrapes, and burns. Drunks got in fights, slashed with knives, and shot each other with revolvers, semi-automatics and the ever-present shotgun. Diabetics needed treatment and kids still caught the measles, mumps and chicken pox. New technologies and modern concepts were employed by doctors and nurses who smiled appropriately, clicked their teeth, shook their heads and occasionally wiped away tears. Still, the new had not completely won its battle against old ways and ancient concepts.

"You don't have a doctor's appointment?" I said, somewhat incredulous.

"She will see me when it is time," Prospect said.

Indian time. A task is begun when it should begin and it lasts as long as it takes to complete. If you need to see the doctor, you go to see the doctor. When it is time to be seen, he or she will see you. If you have to spend the entire day in a waiting room, well that's okay, because that is the way of the world.

"I saw the shaman this morning," Prospect said.

"Your shaman is okay with this?" I gestured to the clinic and the white uniformed professionals buzzing up and down the halls.

"Of course. My doctor is very good at her job."

"There's no... conflict of interest?"

"You have been watching too many western movies, Robert. There is no conflict when the interest of the patient is paramount."

A young nurse walking by paused to reassure Prospect that the doctor would be available in the relatively near future. The old man didn't ask for a time frame. Indian time.

"Do you feel like talking?" I asked.

"I enjoy talking with you, Robert. I find it a pleasurable task."

"Task?"

"At my age I must work at it."

"I don't mind just sitting."

"There are many worlds, Robert. I think we must know each other in some of the others."

"Why would you say that?" I wasn't up on my Indian mysticism.

"I feel as if I have known you a long time."

"Do you feel up to discussing Caldera?"

"Is there any other subject?" He smiled and flew his mind into the past.

Prospect traveled again from the world of glass and tile to the world of rock and sand. He was soon riding a mule across the Gila River bed, dry and dusty, looking more like a wide, flat wash than the lifeblood of a people. Anglo dams up river had diverted the water to Phoenix, the surrounding communities, and the growing number of agricultural fields. The great Pima farms were now more mesquite forest than melon fields. Prospect gave no thought to the matter. What was simply was, and what was to be would be. This was the time of the men with the shining faces. Elder Brother had warned against them back during the ancient days and now his prophecy was being fulfilled.

He had been summoned to the home of Bull McKenzie, still Privy's most prominent resident. Neither man had spoken to the other in many years. He wondered at the outcome of the confrontation, for surely a confrontation it must be.

Bull was waiting for him on the great porch that surrounded his massive adobe home. "I see you bought yourself a new mule," he said.

"It is time for one."

"Get down and pull up a chair. We got matters to discuss." He poured a double shot of whiskey in a thick glass tumbler and refreshed his own. "Here. I know you drink it." Prospect accepted the glass as he sat down, but he did not drink. He noticed a third, empty glass on the table. "It's the good stuff, Prospect. For Chrissakes have a drink with me."

Prospect killed the whiskey with two swift gulps. He had never been drunk a day in his life, but he had always enjoyed the fire of good whiskey. "Thank you."

Bull chugged his own glass of fire and poured again for each of them. They remained silent. It might have appeared curious to some, but neither man felt awkward at what would have been a terrible and potentially dangerous moment for most people. Bull did not think of such things. He had specific goals in life now and awkward moments were side trips he chose not to make. The few quiet moments on that porch were a tool, not wasted time.

Prospect waited.

"I guess you got that new mule 'cause you're planning on doing some traveling."

"Much better than a horse."

"I agree. Where you going? And when?"

"Do you intend to stop me?"

"Don't have to, Prospect. If I wanted you dead, you'd be a pile of dust right now."

"Perhaps." Prospect would not be an easy man to kill, not even from ambush. How strange, he thought, that two fathers would duel over a son, one for the right to let that son live and the other for the burden of killing him.

Bull finished his drink and then refilled the glass, only half full this time. Prospect noticed the large liver spots dotting his hands and for the first time realized Bull McKenzie was getting old. That was something of a revelation, not so much of the effects of age, but of the effects of image on reality. No one thought of the big man in such a fashion. Bull McKenzie an old man? Bull, indeed!

"You really think he's this fella' they called The Lynx?"

"He is."

"Yeah... I spoke with that A. Noye about it a couple of years ago. He thinks the same thing. I got him running the Privy Portal for me now."

Prospect sipped his whiskey. He didn't know where Bull was taking him, but he wanted his wits about him whenever they landed.

Bull continued. "Ain't been a peep out of him in two years. It's like he fell off the Earth. You heard anything?"

Prospect loosened his shirt to reveal a necklace made of chain links. He tugged on one. "This one arrived a year past. I think he has almost slain the dragon."

"How many?"

"This chain has eleven links."

"Sounds about right. Malon pretty much traveled with an even dozen, give or take."

"I believe there should be twelve. I believe he is nearing the end of this trail."

"And now you're gonna' kill the dragon killer?"

Prospect unclasped the necklace and laid it on the table by Bull's bottle of whiskey. "This is as much yours as it is mine."

"Damn it, Prospect!" Bull took a deep breath and then pounded the wall. "Get out here!"

The front door opened and a young woman stepped out. She could not have been more than 30 years old, but she had the bearing and the hollow look of someone twice her age. Her hair was short, curly and dyed a cheap-looking red. Her dress fit poorly and was probably a recent gift from one of the whores in Bull's stable.

"Meet Shella Fischer, Prospect. She is an... opportunist."

Prospect nodded. Neither man offered to give up his seat. Bull did pour the third glass full and offered it to the woman. She accepted and drank about half of it in a few swift gulps. "Thank you, Mr. McKenzie."

"Have some more. You earned it." He filled the glass nearly to the brim. "Tell Prospect what you told me."

She took another drink, obviously nervous. "You promised a reward."

Bull opened his shirt and pulled out a wad of bills. Shella Fischer's eyes bulged. Bull counted out about half of the money and slapped it on the table, placing his glass on top to keep the bills from joining the little dust devils swirling in the street. "Tell him."

She reluctantly pulled her eyes from the small fortune and looked at Prospect. "I was with a man who used to bartend here at the Armageddon."

"Jimbasco," said Bull.

"Yessir. Well, we was livin' up in Solomonville. I was workin' a house next to the saloon. Sneak—that was what I called him—he was tendin' bar and we was both gettin' along real fine. I mean there was no trouble and we was payin' our bills and all."

Bull said what Prospect was thinking. "Get on with it." For once in his life, the Indian was impatient. He had a task to perform, a deadly, unpleasant, heart-breaking task, and he wanted to get it over and done with.

Shella glanced quickly at the money and then back to Prospect. "Sneak, he was always talkin' about gettin' a stake, a big one, from Mr. McKenzie here. He seen somethin' he thought was worth a lot of money... a *lot* of money, Sir."

Bull grinned and added a large number of bills to the pile. "You keep piling it on and I will too."

Shella finished her whiskey and extended her hand. Bull complied and filled it again. She wasn't showing the slightest effect. "One day Johnny Ringo hisself just stomps his way into the saloon and blows a chunk of poor Sneak's head halfway across the room. Just shot him and walked away like he'd killed some old dog. Don't nobody know why neither." She actually managed a tear. Prospect thought it genuine, but Bull knew better.

"The stake, Shella," said Bull. He sweetened the pot with a few more bills.

"Yessir." She began talking a little faster. "So before he got his head blowed off, old Sneak, he done told me about what he seen one night behind the Armageddon."

Prospect leaned forward, slightly and almost imperceptibly, but Bull noticed the movement. *Good.*

Shella kept drinking and glancing at the growing pile of money. "He was draggin' some drunk out to the back door when he seen some girl, she was pregnant, and a boy and a woman. Sneak called her the 'she-bear of Privy,' he did."

"Belle." Bull needn't have spoken. Prospect was already playing out the tragic scene in his mind.

"So Sneak—he didn't get that name for nothin'—he steps back in the shadows to see what he could pick up. You know, maybe find out somethin' that'd give him an edge." Shella turned to Bull and kicked her head back toward Prospect. "He don't say much."

"Prospect speaks the king's English better than the king himself." He thumped a finger on the pile of money. "If you want me to keep on adding to the pile, you keep on adding to the conversation."

"Yessir, Mr. McKenzie. So they was a lot of shoutin' back there, but this boy was too drunk to know what the hell was going on." She looked at Bull. "That was your boy, Mr. McKenzie... that Caldera fella'." She paused, wondering what kind of hornet's nest she'd stirred up.

Neither man made a move or uttered a sound.

Shella forced a weak smile. "This boy fell down all laughin' and ever'thin' and then that she-bear woman shot the girl. She shot her good a coupl'a times, maybe three, and then started screamin' about Apaches."

Prospect's face was a mask of indifference. He finished his drink, poured himself another and began working on that one. Only Bull Caldera knew how the news had stunned the Indian. Stunned? Shattered might have been a better word. Prospect looked at the woman. "This is the truth?"

"I wasn't there, Mister Indian." Telling the story had rattled the young woman or perhaps the whiskey was taking effect. She was ever so slightly shaking. "But Sneak, he swore by it and Sneak did a lot of things, but he never once lied on me."

Bull had already made up his mind. The question was for Prospect's benefit. "You believed him?"

She nodded. "Sneak believed it. We was gonna' start a new life with that money. 'Sides, he wasn't the kind of man to stack no deck on somebody big as you, Mr. McKenzie. It wasn't in him."

Bull handed the pile of money to Shella Fischer. "Before you get drunk, you go over to the Privy Portal and tell this same story to my man. We call him A. Noye and it's a damn appropriate name. You got that?"

"Yessir."

"Then git!"

She paused for half a second.

Bull popped a cork in the bottle and handed it to her. "Take it with you. You earned that too."

She grabbed the bottle and moved quickly down the street. Bull kept his eye on her until she entered the Portal's front door.

"That story'll be all over Arizona and New Mexico Territory by the end of the week... West Texas too," Bull said.

"California," Prospect said.

"Hell yes... California, too."

"And San Francisco. Will you send a telegram to San Francisco?"

Their eyes locked. Bull's voice was low and cold and, most frighteningly of all, completely without emotion. "Yes... San Francisco."

The two men remained silent for several moments. A couple of riders came up the street. One made a move toward the porch. A short, almost invisible swipe of Bull's right hand sent him on his way. He spoke without looking at Prospect. "Your mission changed any in the last couple of minutes?"

"I think it must," said Prospect. Half a minute later he was on his mule and once again the eyes of the two men locked.

"Bring him back, Prospect."

"I will."

"Bring him home."

Chapter Sixteen

Quiller reflected on the direction his story was heading. The tale was far more powerful and heart rendering than he had ever expected. The story of Prospect's journey in search of his sometimes son should have a Homer, a Shakespeare or at least a Louis L'Amour to relate that epic. His journey might not be as grand as that of Odysseus, Henry V, or the Sacketts, but it was as determined, as eventful and as dangerous as any of those tales. Sadly, the quest of an aging Indian from a little-known tribe has not found its way into popular American literature. *And we are the worse for that loss*. Prospect's journey took him through Arizona and New Mexico Territories, much of Northern Mexico, and parts of Texas. Like the object of his quest, he became obsessed to the point of self-destruction.

He spoke with a marshal in Tombstone, a man who laughed off the "Legend of the Lynx," but who took seriously the reality of the killer behind that legend. A victim of cruel fate or not, the mysterious figure was a wanted man. If he came near the marshal's realm he would be brought to justice. Other law officers in the territory were more understanding and provided what limited information, rumors and guesswork they could. Any man who could kill, bring in or make the man known as the Lynx disappear was a welcome ally.

Prospect continued following the slim leads and obscure references without success. He met with Apache scouts south of San Carlos Reservation. Lynx was something of a hero among the tribes. He killed Mexicans. Malon and his men had also traded in Apache slaves. Lynx was known and would not be knowingly killed. Word spread throughout the tribes about Prospect and his great search. Little was accomplished save that the Pima was given something of a free pass through Apache lands. Ancient enemies found common ground in a mad man.

His travels took him from desert sands to mountain snows. He fought Mexicans, Indians and Anglos and he found friends among all three groups. He was shunned, laughed at, shot, aided and even saved by strangers. He gave as good as he got. And still he could not strike a fresh trail. His journey became a series of events, some funny, some tragic, and all fruitless. Tattoo suffered the toil and loneliness stoically. She welcomed him home when he arrived, tended to his wounds and his aching spirit, and then shed tears within when he inevitably took up the trail again.

Prospect found his way to as near the end of the line as a man could be and still continue a mission. He was threadbare, down to his last bullets for his pistol and rifle, and his mule was in a pitiful shape and needed shoeing. Most of his supplies were gone and his equipment was worn out or near useless. He needed work and the pay that came with it if he was to continue without a long trek back to Privy.

The cavalry came to the rescue.

Prospect was attempting to barter labor for goods at a small "wide place in the road" of a town miles east of Tombstone. The owner of the only store, Swig Halen, would have none of it. He neither hated nor cared for Indians. He just wished they would all vanish from the face of the Earth. A Lieutenant Scott, who had just brought his small patrol in for water before moving northwest to Fort Bowie, heard the tail end of the conversation from outside the door.

"I got all the men I need right here, and I got a long line of good white men just waiting for one of them to get killed or run off to take his place," Halen said.

Prospect normally accepted a situation as he found it and either joined in or moved on with little or no comment, but that day he was desperate. "You need meat. I know the desert and the mountains. I know the animal trails and the places of water where they come to drink."

"I get my meat out of Tombstone. Be gone."

Scott entered. "Halen, you know this man?"

"I heard of him. Name's Prospect. He speaks real pretty."

"Is he a man of his word?"

"No one has ever caught him in a lie."

Scott turned to Prospect. "Do you really know this country as well as you say?"

"Better."

Scott looked at Halen.

The man nodded. "That's what they say, Lieutenant."

Scott turned back to the Indian. "Mr. Prospect—"

"Just Prospect, Sir."

"My scout just quit on me. I need a replacement. Think you can handle scouting duties?"

"Yes, Lieutenant. I can furnish references if you'd care to use your telegraph."

"That won't be necessary. Swig here is no fan of the Indian race. If he says you're qualified, then you must be that and then some. You will accept the position then?"

Prospect wanted to establish a strong position with his new employer. He threw a line of Shakespeare as his answer. "'As I am a soldier, a name that in my thoughts becomes me best.'"

"By God! An Indian who knows the Bard. 'A soldier firm and sound of heart.'" Scott grinned. He seemed genuinely delighted. Most white men resented the Indian's command of the language. "We shall have many a conversation around the fire when you return from your scouts. My men are uneducated and half of them can barely speak English."

"There is the matter of my payment," Prospect said.

"Oh. Well, I have some discretion here. Twenty-five dollars a month. That's less than a lieutenant, but more than a private. Done?"

"Agreed. I shall serve 90 days. Then I must move on."

Disappointment showed on Scott's face. "Just like my last scout. Well, I'll work your ass off for three months and then we'll talk."

As they walked out Halen said, "Watch your back, young sir. Watch your back. An educated Indian is still an Indian."

The half-day ride to Ft. Bowie was full of conversation, frequently punctuated by appropriate quotes from Shakespeare. Inexperienced in the West, Scott sought as much information as Prospect could provide. The new scout liked the young officer. He was willing to learn. He was also nervous, jerking slightly at the most innocuous sounds.

Without any implied criticism, Prospect offered a bit of Arizona wisdom. "Out here every lizard rustling through the brush, every bird taking wing, every animal scurrying along out of sight is an Apache... some think."

"From what they tell me back East that could be true."

Prospect shook his head. "If you hear something, it is not an Apache. No one hears them. You *feel* them. And then it is too late."

"Jesus!"

"You will learn, Lieutenant Scott."

Prospect had not seen Ft. Bowie in many years and the changes were startling. The rough outpost was now a legitimate fort. A dozen or more wood or adobe structures, one three stories tall, surrounded a square parade ground. A large number of tents were set up in good order inside the square. He also noticed several outlying buildings and other clusters of tents.

The fort was located in a relatively flat plain, a pass between low and desolate mountains. Its every function was based around one simple command: protect Apache Spring, one of the most important water sources in southern Arizona Territory. It was a necessary resource for Indians, Apaches, Mexicans and bandits. Fort Bowie was built on ground soaked in blood.

Despite the heat, the fort was a busy place. Men were drilling on the parade ground, making repairs to the structures or at work in some other way. The officer in charge knew soldiers and soldering in a fort. Prospect wondered whether he would prove as adept in dealing with the desert and the Apaches. Prospect's knowledge of the land and its people told him that he would soon know.

"We'll find you a tent on the parade ground, Prospect. I'm afraid the barracks are at capacity."

"I will stay out there." He pointed a horizontally moving hand toward the mountains.

"Oh, that isn't necessary. You're not an Apache. You will be welcomed here."

"Perhaps, but I will be a better scout out there. I am best alone... of better service."

"But the Apaches—"

"They once called me Destrozo Calavera. It means skull smasher. They have more to fear than I." Prospect was referring to the distant past and his days of revenge. An Apache raiding party had killed many of his village, including his young sister. Prospect, then known by the Pima name of Keli'hi, had taken the war path as a single warrior. He fought beside his people in pitched battles, but he also hunted alone. He had become feared and honored by his enemies, who gave him that all too descriptive title.

The look in his new scout's eyes was all the proof of his words Scott needed. "All right, Prospect, but you will report to me first thing every morning for assignment. Understood?"

"Yes, Lieutenant."

Prospect's first couple of weeks were uneventful. Scott, following orders from his commander, kept him circling the fort and looking for signs of any impending attack. That restriction kept him always close to the fort. He pushed his orders and his patrols to the limit, reporting early in the morning and late at night.

"I should scout a greater distance, Lieutenant. At least two or three days."

"Out of the question."

"Apaches can run 75 miles a day and then outfight any troop in your army. What you call 'intelligence' can keep you alive, Lieutenant."

"I agree, but I have my orders. I think the captain is testing you."

"What better way to prove my value?"

Scott tapped his fingers on his small desk. "Of course, you are right. I will make another request."

"Then you will kill Apaches and save lives." Prospect nodded and left.

Prospect spoke English better than most men in all of Arizona, but he had never mastered the skill of writing. His reports were taken by a sergeant. They were detailed, up-to-date and so accurate that Lt. Scott gained a fair working knowledge of the flora, fauna and surrounding terrain without ever leaving his desk. He proved to be a fair and competent officer and a good student.

The scouting reports were usually based on the same events, or in most cases, non-events. A typical day saw him leaving the fort before most of the men were out of there tents or their bunks in the barracks. Only one day broke the monotony of his schedule. He had ridden north and slightly west toward a notched peak men were calling Dos Cabezas, or "two heads." He followed a dry wash and skirted the north side of the mountains to his left. Apache sign, mostly footprints in the sand, was everywhere. They were many days old.

At the half-way moment in the day's scout he turned east and circled back toward his post. He wanted to ride on, but he considered following orders a pledge.

He had come across valuable intelligence and that information should be reported immediately despite his personal desires.

Late that afternoon he came across fresh footprints in a narrow valley not more than half a mile from the fort. He dismounted and followed them to a break in the rocks through which Fort Bowie could be observed. Two Apache warriors were playing cards. Apaches were famous for their addiction to gambling and their willingness to bet everything on a single game. Between the game and frequent glances at the fort they were distracted. Their only weapons were knives and their bows and arrows.

Many years had passed since he had encountered Apache warriors in their element. Memories of his village and his sister flooded his mind and he fought to control Destrozo Calaveras and remain Prospect. He crept closer until he could hear their conversation. They discussed only the game and events back at their temporary camp.

The part of his mind that was still Skull Smasher overcame the army scout.

He stepped into the narrow slot of the canyon, his large knife in his left hand and his pistol in his right. The warriors stood up slowly. They glanced at each other and dashed off in different directions. They were so fast Prospect had no chance to fire. He took up a defensible position and waited for an attack from two directions. He was as confident as he was bloodthirsty. He had baited this kind of trap many times before.

In less than a moment he heard the sound of ponies retreating north. The Apaches with a two-to-one advantage had chosen not to fight. *When warriors run away, death returns.* Prospect doubled his speed back to the fort.

"The Apaches did not fight, Lieutenant. Such actions are foreign to their way of thinking. Their band is planning an attack, Sir."

"When? Where?"

"I do not know. If I could scout farther out—"

"We've been over that."

111

"Yes, Lieutenant."

"I don't suppose you have any idea how many are in this band?"

"Fifteen."

Scott was dumbfounded. "How can you possibly know that?"

"Fifteen, no more than twenty. The warriors are led by the man you call Black Charley. You cannot pronounce his Apache name."

"You are certain?"

Prospect nodded. "I know them well, Lieutenant."

Scott paused. He knew how Prospect had gained his knowledge of the Apache. "I'll report this to Captain Armstrong immediately. Stay close in case he wants to hear it from you."

"Yes, Lieutenant."

The two men walked out of the office and across the parade ground. A private marching quick step from Armstrong's office met them halfway. "Captain Armstrong wants to see you immediately, Lieutenant Scott."

They knocked, entered and found the captain looking at a territorial map hung on the wall. "That was quick, Lieutenant."

"On our way to see you, Sir. Prospect has a report I think you should hear."

Prospect outlined the basic elements of his scouting mission, focusing on the unusual encounter with the Apache braves. Armstrong considered the matter for a moment. "I believe I know what they're up to. You have an urgent mission, Lieutenant. You too, Prospect. Scott will need an experienced desert fighter."

"No argument there, Sir," Scott said.

Armstrong took another long look at the map. "Fort Bowie is too well defended to attack. No troop movements or supply trains are scheduled. The settlers seem to be avoiding this part of the territory as much as possible. But there is one valuable and, sadly, vulnerable target."

"Redbird, Sir?"

The captain nodded. Redbird was a small mining outfit that had hit a big silver vein. Several other mining operations quickly moved in and a small community grew up virtually over night. Some women and children had joined their husbands. Two weeks earlier Armstrong had sent a small detachment of privates and one sergeant there. Redbird was in need of protection. Additionally, the town protected a small but generally reliable spring. The community was also a military asset. He had sent extra weapons and more than the usual amount of ammunition. Captain Armstrong looked at his scout. "The Apaches have certainly been watching, especially now that weapons are available. What do you think, Prospect?"

"They know the number of fighting men in camp, the number of pistols, the number of rifles, the number of ammunition boxes and the number of bullets in each box. At this moment they know more than you, sir."

"Scott, have your men fed, supplied, mounted and moving by midnight."

"Yes, Sir."

As they rode out Prospect knew that the Apache braves were heading to their scouts keeping an eye on Redbird and to their band's camp. The fight was on.

Scott looked at his column. "'Tis the soldier's life to have their balmy slumbers waked with strife.' Othello, I believe."

Prospect took a deep breath. More than any man in the column he knew what lay ahead. His voice showed no enthusiasm, only resignation. "Cry havoc. And let slip the dogs of war."

For the first time since their meeting, Scott did not enjoy dueling Shakespeare with his new scout.

Chapter Seventeen

Scott's command consisted of 100 men, two cannons, and just enough food and water to make the journey. Ten mounted cavalrymen accompanied the column.

The enemy force consisted of 15 or so warriors. Only Prospect knew that the odds favored the Indians. The Apache brave was the finest guerilla warrior in the world. He could cover vast distances by foot faster than mounted cavalry and still have the strength and will to fight a pitched battle. A warrior could survive off the desert for weeks on a diet that would starve other men. Until they wished to be seen they were invisible, and after a battle they disappeared, leaving only footprints and the blood of their enemies on the ground.

The column had the advantage of superior firepower, greater numbers and reinforcements within riding distance. Still, Prospect was burdened with a clear knowledge of their deficiencies.

Scott was a good man and would, if he survived, become a fine officer. But his lack of experience was combined with a youthful overconfidence. He was willing to learn, but he had much learning to accomplish. He was correct about his men. Nearly half of them were from Europe and could speak very little or no English. The others were at best illiterate. *How do you issue commands in battle to men who cannot understand your words?*

Armstrong trained them hard and well on the parade ground, but the well-tended center of a fort was far different from desert fighting. Only the sergeants and the cavalrymen had any real fighting experience. Perhaps they would do, provided they lived through the inevitable ambush.

"If they try a frontal assault up the road we could easily cut them to ribbons in the first charge. If they attack from the rear, we merely pivot and accomplish the same thing," Scott said.

"They will not attack in that way, Lieutenant," Prospect said.

"Bah. I have read that the Apache is a brave warrior. He will want to attack us bravely. And that is how he will die. Bravely."

"Look around us, Lieutenant. Look carefully."

Scott slowly scanned the low, rocky hills on each side of the road. "What am I looking for?"

"When you see rocks, you see Apaches. I count two, one on each side of the road."

"Impossible!"

"Inevitable, Sir. Before they attack Redbird, they will attack this column. You must understand. They will attack from high ground, from excellent cover and with surprise that will kill a large number of men in the first seconds. They will enter the road only to collect our weapons and ammunition."

"And our scalps, I suppose."

"Apaches do not take scalps. That is a Mexican tradition."

Scott's confusion registered on his face. He was out of his element. "But you say there are only 15 of them."

"'Only' is a misleading word when one discusses the Apache."

They pressed on. Prospect knew what to expect. The lay of the land would tell him when and where. *They will strike just when this young man feels most confident, when he will be most unaware.*

The day passed without incident and they made camp in an easily defendable wide spot in the road. Scott allowed the men to build small fires provided they did not hover close to them. "There's nothing to hide if the Apaches have been on our trail."

Prospect nodded, but said nothing. The Apaches would learn much from a well-lit campsite. He spent the night at the edge of the encampment away from the others. The men ate well and drank all the water they desired. After all, Redbird and re-supply was less than a day away. They slept well. Many of them found an excuse to walk past their two cannons. Each gave the weapons a gentle touch, as if they were family pets.

Prospect made a short scout around the campsite in the gray light before sun up. He arrived back in camp just as the men were preparing breakfast. Their food supplies were nearly gone by sunrise, but the water barrels carried just enough to get them to Redbird. *We are traveling too slowly.*

He went directly to Scott and made his report without emotion, merely stating fact. "The Apache warriors have left to join the rest of their band. They will attack us today, Lieutenant." The sun rises. Rain falls. The stars come out at night. The Apaches will attack.

"You are that certain?"

Prospect pointed to the men in camp. "Many of these soldiers will not see the sun rise again."

Scott squatted down and used a dry twig to draw meaningless images in the sand. He was devising the day's strategy, at task for which he was woefully unprepared. "I'm splitting the force."

"That is unwise."

"We need men at Redbird as quickly as possible. They have women and children there. I'll leave half the force here with the remaining water. The rest of us will ride on to Redbird. Quickly" He was evaluating his plan as he outlined it to his scout. "If they attack on the road we can crush them between two forces. If they wait until we're set up in Redbird, we will annihilate them there. And if they refuse to fight—"

Prospect couldn't keep from sounding a warning. "They will not refuse."

"If they refuse we will be sufficiently provisioned to move out and track them down. You can find them in the desert, can't you?"

"That will not be required of your scout." He was already fighting the coming battle in his mind. At the moment it was a toss-up as to the victor.

"What do you think, Prospect?"

"I hope Lieutenant Scott has made peace with his god."

Scott tossed away the twig and stood up. He wiped out the meaningless doodles with his boot. "I'll lead the first force. You will ride with me. Understood?"

"Yes, Lieutenant."

"Send Sergeant Heintzelman to me. We move out within the hour." He turned, but paused. "Prospect, I may not always agree with your advice or take it, but I do want you to always speak candidly." He turned and left without another word.

Prospect's thoughts were dominated by a more personal concern. *How can I find Caldera if I am killed in this place?* He saw Heintzelman and passed along Scott's orders.

"Is he gonna' get us kilt, Prospect?"

"He is trying, Sergeant... he is trying."

Within an hour Scott and Prospect led fifty infantrymen, five of the cavalry detachment and the cannons down the road toward Redbird. Heintzelman was left in charge of the second unit. A rider would come when the first unit was set up in Redbird. He was ordered to ration the water and remaining food.

The morning was uneventful. Scott allowed his men a break around midday. They ate their meager rations and were soon back on the road. Every now and then Scott would look to Prospect. "They are not here, Lieutenant." Scott's confidence was reflected in the way he sat in the saddle—straight backed, head erect and eyes to the front and the perceived challenge. Prospect sat just as erect, but his face was an unemotional mask. The column rounded a bend in the road to see Redbird about half a mile away. A hoarse shout rose from the troopers. Scott let them cheer while he straightened his hat.

Prospect wasn't cheering. The mountains rose some four to five hundred feet above them on each side of the road. Something was wrong. About half the column was through the bend before Scott realized the problem. It was a deadly one. He had taken Prospect's advice and had kept en eye on the mountains. He noted prominent outcroppings about two-thirds of the way up each mountain. The rocky formations would make excellent breastworks. *Breastworks!*

The outcroppings seemed to explode with gunfire aimed at the rear of the column. Five men were killed instantly and nearly a dozen were wounded, some mortally. Prospect saw a slight movement above and just ahead of them. Another volley took out several more men. Scott was hit with a through-and-through to the arm. He would live. How long he would live was a matter for conjecture. His column, so near the perceived safety of Redbird, was trapped between two enemy forces that held the high ground. Escape was impossible. Scott ordered his men into the rocks as Prospect helped him to cover.

When the men who could move were all behind cover, a few fired, uselessly, at the enemy, but most awaited orders. Sgt. Heintzelman crawled over as Prospect was binding Scott's wound.

"Orders, Sir?"

"Have the men on the north side of the road fire at the Apaches up on the south side. The men on the south are to fire on the north side. They'll have a better chance of hitting one of those braves than by firing straight up."

"Good," Prospect said.

Scott ordered the sergeant to send two men to the rear column and bring them up immediately. Two more riders were to dash to Redbird and assess the situation there.

All four riders tumbled and were flat on the ground less than a hundred yards from the battleground, their blood a marker in the sand. The one survivor, his leg shattered at the knee, crawled toward his comrades, but was killed by a shot that tore open the back of his skull.

The Apaches quickly dispatched the troop's animals. The only way out was by foot. Redbird, which had looked so close just minutes earlier, seemed an impossible distance away.

Scott assessed the situation. Rushing the enemy was out of the question. A few well-armed Apaches could hold off his entire force as long as they wished. A scramble up those rocky hills against rifles on the high ground would be suicide. A forced march back to the rear force was unthinkable. "We have to rush the town."

Prospect nodded. "You have no other choice."

"Get Sgt. Heintzelman over here."

"He will not be joining us."

"Sergeant Mitchell?"

Prospect nodded.

"Bring him."

A shout down the line soon had the sergeant dashing to the front.

"Sgt. Mitchell, what is our situation?"

"Poor, Lieutenant, damn poor. We're low on ammunition. We can hold off maybe one charge. A second would see us going hand-to-hand." He paused to look back down the line. "The boys ain't up to Apache standards, Sir. It would be a slaughter."

"Pass the word. We're going to Redbird."

"Yes, Sir."

"If you will forgive the terminology, Sergeant, we will be making a dead run. Tell the men to drop everything but their weapons and ammunition. Everything."

"Lieutenant." Prospect pointed to the two bronze cannons shining in the middle of the road. Each was mounted on a four-wheel limber that carried shot and shell and equipment. The two mules that carried the load were dead.

"Assign men to the cannons with additional runners along side to pick up the slack if—"

"I understand, Sir."

"Make sure the men understand; we're running, not fighting."

"And the wounded, Sir?"

"Help those who can walk. Carry those who can't. I want volunteers only for that duty. Volunteers, sergeant."

"They're a good lot, Lieutenant. We'll get the men through." Mitchell crawled back down the line. An occasional bullet struck nearby.

Scott turned to his scout. "How fast can you run?"

Prospect smiled grimly. As a youth he had been a champion runner of his village. He was no sprinter, but he won most of the distance races. "Fast enough, Lieutenant."

"When you get there, tell them we'll be making a run for it in about an hour. We'll need covering fire. If they can send out support to meet us, even better." Scott surveyed the scene and the situation. Almost as if he were thinking aloud, he said, "The Apaches can't move very fast up there in the rocks. Once we're out of this bend we have a chance. Ready?"

For the first and only time during his period as a scout, Prospect saluted. A second later he was already running. Scott was amazed at the erratic way he ran left and right while still dashing forward. Bullets kicked up small eruptions of dust around him. None struck their target. Prospect reached Redbird in less than five minutes. To Prospect it appeared that half the town was watching his run. Then he heard it:

"He's a damn Indian. Kill him!"

Chapter Eighteen

Prospect was saved by Sgt. John Perez who stepped between the miner's rifle and Prospect's face. "He's our scout, you damn fool!" He turned around. "What are Scott's orders, Prospect?"

"You gonna' take orders from a damn Indian, Sojer Boy?" the miner said.

Perez smashed the man's face. Blood formed a red halo as he fell to the ground. He looked at the others. "We don't have time for this!" No one helped the miner get up.

Prospect outlined the situation and Scott's desperate plan. Perez glanced at the sun and estimated the time till the escape from the bend. "We'll be ready."

The scout soon acquired a spare rifle and ammunition and took up a position with an excellent view of the road. The rush, with Scott leading the charge, began precisely on time. Eight men per cannon grabbed the carriage tongue and began hauling. More than a dozen men acted as escorts, drawing fire and replacing fallen men dragging the limber. Once rolling they made surprisingly good speed on the hard-packed dirt road.

The Apaches focused on the wounded who were struggling at the rear of the force. First to die were the men carrying the wounded too injured to move under their own power. Next to fall were the walking wounded and the men helping them. They were easy kills and their deaths bought the rest of the force more time to escape the trap. Men in the column fell also, but as the Apaches struggled through rocky hills that had no paths, the force moved closer to Redbird and safety.

As they reached the half-way point the soldiers and some well-armed townspeople rushed out to provide covering fire and help drag in the newly wounded. Prospect was in the forefront. Covering fire also came from within the town. Scott reached Redbird with about two-thirds of his force. Most were exhausted and immensely thirsty, but in good shape and ready to continue the fight.

Scott wasted no time. While a soldier cleaned and dressed his wound, he sought reports from Perez and Mitchell and advice from his scout.

"There are a hell of a lot more than fifteen warriors out there," Scott said.

"They have been joined by at least three other bands," Prospect said.

"Do you think they'll attack the town?"

Prospect nodded. "Before sundown."

Perez and Mitchell agreed.

Scott stood up. "Sgt. Mitchell, place the cannons where they will do us the most good. We will blast them out of those hills before they can organize an attack. Move!"

Within minutes the cannons were in place, loaded and aimed at the nearby hills.

"Fire!"

Two explosions followed by two echoes were followed by two powerful direct hits. Scott had aimed his cannons just above the Apaches. Rock exploded in all directions like shrapnel. Small landslides followed, raining rocks and boulders down on the enemy. The flat road was more of a trap than a route to escape.

"Fire!"

The soldiers slapped wet flower sacks on the barrels to keep them cool. Prospect watched with detached interest. An hour or so earlier they were dying of thirst. Now they used buckets of water to cool hot metal, spilling the precious fluid into large puddles on the ground beneath the weapons. *It is curious how the rules of survival can change so quickly.*

"Fire!"

The cannon teams were well trained. They moved quickly and with efficiency and dedication to the bloody task at hand. Scott was firing at one end of the narrow road and then at the other end. The Apaches were being forced into an ever more concentrated area. When they began appearing from behind their rocky defenses, he switched to canister fire. The lead balls were as effective as a shotgun at close range. Most of the townspeople and soldiers cheered. Veterans of the War Between the States were mostly silent. They shared in and were damn glad of, but did not enjoy the victory.

The Apaches were gone.

Chapter Nineteen

"'We band of brothers,' eh, Prospect?"

"You brought us through, Lieutenant. You are learning."

"You were right. I should not have divided my command. I'm no Robert E. Lee."

"Who?"

"Someone I wish we had with us at the moment. "Do you think they will attack the town?"

"I do not think so. Many are dead and many more wounded. And I think your cannon were something they had not...." He searched his memory for the word. "Encountered before."

They stood at the edge of town looking toward the bend in the road. The scars on the mountain showed where rock had been turned into shrapnel. "Are they gone?" Scott said.

"The Apache is never 'gone,' but I do not think we will see these warriors for some time."

"I want you to bring up the second force. What do you need?"

"Five men. Five better horses."

"Take whoever and whatever you need. Requisition anything you do not have from the town."

"I will leave within the hour."

"Prospect."

"Yes, Lieutenant?"

"I'll put Sgt. Mitchell in charge, but you may scout whenever, wherever and however you wish. Just bring those men in safely." Scott leaned against the building at his back. He was weak from loss of blood.

Prospect nodded. "Within the half-hour." He jogged off.

Ahead of his self-imposed schedule, five well-fed and well-armed troopers and five better horses followed Prospect through the bend in the road. Many of their fellow troopers were loading the bodies of other troopers on wagons for burial in the town cemetery. Although the death toll among the Apaches had been terrible, no Indian bodies were found. The small force passed through. Most of the men looked straight ahead, as if on parade. They were for the most part inexperienced and unprepared for such slaughter

Sgt. Mitchell rode next to the scout. "Prospect, you been fighting these bastards a long time, ain't ya?'"

"Since before what you call the time of changing voice."

Mitchell thought for a second. "Oh, hell... you mean puberty."

Prospect made note. He had learned a new word in English.

Mitchell cleared his throat. "I been at it a while, but not that long. Look, that young lad put me in charge of this thing. But if you get any ideas I damn sure want to hear them."

"I should scout ahead."

"You ain't waitin' on me. When will you get back?"

"When you see the moon clear the mountains you will soon see me."

"I done most of my fightin' back east, Prospect. That and trainin' recruits. I ain't been out of the States very long. You got any words of advice?"

"Do not trust what you see. Do not trust what you hear. Believe that the Apaches are always near. You will be wrong most of the time, but when it is important, your belief will save your life." He started to move out, but then halted. "Do not make your water alone."

"What?"

"Make water. You call it... to pee."

"Damn it, I know what it means. Why, fer' Chrissakes?"

"While you hold your pride, the Apache holds a war club."

Mitchell watched as Prospect rode his horse up the side of the mountain, a place where neither man nor horse should be able to navigate. "Damn!" Within a minute their guide was gone. He joined the other four mounted troopers.

"What are our orders, Sergeant?" asked one of the men.

"Survive, private. Survive."

Prospect had no trouble finding and following the band. They were moving so fast they didn't take time to disguise their trail. Blood stained the ground along the path. When he was satisfied that this bunch would not return for a fight, he turned west to join the troopers. He thought other bands were surely in the area and he was soon proven right.

Sporadic gunfire brought him to the crest of a small hill where he observed the situation from behind a couple of mesquite trees. Another band of Apaches had crept up on Mitchell's small party. They had stopped for rest in a defensible position and were mounting up for an organized retreat. None of the men panicked and therefore none of them were dead. Mitchell knew his work well.

Prospect fired and brought down a warrior. The shot proved just enough distraction to give the rest of Mitchell's troop time to mount up. They fired a volley. Just before turning and riding away they saw Prospect's horse take a fall. Their scout fell out of sight with it. Ten well-mounted and armed Apaches made any rescue effort futile even if Prospect were still alive. Mitchell led his men down the road toward the second force. They wasted no time looking back.

The scout was down, but aside from painful bruises was not wounded. He crawled back to his horse, the only cover nearby, and grabbed his rifle. *I should have chosen a mule.* The Apaches peppered the horse with shots. They were toying with the trapped enemy. Prospect could hear their laughter. He checked his weapons and waited.

Apaches could be patient, but like all men, not when their blood is up. Within an hour they had tired of wasting bullets on a dead horse. They wanted a kill and then to move on to other killings. Three warriors rode forward, the man in the lead a magnificent image. He knew he would be first to die or to be wounded, but he also knew that once the enemy had fired a shot his companions would get him in a rush. Death or injury was a small price to pay for glory.

With a shout the leader charged and that shout died in his throat as a bullet smashed into his chest and blew a fist-size hole through his spine. The other two warriors shouted and charged, knowing they would reach their target before the man had time to reload. Their knowledge was deficient. Prospect carried a repeating rifle. Two shots quickly brought down the two warriors. The remaining braves watched in shock. They had not expected this. One of the braves, a young man on his first raid, eased forward for a better look. Before wiser men could call him back he was struck in the belly by a round from Prospect's rifle. The bullet struck bone and began spinning within his body. Like a buzz saw loosed from its mounting it ripped through muscle, organ, vein and artery. All this violence occurred in seconds. The Apaches backed off and rode away.

Prospect did not move until dark and then he moved silently along the edge of the road. Just before dawn he saw the glow of campfires and heard the nervous chatter of men unsure of their future. He stepped close, but remained in the shadows. Softly he said, "Hello the camp."

Metal coffee cups clanked to the ground, boots hurriedly shuffled in dirt, a pistol or two cocked.

"Who goes there?" The voice was loud, but fearful.

"Prospect, the scout."

"I don't know that."

"Call your Sergeant Mitchell." Prospect moved silently several feet to his right. He didn't want to give a nervous man a good target.

Another man arrived at the guard's position. By his voice Prospect could tell it was Mitchell. "Prospect, is that you?"

"'A victory is twice itself when the achiever brings home full numbers.'"

"What the hell was that?" said the guard.

Mitchell laughed. "Come on in, Prospect."

The reunion was a happy one. They believed him dead or a prisoner of the Apaches. He did not want to talk, but the men made him tell the story several times around the campfire. Later, Mitchell said quietly, "Your tale gives 'em some courage and a little bit of hope." In the morning the entire force moved out and, without resistance, made an easy ride into Redbird.

Prospect wasted no time in speaking with Scott. His 90 days enlistment was up by several days.

"I'm not sure this troop or this town would be here today if it weren't for you. We could sure as hell use you," Scott said.

"No man uses me, Lieutenant."

"Hell, Prospect, you know what I mean. I'll see that you get a bonus for signing up again."

"You are a good man, Lieutenant Scott, and there are other good scouts. I will take my pay and my leave now."

Scott counted out the payment. "Where to now?"

"I have killed and I must be cleansed. I will go to our desert brothers, the Papago."

"If you change your mind—"

Mitchell stepped into the makeshift office. "Excuse me, Sir, the men will be ready to move out whenever you want, Sir."

"Just in time to bid our scout farewell."

"Sorry to lose you, Prospect." Mitchell took off his glove. "I'd like to shake your hand."

They shook. Prospect nodded to Scott and was gone.

"We have the damnedest luck with scouts, don't we, Sir?"

"I hated to lose that last man, too, the cold one."

"Yes, Sir. A good hand, but he had the coldest eyes I've ever seen."

Scott stood up. "We'll leave first light tomorrow, Sergeant. I have reports to make and you have men to train. And we have to find a new scout. If we're lucky we'll find someone as good as Prospect and—"

"Caldera, Sir. Called himself Caldera."

Well, let's get a move on, Sergeant."

"Yes, Lieutenant."

127

Chapter Twenty

As with Caldera, Prospect was driven by guilt. Desperate after years of failure, he at last realized what he must do. Before finding Caldera he would have to seek a vision. The pathway to a mind lost in madness could not be found in this world. He must enter another reality to find the way.

After completing his cleansing ritual Prospect made the journey to the chief village of the Papagos. After a brief reunion with several friends, he approached the elders of the village. Preparations were made for the vision quest. First he set off to the nearby mountains to kill a god.

To take the life of a god is an act of boldness and bravery. The act brings power and magic, and Prospect needed all he could get to track down and rescue his sometimes son. He had demanded that Caldera destroy Malon's gang, to slay the dragon. That drastic necessity had been forced on him by events. That he had misread the events due to Belle's treachery did not alter the facts. Lives had been shattered by his act. Guilt, as much as love, drove him on. After many silent days he found the nest of an eagle, and through stealth, patience and courage he killed the great bird, the god who had long ago taken this form.

"You have brought much magic," said one of the elders upon Prospect's return to the village. The elder pointed to the sky and then to the great bird. "See how like clouds are the downy feathers. They will help us bring rain. The medicine man will make much use of the wing feathers to brush away the white man's diseases that plague our people. The bravery of this eagle will find spirit in his tail feathers as they guide your war arrow." Prospect had heard these words many times before. Still, like cool waters he drank them in.

He journeyed into the desert. Not too far from the village he found shade beneath a large cottonwood tree near a reliable water source. He gathered wood, made a small fire as night fell, and settled down into a state of magic. He ate very little, just short of a complete fast, for sixteen days. "Four is a sacred number, Keli'hi." His uncle had said that decades earlier in what seemed to be a different and at times unreal world. "Four times four brings special magic."

One of the elders came every day. The old man would sit with Prospect and recite great stories of the visions sought and found by other warriors. He heard of great hunts, fierce battles, and mysterious visions. The old man sang songs and recited poetry. This process continued unceasingly, day-by-day as the magic grew stronger.

On the sixteenth evening his vision arrived with the silent ringing of a great bell. It was a huge metallic thing like the bells hanging in the Catholic churches and church ruins that had dotted the landscape for hundreds of years. He felt the vibrations before he actually saw the great instrument. He heard no sound, but he knew it was ringing. Great waves, like heat waves off the flat desert sands, rippled outward as the bell swung back and forth. Dust devils swirled through empty corridors of some abandoned and worn corridor   And still the bell rang. Soon the walls shattered and crumbled, unable to resist the silent wave after wave onslaught of destruction.

"Iagchulitha!"

The voice was clear and it spoke with authority. Prospect opened his eyes and looked up. The eagle he had killed had returned. The god who became bird stared at him and spoke again. "Iagchulitha!"

Prospect knew the word. In the Pima language it meant sacrifice.

The eagle grew until it was nearly the size of a man. It spread its wings and flew through Prospect and on to the heavens. Prospect closed his eyes.

"You must return to the elders now." The voice was that of a village elder. Prospect opened his eyes to see that the sun was rising.

"Have you a vision?"

"Yes."

"Do you understand its meaning, Keli'hi?"

129

Prospect's life in the white world made him think of the phrase "clear as a bell," but he refrained from using it. He merely nodded.

"Good. We must discuss it with the elders."

Discussions were held, visions revealed and related, stories told, poems recited and songs sung. Prospect was anxious to continue his quest, for he had interpreted his vision and knew where to find Caldera. Two days later, tradition having been honored and preserved, he rode south.

The bell that shatters worlds had to symbolize the Catholic churches. There were no other such great bells in the territory. The dust devils dancing through the corridors told him that the church was long abandoned and left to the care of the winds and the torments of time. Tumacacori! It could be no other place. There he would find and save from madness the lost soul he had sent on a journey to hell.

When he straggled into Tubac there was very little left to stumble into. What structures the rampaging Apaches had left were being finished off by the ravages of wind, sun, summer downpours and drunken shooting sprees. He'd have preferred to pass by the town. He had little need of most store-bought goods for the moment, but he was short of one essential: bullets. For those he needed the white man.

A rough looking young man was loading a small wagon parked in front of the town's only store. He smiled and nodded, then re-entered the store. Prospect nodded back and followed the man in.

Prospect requested several boxes of shells. The grizzled worm of a man behind the counter curled his lip. "Injuns ain't welcome here. Git."

"I have funds to match my needs," said Prospect.

The worm seemed startled. He turned to the other customer. "Hell, Preacher, he speaks prettier n' you. 'Funds' he has." He turned back to Prospect. "Go eat a turd."

Having encountered this attitude before, the Indian was about to turn and walk away when the man called Preacher stepped up. His face was all smiles, but his eyes were cold. "Bob, that' ain't no way to treat one of God's children, especially one that's a paying customer."

Prospect looked the man over. Was he being friendly or was he just a troublemaker looking for sport?

"Hell, Preacher, them Injuns killed D.J. last week. And Bailey the week before that."

"This man's no Apache." He turned to Prospect and offered his hand. "They call me Preacher. I guess around here a man's known for what he does more than what he is. At least I hope so."

Prospect accepted his hand. "I am called Prospect."

"What can old Bob here help you with, Mr. Prospect?"

"Shells. Forty-Fours. And I am just Prospect."

"You heard the man, Bob."

"Damn it."

"Last year I pulled a bullet out of your neck, Bob. Don't make me regret that."

"Hell, Preacher. Never mind."

"Just sell him the goods, Bob."

"And I will be gone," said Prospect.

Once the transaction was completed nothing else was said. Prospect helped Preacher carry out and load up the rest of his goods.

"Don't think too much about old Bob, Prospect. He would have sold you the goods sooner or later. He just wanted you to work for it."

"That is the white way."

"How do you mean?"

"You make the simple complicated."

"Well, spoken, my friend. Where are you headed?"

"Tumacacori."

Preacher smiled. Well, looks like you got a free ride. Tie your horse to the back of the wagon. That's perzactly where I'm heading."

Prospect complied. The white man talked a lot, and in this instance he didn't mind at all. Maybe he knew something of Caldera. "Are you a priest?"

"Nah, more of a Methodist. The Catholics quit on the old mission a long time ago. I just... inherited the property. I was a hospital steward in the war. When I found God I all that training came back and I found a calling. I'm the closest thing to a doctor in more than a couple of hundred miles."

"The store man called you a preacher."

"That I am, as you will learn along the way."

Prospect nodded and smiled. Inside he grimaced. He was about to be saved.

A low funnel of dust approached from the west, whipped into a frenzy by a hot wind. The wave caught up with them, swirled light colored dust and debris about them, and then moved on down the road. They followed its movement across the desert as if looking at a fleet of ships disappearing over the horizon. Through it all, Preacher preached. Prospect took it as God's blessing or His mercy that the man's mouth did not fill up with dust.

Preacher's tone of voice became more serious the longer he spoke. "I was among the worst of the worst. If there is a commandment in The Good Book or a law on mankind's books that I ain't broke, then I never heard of it. I have committed rape and robbery and I have killed men. I—"

"You do not have to tell me these things," said Prospect.

"But I do. My confession is part of my penance." Preacher's voice droned on as if he were reciting a well-practiced prayer. "I rode with a gang of cutthroats, Prospect." The man was filled with shame and remorse and Prospect could see that his feelings were sincere. He continued uninterrupted for some time until a particularly haunting story grabbed Prospect's attention. "When we were through they left to me to finish her off. The others rode away and it was just me and this little mouse of a girl in the desert up near Privy. I carried a Baby Dragoon in those days. When I cocked the hammer, the sound of it must've brought her around. She just stared into heaven and said, 'Why me?' That's all. Why me?" Preacher stopped talking for a moment, overcome with memory and guilt. "I blew her brains out and left her there to rot."

"You shot her in the back of her head?"

"No. Forehead. Why?"

He lied. "I am just trying to see what you saw."

"She said that 'why me' to God I think. She sure as hell wasn't talking to me. But I couldn't get it out of my mind. It was so... like she'd long ago given up on life. I think she just wondered why God treated her that way."

Another hot dust devil rolled by. It buffeted the wagon, stinging the passengers with rock and sand. Prospect said, "You Christians have a saying that your God works in unusual ways." He wanted to keep the Preacher talking, not a hard task, because he needed time to think.

"That girl's words, they worked on me, wouldn't let me go. They haunted me something fierce. Finally they drove me out of the gang and into God's arms." He described his wanderings, not unlike those experienced by Prospect or Caldera, and his eventual encounter with God and salvation.

Prospect heard and he nodded occasionally to show that he was listening, but his mind was to the north, not far from Privy and many, many, years in the past.

"Then God led me to Tumacacori. I been there ever since. I set up a little hospital in the old church. Hell, they wasn't using it. I been serving my little flock of farmers and some of the Papagos and Pimas ever since." He stopped again, content to drive the horse, keep an eye on the road, and to reflect on his thoughts.

Prospect was grateful for the respite. He has his own thoughts to contend with. The "little mouse" raped and murdered by Preacher and the others could only have been poor Alice Chacon. Malon's gang had not been completely wiped out after all. Despite his best efforts, the ways of the white man were intruding into his life. Once again they were making the simple things most complex.

Preacher's body jolted ever so slightly. "I just realized who you are, Prospect. You're the man looking for that Lynx Killer, ain't you?"

"I am looking for my... son."

"Well, one way or another I hear about near anybody who comes through these parts. What's he look like?"

Prospect described how he thought Caldera would look after hard years of killing the dragon.

"Shoot, Prospect, you just described only about half the men in Arizona Territory."

"You would know him, I think by his eyes. Something is... lacking." Although he hadn't seen Caldera in years, Prospect could visualize those eyes. He'd seen the dead, cold stare in the eyes of Apache warriors, the scum that inhabited the saloons of Privy, and in the eyes of Bull McKenzie and he knew it had been a part of his own countenance when he lived as Two Worlds.

They rode in silence for a moment. The abandoned mission of Tumacacori appeared on the horizon. Majestic and beautiful, it made a regal presence in the barren landscape. Its brown brick had decades earlier been painted bright colors. Great swaths of yellow, red and black still remained on the exterior of the three-story structure. There were brick half-columns, arches, a tower, and niches built into the sides where statues must have been placed. There were walls, other smaller structures, and even a substantial garden.

"I might have good news for you, Prospect. That man you described, your son, could be any of dozen men I seen in the last year. But those eyes. I definitely saw 'em, and not too long ago."

Prospect sat up.

Preacher continued with a voice filled with an expectant joy, as if he realized he was about to create his own miracle. "A man showed up a few weeks ago, all shot to hell. We didn't think he was gonna' make it."

"Who?" Prospect asked.

"Don't know. He couldn't even groan for days. We couldn't find nothing with a name or address on it."

"Why do you think he is my son?"

"Those eyes, Prospect. It's like he's hollow. There just ain't nothing there." His face showed that the image was not one that brought him comfort. "I have never seen a man so empty."

"He is dying?"

"No Sir. He's coming around nicely. I got me a wife these days. More than anything he owes his life to her. She ain't left his side since he showed up. He's going to hurt for a long time, but he's gonna' make it."

They arrived at the old mission where glory had given way to ruin and disrepair. Time, the elements, Apache revenge and Anglo drunkenness had taken their toll on the great building. Yet, as with all things in the desert, new life had sprung forth. Preacher had made the old ruin live again. He pulled the wagon up to the side of the old building.

"I would see my... this man now. If I may," said Prospect.

"Of course. I'll unload and then join you."

"Where is your hospital?"

"My wife will escort you. She's probably there now." He raised his hand to his mouth and shouted. "Deanna, we have a guest. Deanna!"

Chapter Twenty-One

Prospect caressed Caldera's forehead. He had always believed Caldera's vengeance trail would end in death, but only after a confrontation between a sometimes father and a sometimes son. He had lived with the sure knowledge that he alone would kill Caldera, that justice for a murdered wife and child was in his hands and his alone. But now he wondered, *What have I done? What have I created?* He looked up to Preacher. "Will he live?"

"I think so. He's got the spark."

"Has he spoken?"

"Naw. He's been out since he stumbled in here three days ago."

"His wounds?"

"Damn bad, Prospect. Damn Bad. Back during the war I saw canister fire so thick whole rows of men disappeared in a single blast. This is the worst I've seen since. Damn, he's tore up." He saw worry cross Prospect's face. "But like I said, he's got the spark. I think he'll pull through."

"How bad?"

"Seven wounds, gunshot. Four of 'em would have killed any normal man."

"He is not... normal."

"Must have been one hell of a fight. He was as near death as a man could be. If it weren't for Deanna, I don't think he'd'a pulled through." His head turned at the click of footsteps in the nearby hallway. "Ah, speak of the devil. I mean angel, an angel of mercy."

A young woman entered the room with purpose. She carried a wash basin and some clean rags. Her flash of a smile said that she appreciated the effort at a joke even if the results were less than funny.

"Deanna, meet Prospect. Prospect, this is my wife."

135

"Ma'am."

"Mr. Prospect." Her face was pretty and her smile would have lit up any room. Her sad eyes would have brought the darkness right back.

"He'd rather you just use Prospect, I think."

"It is my name."

"He can pin a name on our patient." Preacher beamed as if he'd discovered a cure for the common cold.

Prospect noted just the faint flicker of muscle movement around Deanna's eyes. *Curious*, he thought. *My news is not news at all. The young woman knows something of Caldera.*

She placed the basin and the rags on a rough plank stand beside the bed. "You gentlemen may discuss problems of identity outside. I have wounds to clean. It is pleasant to meet you, Prospect." She dismissed them by quickly turning to her task.

As with all men so ordered, they left the room.

The courtyard of the old mission had once been the hub of salvation, business and what passed for society in the area. Not much of anything had been happening in the recent past, as was evident by the dust and disrepair. Prospect stared at the ruins of shops that ringed the dusty, hollow center of the old structure. Whatever society had ever been here had long since departed for greener and safer pastures.

Preacher started to speak, but the clanging of metal against metal from outside the walls interrupted him. He glanced toward the gate, then back at Prospect. "We have guests, a rare event these days. Come with me."

A hunk of rusty iron hung from a small tree outside the church. Next to the iron hung another metal bar on a rope, and next to the bar was a thin man with a thin smile. He nodded to Preacher and glanced at Prospect with suspicion. A small boy of not more than ten sat in the back of an overloaded farm wagon. Prospect figured everything of value the poor man owned was stuffed into, onto or hung beneath that wagon. The boy cradled a shotgun as if he was well versed in its use.

"Johan, welcome," Preacher said.

"Afternoon."

Introductions were made and the usual small talk was completed before the real conversation started. "Me and the boy are pulling up stakes."

"I'm sorry to hear that, Johan."

"Well, we done raised nothing but tombstones on that damn farm. I don't aim to see another crop this year."

"Where you headed?"

"They still got land in California." He removed his hat and wiped the sweat trickling down his forehead. He seemed to be wiping out a substantial portion of his life with the same motion.

"You're the last, then," said Preacher.

"No, sir. You're the last, and if you're smart you'll not waste time following my damn tracks."

"My work—"

"Is finished, Preacher. They ain't nobody left except the Apache."

"We have an understanding."

The farmer spit. "You ain't no holy man to Geronimo and his band, and Geronimo raids where the hell he pleases these days, by damn."

Prospect nodded. Whatever arrangement Preacher had made with the nearest tribes wouldn't mean spit to the old warrior's band of Chiracahuas.

"I come to say goodbye to Deanna."

"She's with my patient."

"I'll be saying my goodbyes to you, then." He paused to look Preacher right in the eyes. "You believe in hell, Preacher?"

"Yes, Sir."

"You believe in salvation, then?"

"I do."

"Well, I'm here to tell you, right now this Arizona is the middle of hell. And your salvation is at the end of that damn road there."

"Johan, I think you—"

"God don't need nobody preaching to an empty desert, Preacher." He stretched out his arms to the nothingness around them and then walked into the church.

"Deanna's always been special to Johan."

Prospect nodded as if he were interested. His eyes scanned the low, rugged hills around the old mission. Apache eyes would be watching any movement around the settlements. Runners would soon report how few members still inhabited the old place. Johan was right. It was time to move on. He hadn't searched for Caldera all these years just to watch him die at the hands of an enemy.

Preacher continued droning. He looked toward the setting sun. "Come on. Let's see what we can scrounge up for supper."

A quizzical look crossed Prospect's face.

Preacher smiled. "Deanna's a good wife and I love her, but the Apaches could learn something about torture from her cooking."

Prospect had seen too many victims of such tortures to find the joke funny. Still, it had been some time since he'd had a decent, home-cooked meal. "I will visit my son briefly, and then I will join you."

"Fair enough."

As he turned, some slight movement behind a scrub brush on a far hill caught his attention. A mule deer? A javelina? Perhaps it was just an illusion in the corner of his eye. Whatever it was, it set his course for the immediate future. He and Caldera were leaving this place at the earliest possible moment. Safety and refuge could be found to the northeast. Privy wasn't much, but it was all they had left.

He found Deanna tending to Caldera. His bandages had been changed, his head and arms bathed and, as he was still unconscious, there was no reason for her to remain at his side. Although he did not employ the tactics of stealth, he was Indian and walked soundlessly through the world. The woman did not hear him approach. She was humming a lullaby, a tune he knew. It had been popular among many of Belle Delcour's whores. As she felt her patient's forehead for his temperature, Prospect noted that her movement was more of a caress than a medical procedure.

"Is he well?" he asked.

She jumped ever so slightly, but pretended not to be startled. "With care and attention I believe he will recover fully, Mr... I mean, Prospect."

"I—" And Prospect was overcome. The stoic image of the American Indian, the emotionless hunter, the warrior with the cold heart, the man beyond caring was a myth created by misunderstanding miliga'n such as the ambitious writer A. Noye. Prospect was moved deeply, but emotions were not shared with members of another race. He could not speak, but he remained in control.

"He will come back to you," she said.

He wondered. What would Caldera do when told that his long vengeance trail was based on a falsehood? Once a man strikes out on the pathway of violence, for many it is impossible to strike out in another direction. He wondered too how the many hard years of killing had changed Caldera. Prospect had set a whirlwind in motion and men had died for it. Would the man known as Prospect become just another link in Caldera's chain of death?

"I should prepare dinner," said Deanna.

"Your man has already begun. I will help. Please stay and tend to my son."

"Son?"

Prospect smiled at her shock. "I admit that there is not much of a family resemblance. It is, as you white people like to say, a long story."

"I hope you will remain with us long enough for a telling of it," she said.

"Care for my son," he commanded.

"I do," she said.

Kitchen sounds echoed through the empty hallways. He followed the noise and sought productive work. His sometimes son was a killer. Once he knew the truth, would he turn on the man who had started all the killing in the first place? As he turned to leave, movement from the sickbed caught his attention.

Caldera stirred. His eyes flicked open and he stared into Deanna's eyes. A confused look crossed his face. "You?" He then slipped back into the darkness from which he had come.

Prospect then knew two important facts. One was obvious. Caldera and Deanna shared a history, a history she had chosen to keep from her husband. The other related to the emotions she displayed when Caldera spoke: genuine joy, then anger and then frustration. The woman was conflicted. She did not know herself. He would have to keep a close watch when she was near her charge.

"I'll call for you should he wake again," she said. It was a dismissal, yet a welcome one. He needed time to think his way through the days ahead. That he would return to Privy with Caldera was obvious. What then? Well, he would face that challenge when it presented itself.

He walked about the mission trying without success to organize his thoughts. Things kept getting more and more complex. He could not escape the past. Like a desert whirlwind it kept spinning back upon itself. The present is built on the past, yet that past continued to rip away all that had been built.

He found Preacher lost in thought in the sanctuary. Prospect was not comfortable around the white man's religion, and the musty old structure only reinforced that feeling. The seating had long since been removed for fire wood. Elaborate and colorful paintings had once covered the walls, but they were now faded, burned and even shot full of holes in places. Dried bloodstains in one of the corners flaked away in the occasional slight breeze. This was not a building that had lived up to its name.

"Prospect... I'm glad you're here."

"I did not mean to disturb you."

"Oh, I wasn't praying. Just thinking."

"It is a noble occupation."

Preacher grinned. "And one too rarely employed. But I'm working hard at it now." He paused before speaking again, as if weighing the price of a soul. "I'm a preacher without a congregation, Prospect. Johan was the last. I feel lost... without a purpose."

Prospect looked at the faded images on the decaying walls. He wished he were outside where he could feel the sun, smell the summer rain or see the sky. "The lack is not purpose, Preacher. It is in the finding of it."

"They were right. You do speak well. Maybe you oughta' be the preacher."

"That is not my way."

Preacher stood up and looked around. "This isn't my church. I borrowed it and folks didn't seem to mind. I think I did some good here."

"I don't believe there is any more good to be done here."

"Your right." Again he paused, searching. "Do they need a preacher in Privy?"

Prospect had not laughed in many months. The lone "ha" that escaped his mouth was laced with irony.

"I should take that as a yes, shouldn't I?"

Now it was Prospect's turn to pause. He thought carefully before speaking. "There are some who would oppose your coming. Most would not care. But a few would welcome you, I think."

"Whenever two or more are gathered...."

Prospect shook his head, not comprehending.

Preacher's countenance changed. He beamed with purpose and energy. "Privy it is."

The Indian was startled by the sudden change in the other man's appearance and attitude. The man who had once been called Two Worlds saw both sides of the situation before him. A man seeking absolution for his crimes had found a new purpose late in life. Prospect had seen this often in the white world. Of course, there was another side of the coin. A purpose can be a deadly thing.

"Privy it is," said Preacher. He clapped his hands as if applauding some performance. "Prospect, you'll be wanting to take Caldera—that's his name, isn't it?" Prospect nodded. "You'll be wanting to take him back home. I think we'll tag along, if you don't mind."

What could he say? "Of course."

A cloud seemed to pass across Preacher's face. Suddenly the picture of his future dimmed. "There is something I'd like to ask you." He didn't wait for encouragement. "You know I rode with Malon. I left that life years ago, but it is a part of me... part of my past."

He lied. "What was past is past."

"I'm thinking of Caldera. I know he's been killing Malon and his men. Do you think he will kill me, Prospect?"

The Indian sighed. "If he wants to continue killing I believe he will begin with others."

Preacher issued his own mournful sigh. "The past... I guess you can never escape it."

"I know of only one who has." His thoughts turned to Belle Delcour and her deadly treachery. Belle was living a life of luxury, free of want and worry, in San Francisco. She alone had escaped her past. Had he spoken her name, it would have come out as a hiss.

Several days later, Caldera, still weaving in and out of awareness, was able to be moved. Four people packed their guilt into a rickety old wagon and started on the journey to the northeast and, perhaps, real sanctuary. Privy. No one knew what they'd find at the end of that road. Peace and prosperity? Maybe. Deanna wondered, however, how much could she expect from a town called Privy.

Chapter Twenty-Two

Sheriff Tom Arlen grinned and shook his head. "My, my, my how the mighty have fallen."

The words, dripping with sarcasm and delight, scraped Belle's eyes open.

The sheriff's fingers wiggled on the edge of her iron cage like eager worms waiting to feast. Folks around Tickville called him Spec Arlen because the previous year he'd busted a lens in the tiny round slivers of glass that compensated for his remarkably poor vision. The man was too cheap to buy a new pair, so he stared at the world through one good lens and one badly cracked chunk of glass. The worst of it was that the cracked glass was on the side of his one halfway decent eye. Cheap and sour, he stumbled around the small California town like some clumsy Cyclops, always getting in the way, always embarrassing himself and the tiny town, and always doing jobs no one else wanted.

"Where the hell am I, Pissant?" Belle's breath was fouled by bad whiskey and perhaps a bit of opium. She recognized the flavor of blood, too. She spit on the floor, half as an attempt at clearing the foulness from her mouth, half as a sign of contempt.

"You in jail, Queenie. And from the charges, you gonna be here a long time... Miss Belle Adams or Belle Delotte or Belle Delcour. You been usin' a lot of names since you got to these parts, ain'tcha?"

"What are the charges?" Belle wasn't in the mood for banter, even if it might earn her an easier time with the authorities. Besides, Arlen didn't look much like the bantering kind. He was a withered prune of a man with short hair, a sour expression and a permanent facial twitch created by trying to make one weak eye do the work of two.

"That might take some time, Miss... I'll just call you Belle."

"What are the damn charges? How much do I owe? When the hell can I get out of this piss pot?"

"You owe the community of Tickville—that is to say, you owe me.... He ran up a tally in his head, then smiled. "Let's just round it off at $250."

"You bastard!"

Arlen's grin widened. He rarely got the chance to really abuse his power, that power being limited by cowardice and a strong desire to remain in office. His venom built up over time until some drunken miner, a drummer passing through, or in this case a belligerent whore got out of line enough for him to administer rough justice behind bars and out of sight of the population. On days like this one, he enjoyed his job.

"As to the charges, Belle, there's quite a list: whoring without a license, drunk and disorderly, resisting arrest, assault on an officer of the law, and pissing me off. I could go on if you want."

"To hell with you!" Belle sat up. Her head hurt something fierce and her right eye socket was swollen. Her ribs and her back were sore too. The taste of blood came from her inner cheeks and gums. She'd been beaten. "Call my men in here." She began a poor attempt at straightening out her dress. The effect was less than she had hoped. It was an old dress and it hung off her in unflattering ways. The hard times of recent years had curtailed not only the richness of her diet, but also its variety and quantity. Belle had lost a good bit of weight.

"That old darkie and them two runts? Ha! They skeedaddled after we brung you in."

"They most certainly—"

"They ain't here, Belle.'" He turned to the partially opened door leading from the jail area to the front office. "Conly! Git in here!"

A pudgy man of enormous height shuffled in. Arlen must have selected him as deputy from among the shallow waters of the gene pool. His was the most open face Belle had ever seen. Fear played across that vast, drooping expanse of flesh when he looked down at Arlen. Lust pulsed through the big red veins when he stared doe-eyed at Belle. She'd loved to play cards with him on pay day.

"Anybody to pay off Queenie's charges?"

"Who?"

"The whore in the cage." Arlen raised himself up so he could stare into the deputy's face. The big man backed off.

"No, Sir. Them three ain't been by at all."

"Git out of here."

"I'll do that right now." Conly stood his ground as if waiting for permission to do what he'd just been ordered to do.

Arlen kicked the man's butt and he scurried out the door.

Belle continued to straighten her dress. She made a poor attempt at being regal. "My man, Hephaestus—"

Arlen enjoyed interrupting her. "Well, you see, Queenie, your man Festus done found himself in a bit of a stink after you... ah, bumped your head. Them runts of yours, too. I think they just decided the smart move was on down the road."

Belle shook her head. "I have some money in my room."

"No you don't, Queenie. First place I looked."

She gave him a quick, harsh stare.

"I knew you'd want your fines covered right away. This here jail ain't no place for a lady. You're short two hundred and fifty dollars to the penny."

Belle tried to put things together. The task was monumental. She was suffering from a hangover and a beating. Worse was the knowledge that she'd been abandoned by Hephaestus and ShortRound. Incomprehensible! Whether they or the sheriff had stolen her money was at the moment irrelevant. Belle was in jail, busted and alone. "What are my options?" She was set to make the best deal possible under the worst possible circumstances. She'd seen similar times.

"You're sittin' on 'em."

Belle pulled her stringy hair back tight to give it some semblance of form. "How long?"

Arlen sniffed. "Forty-five days. Two months. And that's just till the trial. Charges like yours warrants a trial. Takes a while, don'tcha know." Small boys torturing small animals had the same look on their faces.

Belle knew where the conversation was headed. She knew the game and she played it well. "Surely there are options." A well-practiced smile that hinted at desperation formed on her lips.

"Queenie, you and me and most ever'body around ends up in Tickville for one reason, just one. This is the end of the line. They ain't no options in Tickville." He spoke as if he had just come down from the mountain after winning a short game of poker with God.

Belle's smile turned overtly sexual. She sat up straight, spread her legs far apart, and leaned forward. "Sheriff, there are always options."

And the game had run its course, each side confident of its own victory.

"Conly!"

The big man bumbled his way into the jail. "You called, Boss?"

"Yes, you damned idiot."

"What you need, Boss?"

"What time is it?"

"Eight or so. Sun's down. Why?" He seemed eager to please, like a child with a favorite uncle.

"Git over to The Emporium and bring me back a bottle of whiskey. And go get Wes." He turned to look directly into Belle's eyes. His grin returned. "I got me two deputies."

"Make it two bottles, then," said Belle. "And none of that rot gut." She slowly closed her legs, but her eyes remained on Arlen.

He waved his arms. "Go on now. And hurry your ass up. We're gonna' lock up early tonight and have ourselves a little party."

Conly looked puzzled. "But what if some—"

"Git the whiskey. Git Wes. And git your ass back here pronto!"

Conly scooted off.

Belle went into her act. "Why don't you open the cell, Mr. Arlen? We can get started a little early."

Arlen tossed her one of his sick grins. He stood up and stretched. "Ain't no hurry, Queenie. We got all night."

Tickville was a quiet town. She could hear Conly stumble down the street. He was laughing like a little girl.

Belle had experienced worse nights, but few with so many men had proven to be so unimaginative. Conly, the whiskey and Wes arrived not more than half an hour after the big man had giggled down the street. They didn't even wait to get drunk. The cage doors flew open and the animals started drinking and rutting. They worked at trying to get Belle drunk, too. She could have drunk them all under the table, but she played along. The sheriff seemed to need the act.

When he finished, Conly jumped in, but Arlen shoved him away and motioned for Wes. He was the least eager to participate. He looked to be what passed for a "straight arrow" in Tickville, and he seemed somewhat befuddled by the whole affair. He even made an excuse to leave, but his boss wouldn't hear of it. So Wes took his turn while Arlen and Conly looked on. Being a spectator sport was a lot more challenging for Wes than for the star attraction, but he managed to satisfy the audience.

Toward the end of his turn, Wes lost himself in the grunting and grinding, and as he finished he almost squealed. Belle realized she'd just been taken by a virgin. He buttoned up and walked sheepishly from the cell. Conly practically ran over him on his way in.

Wes sat down in the sheriff's office. Arlen joined him. "Don't blame you. I don't think I could watch old Conly either."

The men shared a few swigs from the bottle.

"Yeah, git your strength back, Boy," said Arlen. "That whore's got one hell of a lot of charges to clear. You got more work to do in there." He snickered.

"We can do that?"

Arlen didn't know if the young man meant legally or physically. "Well, take another pull or two out of that bottle and we'll see what you can and can't do." A loud "yeehaw" from inside the jail grabbed his attention. "Looks like Conly's done popped his cork. I bet Queenie could use another coupl'a drinks about now." He stood up, staggered a bit from the tangleleg already befuddling his brain, and stumbled back into the jail.

And so it went until nearly dawn, and at the end it was hard to tell who had gotten the worse of the action. Wes had sneaked away in the early hours of the morning. Conly had failed to perform on his last effort. He blamed Belle and was about to strike her when Arlen whacked him on the head with the butt of his pistol. She couldn't tell whether he was protecting his evening's entertainment or whether he just liked to hear the sound of a skull cracking. It didn't matter. He had one more turn and then spent the rest of the night chugging whiskey and offering midnight confessions at the altar of sin. Belle pretended to be drunk and allowed him to prattle on.

When he passed out she considered making a run for freedom, but decided against it. *A deal's a deal*, she thought. She did sneak into the office and rifle the sheriff's desk. She found a few dollars squirreled away and she took them. She also found her purse. It had been rifled, too, but nothing other than a few dollars had been removed. Her medicine bottles were intact and unopened. She replaced the purse and sneaked back into the jail.

Arlen and Conly were still passed out when Wes returned just after sunup. He found Belle sitting at the sheriff's desk. She had cleaned herself up as best she could and actually looked presentable for a whore who had been working the late shift.

"Where the hell have you been?" she said.

"Ma'am?"

"I've paid my fines. I'm ready to be released." Her words didn't comprise a statement. They were a command.

Wes stammered and tried to formulate an answer.

Belle would have none of it. "Are you saying I haven't paid in full?"

"No, Ma'am. It's just that—"

"It's just that your sheriff is as drunk as a boiled owl." She stood up. "Well, that's not my problem. May... I... Go?"

"Oh, yes. Yes, Ma'am."

"I am officially and legally released from this cage you call a jail?" She didn't want Arlen coming back claiming she'd "escaped" just to earn another night of fines.

"Yes. I guess so."

"Guess?"

"You're free, free to go, Ma'am. Released."

Belle grabbed her purse and walked to the door.

"And Ma'am?"

"Yes."

He lowered his head and looked away. "Thank-ee."

Belle shook her head in amazement and stepped into the streets. Freedom smelled like horse dung, but the air was better than the inside of Tickville's jail. Her thoughts moved immediately to the problem at hand: getting some money and then getting the hell out of town.

"Miss Belle! Miss Belle!"

She turned to see ShortRound dashing down the street. "What the hell?" she said.

Short arrived first, but Round was only a second behind him. "We was just coming to get you, Miss Belle," Round said.

Hephaestus followed. He merely nodded. "Miss Belle."

"This ain't no place for us, Miss Belle," said Round. "We don't belong here."

"What the hell is going on?" Belle was tired, angry and confused. "What are you doing here?"

The small men looked just as confused. "That sheriff said we could pick you up first thing this morning," Round said.

"We paid your fines yesterday," Short said.

"Over at the saloon," round said.

Belle leaned against the wall. "Son of a bitch!" That she had been used did not trouble Belle Delcour—that was her life—but to have been so unwittingly used by such a numbskull as Spec Arlen showed truly how far she had fallen. She'd lost her touch. And in the shock of that moment she found it again. In a flash of inspiration a plan descended upon her, as if a gift from heaven. A fog that had obscured her vision for more than a year suddenly lifted. She knew what to do, where to go, and how to get there. And the cold darkness in her eyes showed that she knew what she had to do along the way, too. "Hephaestus, how much money do we have?"

"We have just about enough to leave this hellhole, a course I highly recommend."

"Load everything."

"Anticipating our need for a speedy departure, I have already done so."

"Good. Go fetch it now."

He left in a half-trot. She turned to ShortRound. "You two go to the saloon and get me a bottle of whiskey." She handed them the dollars she'd stolen from Arlen. As they rushed off to do her bidding, Belle leaned back against the building. She had much to do and a long way to travel, but first things had to come first. Her new vision had enlarged the portion of her life dedicated to revenge.

ShortRound and Hephaestus arrived about the same time. She accepted the whiskey with a smile.

"Where to, Miss Belle?" Short said.

"Get in the wagon. And if the sheriff or one of his deputies steps out, you say something and keep him talking. Understand?"

"Yes, Miss Belle."

Belle turned, straightened herself up and, with a smile plastered across her face, walked back into the sheriff's office. Wes was busy cleaning up the mess from the previous evening's activities. "Oh!" He was startled as much by her appearance as by her arrival. He didn't really want to think about what had happened, what he had done, and how easily he had fallen into doing it. "The sheriff's still... ah, you know," he said.

Belle forced a heartwarming grin that would have been the envy of any nun working to save the world's poor and heartbroken. She offered the bottle. "I just wanted to say no hard feelings."

Wes hesitated. Confused and suffering from a hangover, he wasn't sure of proper protocol.

"A hair of the dog that bit us last night, eh?" she said. Without waiting for an answer, she uncorked the bottle and took a belt, then handed it over. Wes's hands shook as he accepted it. "Come on," she said. "I hate to leave a town with bad feelings. You never know when you might pass back through."

The deputy accepted the bottle. He even managed to hold down a swallow. "No hard feelings," he said.

"Thanks, Deputy. Oh, would you mind stepping outside to see if my wagon has arrived? I'm a bit dizzy." She closed her eyes and leaned against the desk.

He nodded, shuffled across the room and walked outside. A couple of minutes later he stepped back in. Belle had placed the whiskey bottle on the desk. She'd also placed two large shot glasses next to it. She was closing her purse when he entered the room.

"I think you've had enough for one day," she said.

"I think you're right, Ma'am."

"I would appreciate a small favor." Belle flooded him with all the charm she'd learned through a lifetime of whoring. He didn't have a chance. "Yes, Ma'am?"

"See that Sheriff Arlen and Deputy Conly are treated with that same hair of the dog. I don't think they'll disagree, but please insist. For me. Again, I just don't want any hard feelings."

"Yes, Ma'am."

Belle patted his hand as she walked away.

Outside Hephaestus locked eyes with her. He glanced down at her purse and then back. Her face remained a blank canvas. He snapped the reins and a pair of tired old horses led them away.

"I presume we had best make haste, Miss Belle?"

"The name, Hephaestus, is Princess." She looked at her companions. "From now on you will address me as Princess Dodu of Lorraine." The vision was in action.

"Of course," said Hephaestus. Nothing seemed to phase him. "Hold tight, Princess. We are about to make time." He snapped the reins again and the newly minted princess and her entourage disappeared in a cloud of California dust.

Chapter Twenty-Three

"Is she Princess Lorraine of DoDo or DooDoo? I forget," Short said.

"Princess Dodu of Lorraine and you know it," said Round. "Where'd she get that name anyway?"

"It's French," said Hephaestus. "Miss Belle—I mean, the princess—picked up a lot of fancy words and such from some whores down New Orleans way." He added a couple of small, dry sticks to the fire. No smoke drifted skyward to pinpoint their position. He stirred the pot of stew he was making and then went back to stirring the coals into a better position. "You fellows know what dodu means?"

"What?" Short and Round answered in unison.

Hephaestus smiled. "It means plump." They all enjoyed a good laugh.

"Well, Dodu ain't so dodu these days, is she?" Round said.

"Shh. She'll hear us," Short said.

"She's heard every word we've said." Hephaestus sat up straight and raised his voice. "Is that not correct, Princess?"

"You want me to finish cooking that stew, you sons a bitches?" Belle boomed from the back of the wagon, and three male minds darted immediately to her purse and the medicine bottles within. Fortunately her voice carried more amusement than threat. "Keep it down so I can get my beauty rest."

"I shall so endeavor, Ma'am," said Hephaestus. His voice was full of confidence, but at a considerably lower volume.

"He sure as hell talks pretty, don't he?" Round said.

"Sure do. I bet he could even talk circles around old... you know, that Indian feller back in Privy," Short said.

"Prospect!"

"Yeah. Now them two, that'd be a showdown sure enough."

"Sure enough."

The wagon shook as Belle sat up and hopped out. She stomped over to the fire and sniffed at the stew.

"We shall dine shortly, Princess," Hephaestus said.

"I gotta' squat." Half-asleep she walked into the desert and sat down behind the partial privacy of a clump of rocks and a bush.

"And that's the reason we went bust in San Francisco." Hephaestus kept his voice low.

"What'chu mean?" Round said.

Hephaestus shuffled around the fire so that his back was to Belle and the bushes. He pretended to adjust the coals in the fire. "The gentlemen in San Francisco know, appreciate and seek out quality, especially in their whoring. Belle, her girls and her house did not meet the... shall we say, community standards?"

"And now she's Princess Dodu," Short said.

"Of Lorraine," Round said.

Hephaestus glanced over his shoulder before commenting. "The men of the mining camps and boom towns have considerably lower expectations."

"Hell, nobody's gonna believe she's a real princess," Round said.

The black man shifted his position, again glancing to the desert before speaking. "Of course not, my diminutive friend."

"I do love the way he talks," Round said.

Hephaestus continued. "No one believes for a second that she is a true princess, but having caught her in one lie, they accept the other: that she is French and therefore exotic and therefore—"

"Expensive," Round said.

"Correct." Hephaestus stirred the stew again. All was quiet for a moment save the thunk of wooden spoon against an iron pot and the occasional grunt from behind the nearby rocks.

"You think we can do this?" Short said.

Hephaestus stood up. He noticed that Belle was doing the same. His words were a bit rushed as he answered the question. "The men out West have an amazing capacity for something known as suspension of disbelief."

"That's like a bridge, ain't it?" Short beamed with pride of knowledge.

Hephaestus smiled. "In a way you are correct, my friend. It is a bridge between that which a thing is and that which men wish a thing to be. Westerners are quite accomplished at making the journey. And that is why we will succeed." He was busy ladling his thick, brown stew into a bowl when Belle returned. He handed her the first bowl with a slight bow.

"That's right." She looked to ShortRound. "And don't nobody call me Belle from now on, not even when nobody's around. I don't want no slip ups in front of folks."

What is our plan, Ma'am?" Hephaestus passed more stew on to Short and Round before helping himself. The twins focused their attention on their appetites. The black man ate slowly and in correct form, but his mind was racing to the future.

"Money, power and control."

Short stopped shoveling food in his mouth long enough to show interest. "I like the sound of them words."

Round nodded, but kept on eating.

Hephaestus tapped his spoon on the bottom of his bowl as if contemplating his next statement. Belle poised herself to come up with an answer. The black man wasn't as clever as she, but he was a hell of a lot smarter. Actually, he was just smashing a bug that had flown into the stew.

"That, Ma'am, is a goal. My question relates to the plan for attaining that goal."

Belle relaxed. She'd thought this out. "We work our way down the coast. And I do mean work." She looked to ShortRound. "You two runts will pick pockets, roll drunks, and steal anything that ain't nailed down. And if you get caught, I don't know ya.'"

They nodded their complete agreement. For them nothing had changed in decades.

She turned to Hephaestus. "You'll pick up whatever odd jobs you can wherever you can. Find out who's the he-bear in town, who's got the money, who's got the weakness."

"Of course," he said. "And the princess?"

"Princess Dodu of Lorraine is a stranded lady in distress. She's hopelessly lost and without funds. Her telegrams to the continent go unanswered." Belle slipped into a mocking version of what would become a standard performance and work of art. "Surely some *rich* gentleman will want to come to her rescue. For certain favors which she will reluctantly, but completely give."

They all shared a good laugh.

"When you want to, Miss Belle, you talk as pretty as Hephaestus," Round said.

"What?"

"Princess. I mean, Princess." The desperation in his voice, not all of it feigned, brought another round of laughter. To help make amends for the error he offered to clean up the dishes. When they finished, he took the bowls away from camp for a scouring of sand. Short packed the dinner gear while Hephaestus put out the fire. They had several miles to cover before bedding down for the night. Belle made sure they always camped miles from where they prepared the final meal of the day. The Apaches, or even bandits, could spot them easily enough, but there was no use in lighting their trail to make the task easier.

"The rest of your plan, Princess Dodu... what is it?"

There was no dodging the question this time. "We work our way down the coast. We build up some money. We invest in the princess and then cut across to the Yuma Crossing on the Colorado. From there it's a straight shot into..."

"Privy." He said the word with a heavy finality.

"Damn straight, Privy."

"And Bull McKenzie."

"And Mister Bull McKenzie hisself. He's got a whole empire out there and I aim to bite off a chunk of it for myself."

Hephaestus finished covering the small fire. He started scattering sand and gravel about so that the ground looked, at least from a distance, undisturbed. "And you believe Mister Bull will accept the affections of Princess Dodu?"

She laughed. "The princess will get us there. Belle will take care of the rest." Round returned with the eating utensils and the cooking pot. "Let's see if we can cover some miles before dark," she said.

Belle sat beside Hephaestus in the wagon. ShortRound road in the back, two aging kids playing follow the leader. Belle soon became lost in her plots and schemes. She carefully worked out clever answers to the tough questions the princess would surely be asked. She ran through different scenarios, some pleasant and some confrontational, exploring every possible conflict and contradiction.

It was like watching a series of short plays inside her head. Regardless of the difficulties provided by the script, her heroine always came out on top. She enjoyed the show.

Hephaestus focused his attention on the horses, the road and on any possible sign of bandits or Apaches. The future seemed to be a difficult one, but it would take care of itself in its own way and in its own time. Bull McKenzie might just be their salvation, but he would also be a formidable challenge. No one could control the man, not even Belle Delcour, not even Bull himself. A thought struck home. In Bull's lack of self-control Belle just might find an edge. He flicked the reins to speed up the horses. And as the sun lowered itself in the sky he found his spirits rising. *Yes, Ma'am*, he though. *We just might have a real chance after all*. He glanced to his left. A hawk dived and within a second captured a cottontail in its talons and flew into the sun.

Chapter Twenty-Four

"Hey, runts!" The voice was slow, low and overflowing with a sick glee.

"Hey, down there. Hee hee!" The other voice was high pitched and just as twisted. "I got something fer'ya.'"

The giggling that followed was childlike, yet malevolent. It reminded Round of the way he and Short used to laugh when rolling drunks or abusing whores back in Privy. Being on the receiving end of such mockery hadn't changed his ways of thinking. He was filled with too much fear for rational thought. "God have mercy! They're gonna' do it again!"

"Back up. Back in the corner."

The dark cell was square and without a window. A wooden door was built into the thick adobe walls that had absorbed years of blood, sweat, excrement and human anguish. What passed for air hung, immobile and foul, sticking to a man's skin like grease. ShortRound's contribution decomposed in a slop bucket that hadn't been tossed in the two days since their imprisonment. A single, tight circle of light beamed from a hole in the roof, a vertical air pipe. It had a metal cover which the guards took pleasure in closing during the hottest part of the day. When open it would allow some of the hot air in to circulate the fetid odors hanging like ghosts in every corner of the cell.

"Leave us alone!" Round's voice carried the terror his guards wanted to hear. More giggles followed the plea.

"Just back up and don't move," said Short.

Both small men tried to meld their bodies into the adobe. Neither could take his eyes off the circle of light.

"No... oh no!" Round whispered.

"Don't move... don't move... don't move..."

157

"Hey, runts, here's yer' supper!"

"No!"

"Don't!"

"Hee-hee!"

The rattlesnake, dropped down the pipe through the roof, landed with a muffled "thump." It immediately coiled and began an angry buzz. The sharp finality of the lid closing on the air pipe followed. The room went dark. The buzzing eventually slowed from an angry threat to a slow, dire warning. Two small men, almost in unison, backed up on tiptoes. When the buzzing finally stopped, the nightmare really began. And not even the pounding of two terrified hearts could drown out the faint giggling from above.

Hephaestus approached Belle with all the show he could muster. "They are in dire straits, Princess." He presented her with a glass of brandy on a linen napkin in his palm. She accepted it with as much of a show. He bent low to converse in privacy. "One, they are being tortured."

"Tortured?" It was a gasp.

"The guards here have a game in which they toss vipers or scorpions into the cells. The prisoners dare not make a move for hours at a time."

Belle paused. She seemed to be savoring the idea and perhaps saving it for future implementation against some enemy. Hephaestus stood erect as if allowing her time to think. The few other patrons in the hotel's reception area continually glanced toward the princess. When in public, Belle performed. She had to meet expectations if she was to execute her plans successfully. She quickly motioned her manservant closer. "I want them out of there."

"You're loyalty is admirable, Ma'am, but there are complications."

"What the hell would they be?"

"This mayor you've been keeping time with is most proud of his town. He is particularly proud of his jail."

She took a polite sip of her brandy. "That ain't all he's proud of." Her face registered scorn.

Hephaestus continued in an overly deferential manner, as if passing along the latest missive from the Province of Lorraine. "His jail is far stronger than most prisons in these parts."

"He's a big one for show, he is. Fetch me another drink."

"Yes, Ma'am." He marched off with all the dignity of his "office."

Belle organized her thoughts. Short and Round had been caught red handed picking the pocket of Reverend Ford Beline, a man who preached, but did not much practice the art of forgiveness. He insisted on prosecution to the fullest extent of the law. After all, he said, the pair of ruffians had attempted to abscond with the funds from the most recent passing of the collection plate. No one thought to wonder why those funds were on the good reverend's person rather than in one of McCloyville's many banks. For whatever reasons, ShortRound had again received the short end of the stick.

Loyalty? She hadn't even thought about that. ShortRound had been with her for years, all the way back to her days before Privy. Did they feel loyalty to her or were they just riding the most convenient meal ticket? It didn't really matter. They knew her real identity and a good bit of her plans. She would not abandon them to a legal inquiry.

Hephaestus arrived with the second drink. He carried a newspaper under his arm. Again he bowed low in handing over the drink. Again he spoke in a low voice. "Ma'am, we should be leaving California as soon as practicable."

"We leave as soon as I figure out how to get ShortRound back. I'll work through Mayor Beline. He's a gullible old fool."

"We haven't time, Ma'am."

She accepted the glass and the napkin with grace. "What's up?"

"A patron just arriving from the west was speaking with the hotel manager. It seems that Sheriff Arlen and his deputies were taken violently ill after our departure. Arlen and that deputy, Wes, are dead. The other one, Conly, survived and is acting sheriff. Belle Delotte and her 'educated negro servant' are wanted for questioning, as are two midgets who are suspected of being traveling companions of said Delotte and said negro. The newspapers from the west arrive day after tomorrow, Princess."

She finished the brandy and stood up. "Come." She marched outside.

Hephaestus bowed and followed.

McCloyville was busting at the seams. Silver had been discovered in the nearby hills just six months earlier. A withered stage stop had boomed to a town of more than 3,000 miners, whores, pimps, thieves, killers, drummers and shopkeepers. Fortunately, too many people were busy trying to make too much money to pay much attention to Princess Dodu and her entourage. The arrival of newspapers would quickly change all that. She stopped and looked around the town as if considering purchasing some or all of it. The performance continued even under stress. She looked at Hephaestus and said quietly, "Have you had a look at the jail?"

"I have, Ma'am, and it is a veritable fortress: an adobe wall two feet thick and seven feet high surrounds the jail building. That wall is topped with strands of that new barbed wire, which adds another two feet to its height."

"And the jail itself?"

"An adobe structure. Two cells. No windows. Iron-reinforced doors. Sadistic guards who are well armed. I do not see how anyone can escape such a structure."

A horse tied to a nearby rail offered a comment on the situation. The opinion splattered in the sand with a modest thump. A number of fat flies made it their new residence. Belle looked at Hephaestus. "Go back for a second look at that jail."

"And what shall I be looking for, Ma'am?"

She whispered the answer. He nodded and moved away. Belle ambled back into the hotel. Princess Dodu needed another drink.

They discussed the situation when Hephaestus brought her meal to her room. She was living on credit that she'd purchased with a few favors promised to the hotel's owner, and the princess was taking full advantage of the man's gullibility. More than ever in her life she enjoyed making fools out of men. And the thought of Spec Arlen in a death struggle with a liquid demon eating his guts brought a warm sense of pleasure.

"You think they can squeeze through?" She spoke softly. The walls were thin and one never knew who was on the other side.

"Their diminutive size makes that route of escape a certainty save for two concerns."

"Those are?"

"One, the exit point is barred by iron. They could conceivably loosen the metal. It's just an adobe wall, but they would need a sharp implement. Two, there are two guards during the day. One at night. Mr. Short and Mr. Round are vicious little weasels, but I do not see how they can overpower a large, well-armed ruffian. Again, some sort of weapon would be required."

Belle cut into her steak. The food was surprisingly good for a town so far from the coast and civilization. As she chewed the rare beef she poked the round end of a baked potato with her knife. A smile formed and her eyes brightened. "You've done some acting, ain't you?"

"Performing talent was one of my many skills back on the plantation. You've seen my work."

She slid the round end of potato over the point of the knife. "You ever had a woman dogways?" Her eyes locked on to his.

"If you mean—" He stopped in mid-sentence as their eyes met. She really wasn't talking about sex. "Oh, no, Ma'am. Not that way."

She spoke as Princess Dodu. "Oh, yes, my good man. Most definitely yes."

"Oh... formee-dibble," Belle said.

"Princess, I told you this wasn't such a good idea." Mayor Sam Redlich was an opportunist of the first magnitude. His wife was back east visiting relatives, which allowed him the time to enjoy the physical charms of Princess Dodu of Lorraine or whoever the hell she was. *Who knows?* he thought. *She might or might not be a real princess, but she could easily have powerful connections which could be of value to a man moving up in society. And if not... well, her charms are certainly a notch or two above those of the other women in McCloyville.* He went along with her request for a tour of his town, including his famous jail.

"I have heard of this facility in many communities." Her faux French required the use of "eet" and "faceel-ahtee." It was a corny performance, but one no one in their long journey down the California coast and then eastward through the mining towns had given a bad review. The show must, and did, go on. "You are quite famous in this land."

Redlich nodded and feigned a modest expression. When he thought she wasn't looking, he took an immodest look at her lusty figure. Belle had gained back some of her weight on their journey. The charms and wiles of the princess combined with the hard work and illegal enterprises of Hephaestus and ShortRound had provided ample funds for rebuilding her frame.

"The prince, my father, is responsible for all the prisons in Lorraine. He would never forgive me if I did not avail myself of the opportunity to visit your American institutions."

"Well, Princess, if you can stand the smell, I can provide the tour."

"Let us begin, Monsieur."

Redlich led the princess and her faithful servant into the compound. There wasn't much to see: two adobe cells in the middle of an empty courtyard, a wooden privy set out from the wall so that it couldn't be used as a means of escape, a narrow trench from the privy lead to a grated hole in the wall, barbed wire that was even more intimidating than she'd been expecting, and a guard making a rare attempt at alertness. The moment she stepped inside, three of her five senses were assaulted: the sight was bleak and hopeless, the temperature was instantly 15 or 20 degrees higher, and the place stunk. The heat of the sun seemed unable to make an escape. It just bounced back and forth between the walls, the buildings and the hard packed earth. She placed a perfumed handkerchief beneath her nose. Even Hephaestus choked.

"The guards say you get used to it," Redlich said. "I don't see how."

"Nevertheless, Sam... Mayor Redlich... we must persevere. Come, Hephaestus."

He walked them around the perimeter, approaching the privy with some trepidation. Hephaestus took particular note of the trench leading under the wall. They passed each of the cells, the one holding ShortRound last. She insisted that the doors be opened so she could get a better look at the construction.

"Oh, little persons!" She pretended a sort of delight, as if encountering a couple of Leprechauns on the heather. Belle moved quickly to examine the prisoners. While her voice said, "How precious!" her eyes said *Pay attention, you little dimwits!*

"Not too close, please, Princess. They are, after all, criminals," said Redlich.

"These little things? Mon dieu!"

"Pickpockets, Princess. A couple of experts."

"You little people really should—"

Hephaestus groaned.

She stopped and looked at him. "What is the matter?"

"I don't feel so well, Princess... my stomach. I haven't felt well all morning."

"We should leave at once and return to our lodgings," she said. Belle stood up and walked to Redlich.

Hephaestus reached out and placed his arm on the wall. "With all due respect, Princess, I do not believe I have that much time."

"Explain yourself!" She was really getting into the imperial act.

"Again, respecting your every wish, Princess, I believe a moment of privacy is imminent... if you understand my meaning, Ma'am." He moved quickly to the slop bucket in the corner.

"Oh! Mayor Redlich, thank you for the tour. Perhaps you will escort me back to my hotel?" She packed a lot of promise in her words and into the blinking of her eyes.

Redlich turned to the guard. "Watch him, then lock up." He turned and escorted the Princess away from the prison. The guard flicked his fingers on the rifle in his hands and looked at ShortRound. "You two, over in the corner. Move an inch and tonight I'll drop a whole nest of wigglers down that pipe." He looked at Hephaestus. "Do your business."

Hephaestus pulled down his britches and straddled the slop bucket. He didn't have to fake going through the motions. He'd spent a significant portion of the previous evening downing massive portions of baked beans and chili peppers.

Even the numbed senses of the guard were stunned. "You ate something that died!"

Hephaestus struggled. He grunted and groaned and sweat beads glistened on his dark skin. Several veins pulsated up his neck and into the sides of his head. At last he made a painful grunt and said, "That's it." He looked directly at ShortRound and made an embarrassed grin. "When you have to go now, you have to go now. Too bad, but that's the only way out." He looked at the guard. "Do you have any paper?"

"Paper? Hell, man, this ain't no hotel!"

"Mon dieu!" He stood up with all the mock dignity he could muster, buttoned his britches, and marched out the door. "The Princess shall hear of this!"

When the door slammed shut Short and Round stared at each other. "Did he mean what I think he meant?" Round said.

"Yeah, and he said 'now' twice. I think that's when we have to make our move—now."

"We don't even have a weapon."

"Yes we do." Short walked over to the slop bucket. "Sometimes I wish Festus wasn't such a smart son of a bitch." He reached his arm down into the warm goo and pulled out something.

"A turd?" Round started to gag.

Short fought back the churning in his own belly and began wiping the mess off the object. It was a cylinder about three inches in length and no more than an inch around. As Short wiped off the excrement, Round could see that the object was coated with rubber. An incision ran the circumference right in the middle. "Belle's beaver blade!'"

"Yeah, only Festus had to hide in another hole." He finished wiping it clean by rubbing it in the sandy floor. He held it up and pulled from each end to reveal a razor sharp, two-inch, double sided blade. "Now we have an edge." His eyes tightened as he ran his thumb along the edge of the blade. "And we'd better be using it tonight."

Short started his ruckus well after midnight so the guard would be less than alert. With luck he'd have been asleep or drunk and would be groggy when approaching the cell.

"What's goin' on?" said the guard. His voice was muffled by the heavy door, but even so the man's slurred words gave proof that he'd been drinking.

Good. "It's Round. He's taken ill."

"He'll keep till mornin'."

"Guard, he's really sick! He's dying!"

"Then die."

"You want that to happen on your watch?"

"Son of a bitch." A key banged against the lock several times before it was properly inserted.

"We'll stand back from the door," Short said.

"Sure, pissants." As with most men just before they are killed by their fellow man, the guard made the ultimate mistake of underestimating the cleverness, if not the size, of his enemy. The massive door swung open and the guard stepped into the darkness holding a rifle in one hand and a sputtering candle lamp in the other. "Now where's that little runt?"

164

Round couldn't resist a verbal answer. "Here!" He was standing on Short's shoulders, which brought him and Belle's beaver blade into close proximity to the man's jugular vein. Round leapt on the guard's back. It was a trick he and Short had played on many a drunk and many a poor whore. He made two swift slashes, one to each side of the man's neck. Both movements severed their intended targets. Round rode the dying man to the ground, his small fist stuffed in the man's mouth to muffle the weak scream that tried to escape.

Short caught the lamp and quickly blew out the light. "Move! Move! Move!" He whispered even though there was no one else in the compound. They dragged the guard from the door and dashed into the darkness. Round took time to grab the rifle and the guard's pouch of bullets.

They scrambled across the compound to the privy and stared at the narrow trench leading from it to the wall. "Like Festus said, it's the only way out. I'll go," Short said. In perhaps the bravest act of his life he slid into the trench and stopped at the iron grate. He retched violently twice before he pulled out the knife and began chiseling away at the adobe holding the bars.

Some moments later Round whispered, "My turn." He hated the thought, but he and Short shared everything, good and bad, and had done so throughout their lives. He didn't intend to welch on a contract.

"No time," Short said. He retched again. "I've... almost... got it."

Round heard a muffled grunt and the sounds of a struggle, then, "Come on!" He took a deep breath that alone made him gag, and followed his partner, quickly adding his own vomit to that left by Short. Only one of the bars had been loosened, but it was enough. Seconds later both men were outside.

Hephaestus had been watching from the night shadows of a nearby building. "Here! Quick!" This was followed by a much weaker, "Christ Almighty!"

"This was your idea," Round whispered. He took only small pleasure in the faint gagging sounds from Hephaestus.

"Can we get the hell out of here?" Short said.

Hephaestus stepped into the empty road and struck a Lucifer, obviously a signal. The wind blew it out. "Damn!" He tried again

165

and again, but the hot desert wind would not allow the flame to catch. "Just as well. The way you two smell a flame might just blow us all to hell and back. "Wait right here." He jogged off into the night.

"That's a bad start," Short said. "Even the wind's against us."

Round jumped down in the dust and began rolling around like a dog. "What the hell?" Short said.

"Maybe we can rub some of this off. Or at least cover it up."

Short, seeing at least the hope of wisdom in his partner's words, joined him.

Within a moment the wagon rolled up, and Hephaestus ordered them into the rear where he'd spread a canvas tarp for them. "No use fouling up our wagon any more than required," he said. "Which way, Princess?"

Belle leaned into the wind and tried for clean air. "To the river. If we don't get these two cleaned up, the posse can track us by their stink."

"We're not too far from the Colorado. Arizona's on the other side and that's another jurisdiction."

Belle thought for a second and nodded. "You know them dire straits you mentioned?"

"Yes Ma'am."

"Well, I think we're smack dab in the middle of 'em. Better haul ass, Hephaestus."

"Yes, Ma'am!"

The wagon soon disappeared into the dark night on a lonely road to an uncertain and dangerous future.

Chapter Twenty-Five

The weary, parched and hungry crew reached the Colorado River at Yuma Crossing several days later, certainly a few days or so ahead of any east-bound newspapers. Wary of the potential disaster of a telegraphed warning, Belle and ShortRound hid beneath a canvas tarp as Hephaestus drove their wagon onto the ferry. When the wheels rolled into the relative safety of Arizona dust, the small group purchased supplies, nearly wiping out their meager financial reserves, and pushed on toward Privy and a confrontation with Bull McKenzie.

They exchanged information with traveling parties they met along the road, not that the information proved of any value. The Apaches were taking a beating from the Army or the Apaches were tearing up the entire countryside, raping, murdering, burning and kidnapping at will. All the major water holes were flowing in record amounts or drought had dried them all up. Geronimo was in Mexico or Geronimo was in New Mexico or Geronimo was behind every rock, bush and sand hill. Smart travelers acted as if the latter were true. Burnt wagons, hasty burials, and the scattered bones of animals were tragic roadside markers commemorating the foolishness of those who ignored that last premise.

They pushed on without stopping except to build a smokeless fire, dig into their dwindling food supplies, and answer nature's call. Belle and Hephaestus took turns driving the horses, napping as best they could between shifts. ShortRound was in charge of cooking, taking care of the horses, wagon repair, and lookout duties. They even devised a way to use the long rife they'd stolen in McCloyville. Short aimed and fired, resting the barrel on Round's right shoulder. They practiced at every stop and became quite an accurate team.

"Half-pint shootout... half-ass shootout..." Belle was mumbling, lost in thought.

"What are you saying, Princess?"

Belle sat up and stretched. Hephaestus, handling the reins, shook his head. He was glad she'd spoken. It was well past midnight and he was dozing off. The weary horses weren't likely to run off, but a careless moment could send a wagon wheel into a rut or a bad hole. A breakdown would most likely be fatal.

"Hephaestus, I was just thinking. When we get set up in Privy we might could earn us a pretty penny off them two runts."

He squinted and rubbed his eyes. "How might that be accomplished?" Something seemed to be flickering in the distance. A star on the horizon? A distant campfire? Spots before his weary eyes? The phenomenon soon disappeared.

"A man's weakness is his pride," she said.

"You could write a book on that, Princess."

"How many of those dumb sumbitches you think would back down from a challenge by a couple of midgets?"

"A gunfight?"

"Nah, dummy. A shooting match with a lot of bets on the side."

"Might work... might work at that." He squinted and leaned forward. The strange light flickered on and then out again.

"What are you glaring at?" Belle's voice was as imperial as ever, but there was a tinge of fear around its edges.

"Look... it's there and then it isn't. Some kind of light out in the distance. Looks to be on the road."

"Apaches?"

"I do not think it likely they would show themselves."

"What do you think we oughta do?"

Hephaestus wiped his eyes again. The light was gone. "Well, I suggest we be prepared for just about anything."

Belle leaned back into the wagon and punched Short. "Wake up. And get that rifle ready. We might have company."

The strange light hovering over the desert floor flared and dimmed throughout the next several hours and then became a steady glow in the early morning darkness. At times it appeared to be hovering against the distant horizon. At other times it seemed to be taunting them from just over the next rise. Toward dawn the mystery faded with the darkness when they arrived at a stage stop. The light that had drawn them through the night was a lantern affixed to a pole above the station, a beacon in the night.

As the wagon pulled to a stop, an old man stepped out to greet them, shotgun in hand. "Howdy, folks," he said. He was ancient, but even a quick glance revealed that he was spry and ready for a fight if necessary.

"Good morning, sir," said Hephaestus. "May I present Princess Dodu of—"

"Belle Delcour McKenzie! Damn glad to see you, Sweetheart!"

For just an instant Belle, Hephaestus, Short and Round stood immobile. The unexpected had just landed on their front porch. Belle recovered first. "I don't recall you, Mister...."

"Monaghan. They call me NoBrains and for good reason. Here let me help you down, Ma'am. I 'member seeing you take that bath o' yours back in Privy. Oh, that must'a been a hunnerd years ago. Lady, that was something to see. So you're a princess now! Don't that beat all!" Monaghan rambled continuously as he helped her off the wagon and into the old structure. The station wasn't much: a small corral, a stone-lined hole in the ground half-full of dirty water, and an adobe shack with a brush roof supported by thin ocotillo branches. Bullet holes and burn marks told a story of frequent battles. The inside was surprisingly clean. She'd expected the interior to be as cluttered and as greasy as the old man's beard.

Short and Round collapsed in a corner. Hephaestus began taking an inventory of the place, looking for supplies for purchase or theft. Belle let Monaghan ramble on, hoping to pick up some information that might help her adjust her strategy. Princess Dodu had served her well, but like much of the litter along the West's trails she had to be discarded when her weight became too much of a burden. Belle dropped the old girl and never gave her another thought. But one thing troubled her: that she had not anticipated such exposure the closer they got to her old stomping grounds was telling. Belle was losing her edge.

"Yes, Ma'am, I'm shore proud to see you again! Ain't nobody out here 'cept me an' old Luther." He turned to the back wall and shouted. "Foote, get in here! We got customers!"

A moment later a man who would have appeared old had not Monaghan been in the room stepped through the door. "How ya'll are?" His Cajun accent was so thick that Hephaestus actually squinted his eyes to help understand the man's words.

Monaghan glared at him. "Fix us some breakfast. And be quick about it!"

"Certinement."

"You folks are welcome to fill up your water barrels from the cistern out there. We have to haul it in from the river every week. It ain't sweet and you'll hafta' strain out the bugs, but you can get it down your gullet." Monaghan offered a chair to Belle.

She sat down with a pleasant smile, which seemed to make the old man's day. "How far is it to Phoenix, Mr. Monahans?"

"You mean Punkin. I don't use that other name. Let's see... it's ten miles to the river, and Punkin... well, the way it looks like you're traveling, I'd say a week or so depending." He launched back into talking.

She brightened. That meant Privy, Bull McKenzie and a salvation of sorts was also within a week's journey. While ShortRound dozed in the corner, Hephaestus began helping Foote prepare the meal. *Good*, she thought. *He'll be able to pump the Cajun for information, provided he can make out what he's sayin'.*

When Monaghan broke his monologue for a breath of air, she jumped in. "Do you have any news of Bull McKenzie?"

"Bull? Sure. Me n'ol' Bull go back 'bout as far back as you can go." He started telling the story of how he and Bull had met back in the days when Phoenix was Punkin.

She let him ramble on. Her history with men had taught her that she learned more when she let them babble than when she pushed. Patience was frustrating, but it worked. She encouraged him with a smile. During the course of their mostly one-sided conversation she learned that Bull continued to build his great empire. He was a force not even the Apaches could stop. She warmed to the thought that she had a future. Beg, barter or bully, she'd climb back to prosperity.

Breakfast wasn't much—fried potatoes, moldy bread and strong coffee—but it filled the empty spots and the travelers were most grateful. They were on the edge of exhaustion, but the need to put distance between themselves and the poison Bell had left in her wake forced constant action.

"We'd better get moving, Hephaestus," she said.

"You're more'n welcome to rest out the day here, Miss Belle. Foote'n me don't get much company. You folks look like you could use some time off your as—feet."

"We have to push on." And that was that. She glared at Monaghan as he and Foote cleared the table. He could connect Belle Delcour with Princess Dodu, and that fact held the potential of endless trouble. She'd have to do something about that. Hephaestus was watching her and their eyes met. He was a good man. He was intelligent, but most of all he was a survivor. A silent agreement passed between them.

"You got any paper?" Round said.

Monaghan paused and then caught the meaning in the question. "Corn husks in the shed over at the corral."

Round left without a word.

"Taters cooked in all that grease tend to go through a man," Monaghan said.

Foote clipped a thumb and a finger to his nose. "Fiare du tracas." Both men laughed.

Belle stared. *I wonder what he's up to?* She'd become so distrustful of men that even the performance of daily bodily functions aroused her suspicions. "Perhaps we'd all best take a squat. Hephaestus, you go strain your taters next." He shook his head to indicate his lack of need. A stern look from Belle changed his mind. He stood up and left the room. She turned her attention to the old man. "Have you ever had a cup of real tea, Mr. Monaghan?"

"Here an' there. Never had much of a taste fer it."

"Well, you have to try some of mine. I had it shipped in special to San Francisco. I'll brew up a few cups before we leave."

Several rifle shots followed by a high-pitched scream interrupted her plans. Monaghan and Foote moved so quickly that they appeared as flashes of streaking light. They produced rifles seemingly from the air and positioned themselves at the open door, each one covering the area not visible to the other. They'd had lots of practice. Round jumped into a corner. Belle froze and waited for orders or instinct to dictate her next move.

"Apaches?" Foote asked.

"Them or McCracken's gang. Ain't nobody else crazy enough to be out this way 'ceptin us." Monaghan and Foote shared a grim smile.

Belle gasped. "Hephaestus!"

She looked through the door to see the black man running from the corral. Fear had given his scrawny legs wings and he was covering the distance in huge strides, carrying the bloody body of Short in his arms. The hard ground around him seemed to be spitting up dust as shell after shell exploded from rifles in all directions. Hephaestus screamed and went down. A bullet had torn through the hamstring muscle of his right leg. Short fell from his arms, landed in an awkward position and didn't move. Hephaestus went down, but he rolled with the fall. Several bullets scattered ground where he would have been had he stayed down. He kept rolling, a smaller moving target, till he reached the door of the station. Monahan stepped out and dragged him the rest of the way in. Foote slammed the door and threw the table against it. Everyone froze and even Belle and Round, who had remained motionless throughout, were breathing heavily.

Belle jumped to Hephaestus. She glared at Round. "Help me, you little coward!"

Round crawled across the floor and they began to treat the black man's wound. He was lucky. The bullet had gone straight through flesh without striking bone or a major artery. He might walk with a limp, but he would walk again. How far he would walk was a matter of conjecture.

"How many?" Foote asked.

"At least a dozen from the sound of it. Probably more," Monaghan said.

"Trap like one 'dem rat." Even through Foote's thick accent Belle understood his meaning.

Monaghan said nothing.

After Hapheastus was patched up Belle turned to Monaghan. "What's next?"

"Don't rightly know." He and Foote exchanged a glance. Each man knew he was lying.

"Guess!" demanded Belle.

"All right then." He was angry at having to explain the obvious. "If they're in a hurry, they'll rush us. If they ain't, they'll burn us out." Either way, we'll be dead by sundown."

"Torture?" A cold shiver snaked down her spine. She'd been abused and beaten by men all her life, but the thought of torture at the hands of Indian warriors was a thought she couldn't face. Round, back in his corner, puked.

Foote left the door and walked across the room. He took a couple of .45 Colts and a box of shells from a drawer in a cabinet. He handed one of the pistols to Belle and gave the other to Hephaestus before setting the shells on the table. "They go on in them dime novels about saving the last bullet for yourself." He made a point of looking her directly in the eyes. "Every once in a while, them books get it right." That cold snake crawled down Belle's spine again.

Hephaestus had already loaded his pistol before Belle started doing the same. "He's right, Miss Belle. In the parlance of the locals, we're screwed."

Belle wasn't one for giving up. "I make a damn good livin' getting screwed."

Hephaestus shook his head, half in resignation and half in amazement. "Well, I intend to make a good showing of myself whatever happens." He moved the pistol around to get a feel for it. "If you intend to get out alive, then it's time for some real desperation thinking."

Belle was desperate. And she was thinking. Something about the way Hephaestus had said "show" had sparked an idea. She drummed her fingers on the table. The black man practiced aiming his pistol. Round sat in his own vomit and remained motionless. Monaghan and Foote stood by the door, leaning their heads against the adobe walls as if trying to pick up the vibrations of silent footsteps outside.

Belle mumbled the word "show" over and over, the drumming of her fingers almost matched the speed of Hephaestus' beating heart. She raised her head and looked at Monaghan. "How much time we got?"

"Till what?" he said. He was trying to protect something beyond protection.

"*How much?*"

"Some. If they ain't rushed us by now, they gonna' burn us out. Takes time."

"Are they a curious people?"

"What?" They were facing a certain and painful death and this whore was asking a bunch of stupid questions.

"The Apaches... are they curious?" Her tone allowed no room for discussion.

"Curious as most, I guess."

"I mean, if something really unusual happened would they hold off shooting us, even for a minute or so?"

"Reckon they would. What you got in mind, Belle?" He was a desperate man and that made him curious.

"Do they believe in witches, Mr. Monaghan?" Her voice was clipped.

"They got medicine men."

"They believe in magic?"

"Most folks do, Ma'am." He knocked on wood. Foote crossed himself.

Hephaestus sat erect. He made his own luck. "What have you in mind, Miss Belle?"

Belle knew nothing of the Apaches, but she did know men and all men are superstitious. Late at night, drunk and in the arms of a whore even the bravest men spoke of ghosts, demons, and the unknown terrors in the darkness. No matter what they say in the harsh light of day, they fear death and they fear the unknown—especially the unknown. That's where the real terror lies.

"I'm gonna' ride me valkree," she said.

Hephaestus smiled. He hadn't a clue as to what plan she had developed, but he already liked it.

Chapter Twenty-Six

"Goyahkla!"

The Apache with the stern face and dead eyes yawned and glanced up from his rifle to the man who had whispered his name. He was known by many others: Sumbitch. Murderer. Red devil. Damn murderin' sumbitchin' red devil. To a few he was called Jerome.

Nonithian, The Limper, was so named because of the curious twist to his walk, a gift from a Mexican soldier who broke a truce and his leg. The soldier died at the hands of man he'd wounded, but the Indian was forever marked with a scar, an odd way of walking and a new name. "What do you think?" he said.

Jerome's square jaw was set. They would kill. The real question was how much time to invest in the process. White soldiers were on the move. They were poor fighters, but they were as numerous as ants in a hill. They kept coming. The Mexicans were the same. A scorpion is a fierce warrior feared even by humans, yet he had seen scorpions overwhelmed and devoured by ants. It was a sobering thought. They should be on the move quickly.

"Burn them."

Jerome surveyed the scene. Two men would be running the station. The wagon meant at least one traveler, perhaps more. A small group of frightened white people trapped in a box. He would burn them out, kill them quickly and then move on. The times did not allow for amusement. He stared at the small, bloody body in the dust near the adobe station and wondered whether it were an omen. Jerome was a war leader and medicine man, but he was no chief. He had true power. He could often read the future in the blowing sands or cloud studded sky. His curing abilities were legendary. All this and more had his people seen, yet this not-man, not-boy weighed on his mind. He had seen his face before killing him. It was small like a child, yet old. What could such a thing mean? His troubled thoughts were interrupted by chanting from inside the station.

"Ay-yah ah-ah-*yah!* Ay-yah ah-ah-*yah!*"

The voice was female and full of fury. It was something like a war cry, but unlike any he had ever heard. Had he been a dandy in San Francisco some five years earlier and had the misfortune to attend Professor Langley Phillips Traveling Opera Show, featuring Belle Delotte, he would have suffered through the god-awfullest production of *Ride of the Valkyries* to ever trod a stage, the human ear and musical taste. But the shriek was unfamiliar music to his ears and therefore suspect.

"Ay-yah ah-ah-yah! Ay-yah ah-ah-yah! *Ay-yaaaaaaaaaaaa!*"

The high-pitched chanting was horrible. Those trapped inside must have thought so too, for screams of terror, the screams of men, soon followed. Behind rock and tree, wall and fence Jerome's warriors leaned in for a closer look. They heard the crashing of boxes, glasswork smashed against the walls, and the ripping of wood as if the small building was trying to burst from within. And through it all were those terrified screams.

The door flew open and an old man jumped out. Jerome knew this man and had seen him here and there for decades. He was wise to the ways of the desert, the Indians and the white man and was not likely to be frightened by common events. The man screamed and cried and rolled in the dirt. He finally stopped moving and formed himself into a ball. The Limper raised his rifle, but before he could take aim Jerome raised his hand. He was curious about the strange behavior of these white people. Perhaps some magic involving the not-man, not-boy was involved.

Another man rolled out the door. Screaming in terror he cowered near the old man. The black man flew through the door as if he had been thrown by a giant. He hit hard, rolled and scrambled to the adobe walls of the building and cowered down. He grabbed a small stick and bit down on it as a man undergoing severe pain might. This was most curious. All three men carried pistols. What could frighten a man so that he could not fight back? An angry god? A demon? An evil spirit?

Jerome got his answer within seconds. A witch, for that is all she could be, emerged from the dark of the building. She was an aging woman, a large woman and her hair splayed out from her head like the rays of the sun. She was without clothing and without shame, for she walked proudly. The veins and arteries within her body were thick and dark. Her face was painted as a skull. She walked slowly and regally out the door.

"Ay-ah ah-ah Yah! Ay-ah ah-ah Yah! *Ay-yaaaaaaaaaaaa!*"

Smoke billowed out the door in her wake. The building was burning. Jerome thought, *Her power must be great indeed, if she can force armed men into an open space surrounded by warriors.* There was much to fear, yet there was perhaps much to learn. He signaled his men to wait and observe.

The white men and the black man continued their cowardly ways. The witch continued walking and singing. She approached the dead not-man, not-boy and sang to it. She knelt down, ran her hands over the bloody mess, picked him up in her arms and carried him back into the burning building. The warriors had never seen anything quite so puzzling, and Jerome, even with all his great power, was confused as to the proper course of action. He chose to wait and watch, which was just fine with the warriors. Witches, too have power and they did not want to be caught in a crossfire between that she-devil and their leader.

They could see nothing inside the dark and smoky building. More smoke billowed and flames began to shoot out the roof. It was as if the witch were engaged in some titanic battle with unseen forces. The singing continued louder and louder at an increasingly higher pitch. "Ah-yaaaah! Ah-yaaaah! Ah-yaaaah!"

A brief moment of silence was followed by a horrible shriek and then silence again. No one moved. The warriors almost forgot to breathe. And then the she-devil emerged. Still carrying the small body she strode proudly into the open, her face beaming with arrogance and accomplishment. She laid the not-man, not-boy down in the dirt, then stood above his feet and waved her hands over his body. She then opened her arms and sang a long, loud command. "Ay-yaaaaaaaaaaaa!"

The not-man, not-boy sat up!

Jerome's warriors could not help themselves. Unconsciously they backed away from the sight. Even Jerome, who had amazing healing powers, was stunned when the little person quickly got on his knees and prostrated himself before the witch. The others from the station crawled to her feet and began worshipping also. Their voices were filled with terror and awe. The black man was even weeping. As the smoke from the burning building swirled around them, the witch sang another command. The men and even the not-man, not-boy jumped up and formed two lines before her. The witch strode between them and began walking down the road, which led north. No queen, no ingénue on the stage, no lady born to wealth and privilege, ever walked with greater dignity and authority than she-devil Belle that day. At the edge of the station property she paused. Her followers seemed startled, but they bowed low and mumbled in fear.

The witch turned back and looked at the warriors. Her eyes fixed on Jerome, for he was the only man standing and the only one not fully cowed. She bowed her head slightly and smiled. A sign of respect? Perhaps, and that is how the warriors understood the gesture. Jerome wondered whether instead it was a warning or a dare or perhaps a riddle for him to puzzle out. He would do that, but on another day.

He led his small band toward Mexico and plunder. He would not follow and kill the witch and her party. The white soldiers were surely around; the ants were crawling. Besides, he had much to think upon. He and his men had witnessed a miracle. Of that he was sure, but its meaning was unclear.

As the old station blazed, Jerome led his men into the desert. He was quiet, lost in thought for some time. The event he had just seen was an omen, but did it portend good or evil? This he did not know, but even in the heat of the day a chill ran down his spine.

"I gotta' hand it to you, Belle or Princess Dodu or whatever you're calling yourself these days." Belled winced at the connection of her names. "You, Ma'am, are one of them geniuses," Monaghan said.

"The lady is a showman... a master showman," Hephaestus said.

Belle nodded in recognition. Her mind was focused on other matters. Once their immediate survival was assured, she had immediately turned to the longer view of things.

They had marched, in step, for several miles before daring to take a break beneath a stand of mesquite trees beside the road. Their hopes had first been raised when the Apaches did not kill them within the station and then again when the warriors held back from riding them down. Still, fearing a watchful scout they had kept up the charade and marched on. Belle's pale skin turned bright red and began to blister. She pulled her long hair down, a mask, to keep the sun off her face. Still she marched as if performing on the stage. It was in truth the performance of her life. Hephaestus, Monaghan and Foote had smuggled canteens and some jerky under their jackets, but no one had dared break stride or pause for a break.

When the rolling desert became flat and they could see no tale-tell cloud of dust indicating riders, they finally stopped. Hephaestus gave Belle his coat and a pair of canvas pants he'd worn over his own. He also pulled out a pair of old shoes tied to a small rope beneath his coat. She was hardly dressed as a princess, but her skin was at last saved from the sun. Round just sat down, lost. In a very real and personal way he had lost half of himself.

After resting a few hours to allow the sun to dip closer to the horizon, the small band of survivors trudged on. Each walked to his own beat and made no pretence of parading. Some time after sunset yet before dark, they reached the banks of the Gila. No promised land was ever greeted with greater joy by pilgrims from the wasteland.

The men made camp while Belle soaked her burning skin in the warm, gently flowing waters. She was burned and blistered, but her skin would recover without scars. Despite the cool night breeze they made no fire.

"You pulled off a miracle back there, Miss Belle. Yes you did, but there ain't no need to go pushin' our luck," Monaghan said.

"Merci bon Dieu," Foote said.

Hephaestus didn't know what that meant, but he agreed with the look on Foote's face. He'd never seen an Apache before. He silently prayed to the African gods of his ancestors, to Sweet Jesus, and to any other gods who might be roaming the desert night that he'd never see another. He tore off another piece of jerky. "How do you men subsist on this pitiful example of shoe leather?" he said.

"It'll hold your insides together, that's about all," Monaghan said.

Foote seemed to agree. "Merde." Hephaestus didn't know that word either, but the expression on the Cajun's face was the only translation necessary.

Belle brightened up. "I can help with that, Mr. Monaghan, Mr. Foote."

"Beg pardon, Ma'am, but can't nobody do nothing with mule jerky," Monaghan said. He'd invested decades in experimentation, but had never found the cure.

"I think you'll like this. Hephaestus, did you bring my purse as I asked?" She already knew the answer. When he said yes, their eyes met. The determination in Belle's eyes won out, of course, and the silent plea in the black man's eyes was replaced with a familiar look of resignation. He handed over the small pouch and Belle removed one of the bottles. She handed it first to Monaghan. "Put about a dime's worth in your mouth." He did so. "Now, just use your tongue to roll it around your cheeks and gums real good." She watched as the old man complied. "It's not what they call cuisine back in San Francisco, but it should help hide the taste of that shoe leather."

"Thank-ee, Ma'am."

She passed the bottle to Foote who followed her instructions to the letter. Belle smiled. The taste was bitter, but she knew men. Rather than disappoint a lady, especially a lady in distress, they'd endure just about anything. She kept that smile on them. More than that, she kept her eyes on them so neither one could turn quickly and spit.

She made an offer of the bottle to Hephaestus, who politely declined as she knew he would. "Just finishing up now, Ma'am," he said. He stood up and dusted himself off. "I think I shall check on Round." He walked to the far edge of the camp where Round was staring at a desert as empty as his heart. And that's how they spent the night: Hephaestus with Round, Monaghans next to Foote, and Belle keeping an eye on them all.

About midmorning the next day a couple of wagons approached from the south. Hephaestus ran out to meet them, and by the time they approached the camp, the lead driver knew of the small company's misfortune, or at least the version he and Belle had cooked up that morning. And it wasn't too far from the truth except there was no mention of Princess Dodu. Belle walked out to meet them some short distance from the camp.

"Sorry for your troubles, Ma'am. We can take you as far as Phoenix."

"That would be a blessing, Sir," she said.

"Hop aboard, then."

"Hephaestus." Belle turned her head as if hiding a tear.

Hephaestus spoke to the lead driver. "Might you have a shovel we could borrow first, Sir?" he said. "Two of our party did not make it through the night."

Chapter Twenty-Seven

Prospect had seen the transformation of the West: from roads to highways, from wagons to automobiles, from arrows to airplanes and more. Yet nothing was as dramatic or powerful as the story of a few people all but unknown to history.

I had a pretty sound knowledge of Belle's arrival back in Privy, and the tragic consequences that followed, thanks to A. Noye and his lively newspaper. My research had even uncovered his unpublished manuscript about The Lynx which, although wildly fictionalized, did fill in a few gaps. What I lacked was a clear picture of the events between the peaceful return of Caldera and Belle's more violent return some years later. Naturally, the task of filling those gaps was put on Prospect's frail shoulders. I marveled at how talking about his sometimes son reenergized his spirit. I also couldn't miss the deep sadness in his eyes. I avoided direct eye contact with him when he wondered about Caldera's fate. Perhaps he suspected that I knew more than I was revealing. Nonetheless, he continued without hesitation to relate those events—events that weighed heavier and heavier on his heart.

Caldera healed quickly and was soon fit for work, which became the first of many challenges. Bull's efforts to spread the word had been one of the territory's most successful public relations campaigns and his son's record was clean as far as the law was concerned. Caldera was no longer a wanted man. The problem was that no one wanted the unwanted man.

Cleared of murder, he was still a known and feared killer. Most people didn't have to read between the lines of A. Noye's dime novels about the Lynx to make the connection. He was a man without emotion, and even the most hardened men found him unnerving. Bull got him a job as a bouncer in the Armageddon and he was good at it. "Efficient," said Bull's manager. "But he gets on people's nerves. Bad for business." A few hard cases had tried the new bouncer. There was no gunplay, but the cold almost mechanical manner with which the troublemakers were dispatched—a pistol swiped across the forehead and a kick out the batwings—was in its way more unsettling than .44 caliber fireworks. Business had dropped off under the cold hard eyes of the watchman.

Bull arranged for the head honcho of one of his silver mines to take on a new man and again Caldera proved to be a hard worker with a surprising amount of mining experience. He took orders well, didn't drink or fight on the job, and on a number of occasions saved a few lives by his swift actions, quick thinking, and total lack of fear. But Caldera hated being confined. He needed open country. His next job provided the wide open spaces from which he drew strength. He was an excellent ranch hand and proved himself capable at a number of tasks, yet the work was not satisfying. After years of violence, danger and a life of constant tension, he found the work dull and unfulfilling. Prospect and Bull feared that he might just pick up and return to the wild life.

Backhand Benny came up with the obvious solution. He had become a trusted officer of the law and had proven his courage and common sense countless times. Bull enjoyed being the head honcho, which is not the same as carrying out the duties of that office. Those fell into Benny's capable hands. Bull finally tired of playing sheriff and one day out of the blue appointed his only constable to the position. When some of the citizens said there had to be an election, Bull complied in his usual fashion. "I hereby elect the son of a bitch sheriff." No one questioned the returns.

Benny contemplated his solution to the Caldera situation for several days and finally took the short walk through town up to Bull's fortress of a home for a consultation. Before stepping onto the low porch he heard a horrible retching noise from back of the house. Being a good sheriff and an incurably curious individual, he went around for a look.

Bull was hunched over, his head between his knees, vomiting into an old bucket. Prospect was standing beside him smiling.

"What's the problem, Prospect?"

"Scorpion bite."

"He looks awfully sick. You want me to get some medicine or something?" He didn't know about the medicine, but he figured a bottle of "or something" would be needed in the very near future.

"His medicine has made him sick. That's good," Prospect said. When Benny shook his head in confusion Prospect held up a small bag. "Vee-ipkam. You call it Rattlesnake weed." Bull retched horribly. Prospect smiled. "We use poison to fight poison."

Benny forced a weak smile and turned his head for a breath of decent air.

"What the hell do you want?" said Bull. The last word exploded with a gut-wrenching force.

"Maybe I should come back at a better time, Bull."

"Spit it out!"

"Well, I've been thinking." He hesitated, wondering how Bull's condition might affect his judgment.

"Stop thinking! Start talking!" He grabbed at his stomach and a pained expression hammered his face. He heaved again.

Benny shifted his position to move upwind. "Caldera needs a job. I need a deputy."

"Your solution is well balanced, Ben," said Prospect.

Benny didn't quite understand his meaning, but he knew the old Indian approved, which might have a positive impact on Bull's temperament. Bull dry heaved over the bucket. His stomach growled and he moaned.

"I'll check in with you later, Bull."

"Do it."

"Sure."

"I mean do it. Hire Caldera." His stomach rumbled like a hot spring.

Prospect seemed genuinely pleased. Caldera had buried his emotions for more than a decade. He'd become a relentless machine of vengeance. Those suppressed emotions were pure energy and someday that energy would seek release. Caldera was like a powerful steam engine with the safety valves tied down. Soon there would be either a venting or an explosion. A job as policeman would provide that outlet. The work would also bring him into the community. Prospect was trying to reinstate his sometimes son into the world of men.

Bull groaned. "Oh God!" He got on his hands and knees.

"I'll tell Caldera the good news," said Benny. He backed away from the scene.

"Christ!" Bull got up and staggered toward the privy at the far end of the property.

Prospect smiled. "Vee-ipkam works both ends."

Benny grinned and turned back toward town.

Caldera was speaking to Privy's new parson when he got the news of his new employment. He'd been invited to Preacher's small home, one of Bull's rentals, for an evening meal. Deanna was nervous and she overcompensated by chattering on in eloquent but meaningless words and phrases. Preacher was also nervous, although his feelings were better hidden. Caldera was just hungry. If he had any feelings they weren't on display. After the meal the two men retired to a couple of chairs on what passed for a porch. The small talk didn't last very long. Caldera looked at him. "You're gonna' get yourself killed, Preacher."

He looked away from Caldera's gaze. "How?"

"You can't go winning souls in the places you been going." In the year he'd been in Privy Preacher had become a missionary obsessed. He'd been beaten half to death several times in confrontations with the heathen rabble in the Armageddon, down at the cribs and even at camps outside of town.

"You don't believe in God, Caldera?"

"Oh, you can't grow up 'round Prospect without finding some kind'a God. Don't reckon I'd find him in your good book though."

"Where would you find him?" Preacher was seeking an opportunity to save one of those souls.

Caldera swept his hand up and out, indicating the hills and mountains, the cactus, mesquite and Palo Verde. The wind flowing through the millions of saguaro spines offered a gentle and ever-changing melody. A recent desert shower filled the air with an earthy and inviting aroma.

Preacher thought, *How can I compete against the desert for a man's soul?*

Deanna stepped out with cigars and a couple of glasses of liquor. "Brandy for the parson and I managed a shot of whiskey for the... what are you these days, Caldera?"

As with all her conversations with Caldera, her voice was sincere, but crried just a tinge of bitterness.

"I got on down at the old ranch."

"Honest labor," Preacher said.

"It don't show me much."

"There's too much of the wanderer in you."

"That's his way," Deanna said. Again, there was just a tinge of bitterness around the edges of her words.

"Leave us for a moment, Deanna. Caldera and I have to talk."

"Gentlemen, their cigars and their brandy... it's the same everywhere."

The men weren't sure whether or not she was making a joke. They chuckled anyway as she stepped back inside. The porch was silent for a moment. Preacher spoke first. "You know who I am, don't you, Caldera?"

"Yessir."

"And you know what I've done? And who I done it to?"

"Yessir."

"Are you going to kill me?"

"Preacher, some men just need killin.' That's all you can do with 'em."

"I understand."

"You ain't one."

Most men would have been relieved. Preacher merely hunched his shoulders and let out a soft sigh. It appeared as if one weight had been lifted, yet another added to his burden.

Caldera glanced up. "If you keep preaching to the sinners where you've been preaching, somebody's sure as hell gonna' send you to glory."

"God calls me to the sinners."

"Well, they's plenty of sinners over at San Carlos Reservation. Indians need saving as much as the next man. And them soldiers can keep an eye on you."

"The greater sinners lie closer to home."

"Ain't nothing you can rely on here except Ben and a few friends." Their eyes met, Preacher's with a surprised look in them. "Ain't nobody can watch your back all the time."

"I ride with the Lord, Caldera."

"I hear that General Custer thought the same thing."

"His will be done."

Caldera spat. "Hmmf. Sometimes I think you're *trying* to get yourself killed."

Backhand Benny's arrival put an end to the conversation.

"Hello, Preacher. Been looking for you, Caldera."

"What can I do for you, Ben?"

"I need a deputy. You need a job. Interested?"

"Don't know." Caldera paused, waiting for his friend's curiosity to stir. "I reckon I couldn't start before right now."

Benny grinned. "Well, right now's when I need somebody. C'mon, we have some work to do."

Caldera hopped up, a spring in his step. He looked to Preacher. "You'd best stay preaching to the choir. Leave them other folks to that God of yours."

Preacher nodded, but both men knew he didn't agree.

Caldera was sworn in about fifteen minutes later. The ceremony was brief.

"Do you still want the job?"

"Uh-huh."

"You got it."

The community of Privy wasn't much on ceremony. When Benny pinned on the badge of office, Caldera noticed the star had been cut from a token from Belle's old whorehouse. His first task was to back up Backhand Benny in a touchy and dangerous situation. They had to collect back taxes from the town witch.

"Old lady Colibri, she got the power," Caldera said. "Ask Prospect."

"She's also got the money and Privy wants its share."

The town hadn't been very concerned with tax collection during the years Bull McKenzie had been sheriff. He'd collected and disbursed taxes as he saw fit, usually to his own benefit. Once the city fathers actually began to exercise a little authority by asking for a strict accounting, Bull lost interest in politics. A good bit was still siphoned off by those same city fathers, but not a cent was lost or unaccounted for while passing through Benny's hands.

Old lady Colibri lived more than quarter mile out of town and she was the only white person who could make such a claim. The Pima respected her power and were on friendly terms with her. The Apaches knew and dreaded her curses. She was a person to be avoided at all costs. She had survived for so long alone in the

Arizona desert that even the good Christians of Privy sometimes wondered whether she really was a witch.

The only power Benny was concerned with was money. The old lady was a land owner and an astute businesswoman. She had money and Privy wanted its "fair share" for its lack of service. She disagreed, passionately. The fact that there were no official town limits fueled both sides of the argument over whether she owed taxes.

Her small cabin was just off the road. A variety of animal skulls hung from every wall. Other skulls marked the extent of her property and perhaps the extent of her mental state. Some in town said the skulls were a smart move, a protection from the Apaches who held strong beliefs about the dead. Others said she was just plain crazy. She was sitting in a homemade chair under a small porch when they arrived. A double-barrel shotgun lay across her lap.

"Knew you were coming. Saw it in a whirlwind this morning."

"Then you know why we're here, Mrs. Colibri," Benny said.

"And you know my answer. Go on."

Caldera began easing away from his partner, putting some distance between the two targets.

"Hold still, Sonny," the witch said.

"Crap," muttered Benny. He'd come for taxes, not for trouble.

The old woman's eyes narrowed. "You two can go on back to Privy or you can go to hell. Your call."

A skull at the edge of the house fell to the ground with a thump. Perhaps the peg holding it was rotten or it had just worked its way out over time. Perhaps the old witch had made it jump. Benny's eyes darted to the sound and the small spray of dust it produced. When he glanced back, the world had changed.

Caldera was in a low crouch. His pistol was drawn and pointed directly at the old lady's heart. Mrs. Colibri was leaning forward, her eyes locked on the man with the pistol. One of the sidehammers of her shotgun was already pulled back. Slowly, and with ease and control she pulled back the other. Standoff.

"I came here for taxes, Ma'am, not blood."

"This just ain't your day, is it, Sonny Boy?"

Benny held his arms out and away from his pistol. A slight, hot breeze kicked up the dust. Cactus wrens chirped. A hammer in Privy beat like a distant heart. Sweat trickled into the corner of Benny's right eye. No one moved. "I don't want any killing, Caldera."

"That might not be up to you n'me, Boss."

"Mrs. Colibri," started Benny.

The old woman screamed in a high-pitched fury. Her voice quavered, but the shotgun remained in steady hands.

"Christ, she's crazy!" Benny said.

"Naw, she's just playing her game," said Caldera.

"It's not one I'd care to lose."

Caldera had been sizing up the old woman. His gaze had locked onto hers from the first moment they had arrived. Each recognized something in the other and a silent, bleak understanding had formed. There was no backing down from this moment.

"You got any ideas?" said Benny.

Caldera thought for a moment. "They say you're a witch," he said.

"Some say."

"Is it true?"

"Some say."

"I'll make a deal with you, old witch."

"Why should I deal with the likes of you, Sonny Boy?"

"Beats dyin' all to hell."

And that was the crisis point. The old woman squinted as if taking aim or perhaps in deep thought. Benny held his breath and prepared as best he could to jump, draw his weapon, or die. He noticed that his deputy seemed to relax. *Hell. Maybe Caldera has some kind of witch power too.*

"Name your poison," Colibri said.

"Read my fortune."

"For what?"

"If you're right, you don't pay no taxes this year. If you're wrong, pay up. You got a month to prove it."

She didn't even hesitate. "Deal."

"Why'd you do that?" Benny said.

"We got a fifty-fifty chance of getting them taxes. Before we had about a hunnerd percent chance of getting killed." Caldera holstered his pistol.

"Yeah, I'll take those odds. What's next?"

Colibri provided the answer. "Piss."

The men spoke in unison. "What?"

The old woman pointed next to her chair. "Make your water here, in the dirt."

"What the hell?" Caldera walked over to the cabin and unbuttoned his pants. "You going to look away?" he asked.

"Depends on whether you got anything worth looking at."

Caldera had never embraced modesty. He did his business and buttoned back up without ceremony or comment. The old witch leaned over and looked at the patterns he'd made in the sand. She took her time, and for a few moments seemed to lose contact with the world around her.

Benny thought it was all part of the act. Caldera, who had grown up around shamans and their trances, knew better. She was touching the spirit world.

She at last sat back and stared at Caldera. "You can have your taxes now, you son of a bitch." She spoke directly to the deputy, not the sheriff.

"Why the change of heart?" Benny said.

"I don't want to be dead or in jail when all the fun begins." She stood up. "I'll get your damned blood money now." She started to enter the cabin.

"What's all this fun you're talking about, Mrs. Colibri?" Benny said.

She paused in the doorway, half in light and half in darkness. Her back was to the men.

"What do you see in my future, old witch?" Caldera said.

The witch turned with a smile. She spoke a single word, slowly and with joy. "Pain."

Chapter Twenty-Eight

Benny slammed his gloves on the rough wood table that passed for the sheriff's desk. "You got to do something about Preacher!"

Caldera had just finished sweeping out the small cell that had replaced the town's jail tree. It was more weather proof, but the awful smell of everything bad about the human body made most guests long for the chain, the stump and the hot desert breezes outside. "What's he got hisself into now?"

"He tried to save a couple of miners down at Hell On Wheels." Benny paused, caught off guard by a new thought. "You ever notice a common theme running through the names of the saloons around here?"

"What about Preacher?"

"Oh, they beat the hell out of him and run off before I got there. The son of a bitch won't give me their names."

"That's Preacher."

"Says 'Forgive, brother Ben, forgive.' He sure is throwing that 'brother' around a lot lately."

Caldera sat down. His boss was in one of his long-winded moods.

Benny rolled on. "He's got Deanna worried sick."

"Deanna?" Caldera's voice was tinged with just a touch of suggestion.

"It's her name."

"I know. It's just that with Preacher out saving every living thing between Prescott and Tombstone...." He let the sentence drop.

"What?"

"Are you... uh, you know?"

Benny grabbed his gloves and stood up. "Damn you, Caldera." He stomped his way across the room.

"They ain't really married you know. They got no papers or nothing."

"I reckon I know that too." He stalked out of the office. A minute later Benny stuck his head back in the door. "Anyway, you got to do something. Now." He finished his sentence and ducked back out, slamming the door for punctuation.

Caldera leaned his chair against the wall, put his hands behind his head and thought over his new assignment. A man who exercised true faith was to be admired, but Preacher had been pushing the limits of faith and man. He'd become something a full-time job for the undermanned Privy constabulary and for Dr. Marcy, the town's only sober medical professional. As he stared at the ceiling an idea floated into his brain.

Bull was whittling a cane—his leg had never fully recovered from the scorpion sting—when Caldera approached. Prospect was with him, having delivered a pouch of medicine from Tattoo. The old patriarch of Privy didn't trust the town's young doctor, and he didn't want word to get around about how puny he'd been feeling. Besides, most of the medicine he'd taken his adult life was Indian medicine. He felt more comfortable with it. Truth be told, he felt more confident in it too.

"Bull," said Caldera. No "pop" or "daddy" had escaped his lips in years.

"What can I do for you, Caldera?" His voice was downright friendly.

"Preacher needs a church."

"I need a shot of whiskey."

"He ain't got no money and what the town gives him and that woman of his is barely enough to get by."

"Ain't my problem."

"Sure it is."

Bull packed the medicine pouch in his jacket.

Caldera said, "Is that moomsh?" A grin made a valiant, but failed effort to access his face.

Bull's eyelids clinched.

Prospect laughed. "Are you stove up again, Bull?" Truly Bull's bowels had not been in the best of condition for a number of years. Moomsh, Pima for the Indian wheat plant, was an excellent way to stimulate activity in the nether regions.

"What's all this crap about Preacher's church? Don't he meet with them new folks?"

Prospect, more aware of the danger Preacher faced, nodded. "A holy man should have a holy place to keep his ass busy. We gotta' do something or he's gonna' get himself massacred."

Bull bent over slightly, his stomach beginning a familiar cramp. "Like I said, it ain't my problem."

Caldera took the half-finished cane and began to work on it. His knife was sharp and his hands skilled. In short order the walking stick was completed, the handle smoothed by the scraping of the edge of a sharp blade. "I bet them Easterners would like a real church."

"Don't you—" Bull's protest was cut off by a stomach cramp.

"Think I'll run it by a couple of 'em. They're a cheap bunch though. I wonder who they'll start pestering for money and supplies."

"Bastard!" Bull meant it as a curse, not a description. His eyes squinted what passed for an apology. Caldera never flinched and if he felt a sting no one would ever know.

"Pestering and pestering."

Then Prospect, whose respect for holy men had grown through the years, had a brilliant thought. "No more moomsh."

"I know plenty of Pima folk," Bull said.

It was Prospect's turn to grin. Tattoo was the best medicine woman in Arizona.

"And *pestering.*"

"All right, damn it! Damn you both!"

So blackmail and constipation formed the foundation of Privy's first Christian church, and it was a good foundation. Bull, horrified at the thought of Easterners constantly dogging his trail, became a generous benefactor. He donated all of the major construction materials and even ordered Omar Whelming, chief engineer for Bull's mining interests, to design the structure and oversee its construction. "Hell, man, if you can build a tunnel 1,000 feet underfoot, you can build a box for the Lord." He'd quickly learned that the world "Lord," with a capital L, moved some men when nothing else would. Banker Chandler, who constantly and proudly wore a waistband made from an old Confederate flag, donated lumber for pews and paint, and the necessaries for making the interior presentable. The Easterners donated modest sums of money and enormous amounts of advice.

After Bull and Banker Chandler, the two largest donations came from surprising members of the community. Miss Rachael from the House of Doves brought in a sizeable amount of money collected by her employees. "We have but two modest requests," she told Preacher. "Any of my girls who wish to attend will attend."

Preacher didn't even hesitate. "Of course. All are welcome in the House of the Lord."

Miss Rachael took a deep breath and sighed. She had expected something of a moral struggle. Emboldened, she pressed on. "Some of my girls are Catholic."

Preacher spoke apologetically. "I don't have any denomination, Miss Rachael. I don't know anything about the Catholic Church and I surely don't speak Latin." She nodded. "Perhaps you can acquire a Catholic Bible."

Preacher smiled. "Well, you can bet I'll try."

The need for Catholic services became obvious when a large contingent of the town's invisible community, the Mexicans, showed up to volunteer their labor. Chino Galleta, their spokesman, was also a master carver. As the walls went up and the roof put down, he invested a considerable amount of time working with wood and knife under a nearby cottonwood. When at last the windows were put in, the pews nailed tight, and the paint had dried, he presented Preacher with primitive, yet emotionally powerful carvings of the Fourteen Stations of the Cross.

Deanna, although not a Catholic, had been raised in large cities and had often attended services with friends. She took the carvings and, with Chino's help, placed them in proper position around the church. That settled it. There would be Protestant and Catholic services in Privy, Arizona Territory.

Not surprisingly, at least not to Bull, Caldera, Prospect, Miss Rachael and Chino, the Easterners pitched a fit, but the matter of contention wasn't Catholicism. It was whores and Mexicans. The first church meeting held in the new building wasn't a service. It was a brawl. Such words as "harlot" and "despicable" and "dirty" and "damnable" were thrown with fury equal to any Apache warrior with a lance and a hatred of someone different.

The matter was finally settled when Bull spoke. "All right, you bastards!" Mr. Gatling's gun could not have been more effective in silencing a mass of humanity. "Let's just tear the son of a bitch down." Banker Chandler stood up in a show of solidarity. He rested his thumbs in his Confederate flag, puffed his chest, and defied any one to charge. Miss Rachael and Chino, who had remained outside the church they had helped finance, nodded their assent.

Caldera, there to keep the peace, saw a claw hammer within the pulpit. He grabbed it and immediately inserted the claw into the frame of a nearby window. "If we're gonna' do this, then let's get on with it." The loud creak of protesting wood that followed brought shouts of protest and peace from the dissenters. Late in the evening a compromise was reached. Regular Sunday services would be held mid-morning till noon. Services for the Catholic folks would be held one hour after dawn. The church would be open to functions for all with appropriate notice.

After the brawl and reconciliation a few men hung around to admire their work.

"All that shouting just to decide what you should'a known to do in the first place," Caldera said.

"We fought a bloody Civil War for the same reason," Omar Whelming said.

"I don't know what scared 'em more, Bull's threat or Chandler's big gut," Benny said.

"It was the power of the Lord," Preacher said.

"And a good claw hammer." Benny grinned.

They laughed a good bit over that and then stepped back to get a better view. The small square building stood alone at the edge of town. The moon had risen high, and in the moonlight the church seemed to glow in the dark.

"I owe you, Caldera. This town owes you," Preacher said.

"It was just my idea. Them other folks did everything else."

"God bless you."

That was the first time in his life Caldera had ever heard that phrase tossed his way, but he gave it no thought. He looked at Preacher. "You seem a little down in the mouth."

"Oh, no. This is marvelous, a miracle. I was just thinking."

"Spit it out, Bub... ah, Preacher," Whelming said.

"Tomorrow's Sunday and our first service."

"Yeah?"

"Oh, I just wish we had a steeple."

"Hell, Preacher. Sorry. We can build you one of those. Take about a day," Whelming said.

"Fine... that's just fine," said Preacher, but they all could hear the disappointment in his voice.

The small group remained silent for a moment. Caldera cleared his voice. "I can get you a steeple for tomorrow morning."

"How!"

Caldera was reluctant to speak. "Why don't you go on home, Preacher. Deanna'll be getting worried. You just leave that steeple business to me, Ben, an' Mr. Whelming."

After the parting, two confused men looked at Caldera. "What are you thinking?" Benny said.

"We're wasting time. C'mon." Caldera dashed back toward town, quickly followed by two confused, tired and very interested men. In less than a minute they had reached their destination.

"You are out of your mind!" Benny said.

"What do you think, Mr. Whelming?" Caldera said.

"I can personally attest that it is functionally sound. Aesthetically, though...."

"Huh?"

"It'll work, but it stinks."

The small structure before them was a four by four square about six feet tall. The bottom half was made of rough horizontal planks. The top half was a crude lattice work topped by a peaked roof with four sides.

"We'd best get at it then," Caldera said.

The three men pulled their gloves up tight, pulled their neckerchiefs around their noses, and began the night's work. That work required some manhandling, a sled and horse, tons of soap and water, and several coats of white paint. Whelming cut the bottom section with precision to match the slope of the roof. "The more of that bottom we cut off the better," Benny said.

The moment the paint was dry, which wasn't long in the arid climate of Privy, they hauled it up the side of the church and nailed it firmly in place. A painted cross of two by fours topped the entire structure. Whelming even provided some improvised flashing to seal the edges. "We can make it pretty later. Main thing is Preacher will have his damn steeple for 'the good folk of Privy' tomorrow."

"It still stinks," Benny said.

"They won't notice it down there," Caldera said.

"Speaking of down there, I got a jug of half-ass decent whiskey over at the hotel. You boys want to howl at the moon?" Whelming had lost his appetite for sleep and Sunday wasn't a work day.

"I'm not attending church with a hangover," Benny said.

"Neither am I. See you next Sunday," Caldera said.

Preacher saw his new steeple during a glorious sunrise. He arrived just as the first rays of orange light struck the top of the cross and he marveled as the glowing light descended upon the new holy place. He said a short prayer of thanks for his blessings, mentioning Caldera by name

Shortly after sunrise the Catholic whores and the Mexicans showed up for early morning services. They were grateful for the moment and the opportunity for real worship services. Preacher did his best at being a priest by talking a lot of Mary and love and overcoming adversity. He even spoke of the holiness of sacrifice and suffering. After the services the two groups dispersed quickly so as not to offend any of the other town folk who might come by the church early.

When the time arrived for regular services a good size crowd arrived with it. The women could only marvel at the appearance of a steeple atop the unadorned church they'd seen just the day before. Most of the men stifled their grins as best as possible. The general unspoken consensus was what the hell. The church needed a steeple and it got one. Just about everyone approved.

After services began Bull and Prospect rode by, headed out for an afternoon of hunting. They both paused to stare at the miracle wrought by their shared son. Privy's privy was now a church steeple.

When astonished, Prospect still mingled his Pima and English. "Biht house."

"Kind'a appropriate, ain't it?"

The two men laughed and rode away to the fading tune of "O'erwhelmed With Blessings From Above."

Chapter Twenty-Nine

"Preacher's gone!"

"Where to now?" Benny was already scouring the streets of Privy for "Preacher's Keeper," Caldera. The distraction provided by his new church had kept Preacher occupied and out of trouble for about six months before his old habits took hold. He'd been beaten six times in as many weeks, and had it not been for the death stare in Caldera's eyes the man of God would have been lynched by a bunch of drunken ranch hands not three days earlier. Protecting the man had turned into a full-time job.

"No, Sir. I mean he's *gone*. Deanna, too." The man was an easterner, a shop owner not given to overstatement. Benny guided him to the shade of the overhang of Hell On Wheels. There were times when Benny's old life called him. The sounds of bottles and mugs, the smell of whiskey and smokes, and the ebb and flow of rough conversation were headwinds hard to buck. Preacher's antics made them downright irresistible. But other winds were blowing too.

"Deanna?"

"He took off and she wouldn't let go. It was the damnedest thing, Ben. She's as crazy as he is."

Why can't folks just get to the point? Benny took a deep breath. He could almost smell the difference in quality of the whiskey shots being poured. "Just start at the starting place."

"Yes, Sir. It's about the dirt."

"Dirt?"

"Yes, Sir. Holy miracle wonder dirt."

"I never took you for a drinking man, Mr. McGloughlin."

"I'm serious. A bunch of crazy Mexicans came through here yesterday morning. I'm surprised you didn't see 'em."

"Me and Caldera had to run a jailbird over to Phoenix. We just got back. About the Mexicans?"

"They're some kind of insane religious folk. All they want to do is beat the hell out of themselves. They do it for Jesus, they say. It's crazy!"

Benny raised his head back and expelled a breath of air. "Penitentes."

"What the hell is that?"

"Mostly poor Mexican Catholics. They think the more you hurt yourself the closer you get to Christ... something like that."

"Well, that's right up Preacher's alley."

"And Deanna went with him?"

"Yes, Sir. I guess she figured she didn't have any choice."

Benny winced.

"It gets worse. The telegraph lines have been cut. Word is Geronimo's back."

The whiskey, the smoke and the conversation, the siren call drew Benny toward the batwings that led to the old life. He took in a big draft of air and listened to the music of glass on glass. *Rot gut. Warm beer. Rot gut. Big spender. Somebody just lit a good cigar.* He shook it off. "You seen Caldera?"

"Yes, Sir. He's over at the Armageddon with Bull."

"Thanks." Benny jogged off the boardwalk and up the dusty street. The contrast between Hell On Wheels and The Armageddon offered a quick glance at Privy's history. The former was small, but featured polished wood, brass rails, mirrors and glass, a pressed-tin ceiling and even wallpaper. The latter was still rough wood planks, dusty shelves, worn tables and chairs, and bullet holes. At least Bull had put in a wooden floor. It was his office of late.

Benny explained the situation as best he could.

"Dirt?"

"Yes, Sir."

"Dirt and a bunch of Mexicans?"

"That's what the man said."

"Good riddance."

"He took Deanna with him."

Caldera looked at his half-finished beer with longing. He killed it quickly and stood up. "What the hell...."

"I'll be going with you," Benny said.

Prospect, who had developed a controlled taste for whiskey, killed his shot and stood up. He kicked Bull's right foot. Prospect had invested a considerable amount of time trying to bring Caldera back into the world, and a considerable portion of that effort was directed at bringing the white father together with his sometimes son.

The old man stood up. Despite his age and bad leg he was still a formidable force. "Yeah, what the hell...."

They gathered a few supplies and headed south on the main road. The wide track left by the procession of believers was easy to pick up and easy to follow: one wagon surrounded by ten or so walkers. Caldera led the small band at a quick pace and they made good time.

Preacher and Deanna were headed south, and that meant they would be on the only road to Tucson. Further tracking might become difficult if the couple were waylaid or kidnapped by an Apache band. The look on Benny's face betrayed his fear and worry, a look partially mirrored in Prospect's countenance. He'd too often seen what horrors could descend on the unprepared. Bull was fierce and focused and the years seem to drop from his face and eyes. The blood hunt was on. Caldera—well, no one could read Caldera.

They made twenty miles before finding Preacher's wagon. It had been ransacked and most of the contents scattered across the road.

"Oh no!" gasped Benny.

"Don't mean nothing... yet," Bull said.

Caldera, in the lead, surveyed the scene, put two and two together, and came up with an ugly answer. He spoke to all, but he looked directly at Bull.

"Apaches. They attacked here and split up in two groups. Looks like they took a bunch off that way." He pointed to the east. "I reckon there's a bit of torturing going on. Don't look like they was in much of a hurry."

"Deanna?" Benny's voice was weak and trembling.

Caldera puffed air through his lips and nodded to the northeast. "Three of 'em. Looks like she was dragged."

Benny's sudden move in that direction was anticipated by all three of his companions. Bull blocked his way while Prospect grabbed his arm.

"That ain't the way," Bull said.

"I'll take a look." And before anyone could object Caldera was into the desert. Prospect gave him a few moments and then moved on, followed by Benny with Bull bringing up the rear.

They'd moved through the scrub brush and cactus less than half a mile when Caldera returned. He motioned for silence. "'Bout a quarter of a mile, down in a wash." He looked to Benny. "She's alive."

"And?"

"We better hurry."

"How?" Prospect said.

Caldera looked at Bull, who spoke quietly and with determination. "It's your call."

Benny asked, "Have they...."

"Let's go."

They dismounted and tied off their horses. Prospect pulled a well-worn hand axe and hefted it, enjoying the feel. The Apaches had been cruel to his people and it had been a long time since he'd killed one. Bull pulled a Bowie knife. He came close to grinning. Caldera led them on foot to the base of a small rise. The wash was on the other side. They could hear whimpering, a female voice. The guttural taunts were harsh and male. A faint trail of smoke drifted over the desert.

Caldera motioned for his war party to wait. He crawled up, as silent as a snake, for a final look. Deanna cowed against the edge of the wash, a ten foot tall prison wall. She was curled almost in a fetal position against the hard, white caliche. Two of the Apaches left one to attend the small fire they were building, a fire designed for purposes other than warmth, cooking, or to bring light to the darkness. The one attending the fire stirred the flames with a large stick. The end glowed red hot even in the harsh light of the sun. He grinned and returned it to the flames.

The other two grabbed Deanna. She shrieked as one pulled her up and the other ripped open the back of her dress. On the other side of the rise Bull and Prospect grabbed Benny and gestured for silence. Down in the wash the Apache who had pulled Deanna off the sand ripped the front of her dress. She fought, but that only gave them more opportunities to tear at her clothing. In seconds she was naked, trying to cover herself and pressing against the edge of the wash.

"Don't," she whimpered. It was a low, weak and desperate plea and it fell on deaf ears.

Caldera turned back and motioned left for Bull, right for Prospect. Benny, confused at not getting any orders, hesitated before moving cautiously toward Caldera's position. By the time he reached his friend the others were in place and before he could whisper, "What now?" his three companions were in motion.

Caldera leaped, knocking the Apache into his own fire. They rolled in the dirt, but Caldera's razor sharp skinning knife was slicing through the man's guts before he could respond. Bull's Bowie knife was embedded deep into one Apache's back. The warrior staggered, still full of fight and looking for an enemy, but found only another knife sticking in his gut. Prospect, moving faster than Benny thought any man could move, took off the side of the other Indian's head with one clean, swift swing of his axe. Prospect swung again and took off the other side for good measure.

The whole affair took less than half a minute. Benny scrambled over to Deanna. She was in shock and mumbling. Caldera scanned the scene to make sure there were no others. Satisfied, he motioned for everyone to get moving. They climbed quickly over the rise and back to the horses before Deanna became aware that she was no longer with the Apaches. She clung to Benny, silent, grateful and still terrified.

Caldera wiped some blood and brain off her shoulder and out of her hair. "For God's sake, put a blanket on her," he said.

Benny started to move, but she refused to let him go. Her eyes were still wide.

"It's me, Deanna," Benny said. "And Caldera, and Prospect and Mr. McKenzie, too."

Prospect pulled a blanket from behind his saddle, cut a slit in the middle and tried to hand it over. Deanna just shivered and held onto Benny. He took it and she allowed him to slip it over her head. Modesty accommodated, Benny turned to Caldera. "Now what?"

Caldera looked at Deanna. "Scream."

She just stared at him, uncomprehending.

"Them other Apaches ain't going to be too far from here. If they don't hear screaming pretty soon, they're gonna' be coming to see why."

Benny took her by the arms. "Scream, Deanna." Wide eyed and still in shock, she just stared and mumbled.

Caldera reached under the folds of her blanket. His fingers grasped the tender skin at her rib cage. He pinched and twisted as hard as he could. Deanna screamed. And then she buried her head in Benny's shoulders. Caldera pinched once more and she screamed again. This time she kept screaming. She screamed out all the terror within her, the horror of the last few hours, the years on the move with Preacher, and the nightmare of captivity before Caldera's rescue. She screamed all the anger, frustration, and hatred within her until she was hoarse and could scream no more. The fit lasted almost a minute.

"That was good, Deanna. Damn good," Caldera said. And with that comment and reassurance she began to compose herself. She tried to speak.

"Ain't no time for that," Bull said.

"Take her back to Privy," Prospect said.

"We'll do what we can for Preacher and them Mexicans," Caldera said.

"I'd better go with you." Benny's eyes darted from Deanna to his companions and back again.

Caldera looked him in the eye. "We might not make it. You want to leave her out here like that? You got that much faith in your God?"

Without another word, Caldera, Bull and Prospect mounted up and were off. Benny helped Deanna onto his horse, climbed on behind her, and headed back to the relative safety of Privy. He glanced once over his shoulder, but his companions were already out of sight.

They found the corpse of a Penitente about half a mile from the wagon. He had apparently made an attempt to escape into the desert. A single shot to the back of his head had ushered the man to his heavenly reward. Tracks in the sand showed that the rest of the party had been herded off the road. They were easy to follow. Again, Caldera rode out alone.

"He's become quite...." Bull searched for the appropriate word.

"Capable," Prospect said.

"Yes,"

They rode on, with no more needing to be said. They were skirting the edge of a dense growth of mesquite when the screaming began. It was a peculiar kind of scream, agony combined with rhythm, and it was very near. Instantly the men dismounted, tied their horses, and pulled their rifles. Each stuck an extra pistol in his belt. Prospect added his bloody axe to his arsenal.

"That's the damnedest scream I ever heard," Bull whispered. He stared through the small forest, but could see nothing through the dense growth.

Prospect stared at the ground, using his ears instead of his eyes. "They're close. There's probably a clearing on the other side of this thicket." He cocked his head. "That's a song!"

"What?"

"What you call a hymn. I have heard the Mexicans singing it at Preacher's church."

The screams became more intense and yet there was rhythm, even a melody to it. "What the hell is going on?" Bull said.

Prospect led as they worked their way to the edge of the thicket. Here the growth was a bit thinner. They crawled into the scrawny trees and moved into position to see what was going on. Both men were stunned. Each man shouldered his rifle, took careful aim, and held his breath.

Preacher and the Penitentes were squatting in the dirt. One of the men, the screaming singing Penitente, had been stripped of his clothing and staked to the ground. Two Apaches had built a small fire and were dropping coals one at a time on the man's abdomen. Their faces were clinched in confusion. The more pain they inflicted the more joy filled the tortured man's voice. One shook his head and walked away.

The sight that most disturbed Bull and Prospect was Caldera. He just stood up, walked out of the safety of the scrub brush and calmly walked into the clearing. He stood face-to-face with the man who had to be the leader of the small band of warriors.

"Sweet Jesus! Does he know who he's palaverin' with?" Bull said.

"He *is* quite... capable," said Prospect. Nonetheless, he took careful aim at the man facing his sometimes son.

Things were not quite as tense in the clearing.

"Been a long time, Jerome."

204

"Long time, Caldera. Why are you here?"

"You talk better these days."

"The white man has taught me much."

Caldera glanced around. The band was in bad shape. The men and horses were skinny, worn thin by hunger and privation and constant running from the army. Two of the warriors were skinning one of Preacher's mules. One was eating strips of raw meat. Even the poor Mexican zealots were in better shape. When he looked at Preacher, the man of God's eyes pleaded for knowledge of Deanna, but he dared not respond. He turned back to Jerome.

"I come to ask you to let these fellers go."

Jerome snorted.

"They ain't nothing to you."

"Mexican." A lifetime of hate and revenge was expressed in the contempt found in that word.

Decades earlier Mexican soldiers had slaughtered most of Jerome's band, including his wife and children. The fury and hatred in the old Indian's eyes told the story.

"I could give you to my warriors," Jerome said.

The staked-out Penitente screamed in agony as a coal burned into his guts. A smile crossed the man's face and he struggled to continue the hymn.

"You n'me come too far together for that," said Caldera.

Jerome's face was a mask of indifference. The young man before him was full of foolish pride, yet there was bravery in him. "Go."

"The Anglo... he is a holy man. And he is a friend of mine."

Jerome barked something to one of his men, who grabbed Preacher and brought him to Caldera. The Indian shoved Preacher so that he fell on his knees.

"Caldera, is Deanna well?"

"Shut up." Caldera never took his eyes off Jerome. "Them others. I'd like you to let them go, too."

"Go. Now. Or we go together no more."

Caldera pushed his luck. "Jerome, them crazies ain't nothing to you. They're holy men, too, but loco in la cabeza. Crazy in the head."

Jerome placed his hand on the pistol in his belt, and a clearer message was never sent, but Caldera pressed on. "There's something else, Jerome."

"What something else?"

"Nantan Lupan."

The words mean Gray Wolf in Apache, a name given to George Crook, general of the United States Army. Several of the warriors stopped what they were doing at the sound of the name. Caldera slowly and very carefully took Jerome's fist and held it between his hands. He released his grip and formed a circle with his hands. He tapped the man's fist and said, "Jerome." He then slowly closed his circled hands around the fist until it was entrapped. "Nantan Lupan."

The Apache leader jerked his hand down in disgust.

"You ain't got the time, Jerome. You'd best be gittin' on down the road. I'm asking you to set them Mexicans free." He had made a valiant effort and on another leader the tactic might have worked. Jerome was, however, a most practical leader. "I will set them free," he said. He took his pistols and one by one executed the Penitentes, one shot to the head of each man. Then he returned to Caldera, pointed the pistol at Preacher's head and said, "Go."

Caldera grabbed Preacher, pulled him up, walked him over to his horse and the two men rode out of the clearing. They joined up with Bull and Prospect, who were already mounted.

"We better make tracks," Caldera said. "Jerome ain't gonna' be so accommodating when he finds out we killed three of his boys." Minutes later they were back on the road and headed toward Privy at a fast gallop.

"Deanna?" Preacher said.

"She's a little roughed up, but she's fine.

"Did they harm her?"

"She got scared. That's all."

When they reached the wagon Preacher made Caldera halt. He jumped off the horse and rambled through the contents. "Praise God," he said as he lifted a clay jar from a box.

"Their holy soil," Prospect said.

"Well, we're likely to catch holy hell if we don't get outta' here," Bull said.

"You got work to do, Preacher," Caldera said.

They didn't slow their pace until they could see the steeple of the church shining above the horizon. Caldera accompanied Preacher to his church and inside where he put away the clay jar for safe keeping. Only after the soil was safe and sound did he ask to be taken to Deanna.

Caldera watched him and wondered. *Strange priorities.*

Bull and Prospect made straight for the Armageddon, and it was some time before either spoke. Bull threw back a shot and poured another.

Prospect sipped, enjoying the slow burn of whiskey through his gullet. "Jerome," he said.

"You think he knows?"

"I do not think so."

Bull laughed. "Life is an amazement."

Prospect laughed, finished his drink and poured another.

"My boy knows Geronimo," Bull said. His laughter was out of control.

Life truly is an amazement, Prospect thought. In all the years they'd been together that was the first time Bull Mackenzie had ever used the phrase "my boy."

Chapter Thirty

Caldera tracked down Benny and the two tired constables entered the Armageddon to join the festivities. Bull had made sure extra shot glasses were at the table. "Figured you'd get here sooner or later."

Benny poured a shot in each glass and handed one to Caldera.

"How's Deanna?" Prospect said.

Benny killed his shot. "Damn. Bull, you brought out your good bottle." He savored the whiskey. "She's gonna' be all right. Shook up something fierce, but give her a couple of days and she'll be back."

"She is a fortunate young woman." The dark introspection in Prospect's eyes reflected just how fortunate she had been.

"Preacher?" Bull wasn't concerned, just curious.

Caldera poured a shot for each man. "Don't know. I mean he's fine, but he ain't all right. He keeps looking at that holy dirt like it was one o'them bags'a gold you used to yarn about."

"He carries the burden of many sins," Prospect said. "As do we all."

"Ain't you the cheerful one," Bull said.

More than two hours had passed since the small war party had entered Privy, but the men were not yet heavy legged with alcohol. Each was savoring the moment in his own way. Bull was celebrating a victory. Rarely in his recent battles with Apaches and bandits had a fight been so fast or so successful. As a deputy, Benny had faced down many a drunk and even a few drunken killers. He'd only had to fire his weapon at a man once or twice and he'd never been in a scrape that could in any way be described as a battle. He too had caught some of Bull's enthusiasm.

Omar Whelming stalked in wanting to wet his whistle while his wagon was being loaded down at Bull's lumber yard. Bull called him over to the table and poured a shot. "By the power vested in me by me I hereby appoint you sheriff for the rest of the day." He took Benny's badge and pinned it on the surprised engineer. "The real sheriff and his posse are going to get rip roaring drunk." And that was that. A *fait accompli* had been delivered by the ultimate power. Neither Benny nor Caldera objected.

Whelming looked at the whiskey bottle and the one remaining empty shot glass. "Seems like most of the desperados around here are sitting at this table."

"Hell, sit down. Privy's done all right without the law before."

Whelming helped himself to the bottle.

The drinking, slow and easy, led to looser tongues, at least with Bull and Benny.

Caldera contributed to the conversation, but showed neither joy nor remorse at the killings earlier in the day. Prospect grew more and more absorbed in his own thoughts.

Caldera was the first to see Deanna. She stood stoop shouldered and with her head down just outside the batwing doors. She searched the interior until her gaze locked on Caldera. She looked as lost as a person could be, and a doe-eyed look of fear marred her considerable beauty. Without a word he stood up, crossed the room, and joined her on the wooden sidewalk. Benny caught the movement and watched. She and Caldera had a bond that he respected.

"Preacher left me."

"Damn it!" Caldera's curse was a frustrated, angry whisper. "Where this time?"

"He said for you not to follow him."

"Where, Deanna?"

She bit her lip as if swallowing the words would make them disappear. "Mexico. He's taking that jar of dirt down where it belongs. He called it a 'holy mission.'"

"Oh, Christ. Deanna, I can't be chasing him down—"

"That's right. You *can't*."

It took a few seconds for her words to sink in.

"He doesn't want you or anybody to come after him."

For the first time in many, many years Caldera felt the numbing effects of confusion. He had a duty to protect Preacher even if it was to protect the man from self-destruction, but he also felt a duty to honor the man's wishes. "What the hell is he doing, Deanna?"

Her face reflected sadness, resignation and fear. "Suicide."

"Damn it, he's paid for them bad years."

As she looked at him tears began coursing down her cheeks. "Caldera, I have no one. Nothing." She grabbed his vest and buried her head in his chest. "What is to become of me?"

"You'll figure out something."

She stepped back and a little strength crept into her voice. "What shall I do then? Miss Rachael's?" At that she broke down again.

Even at this late date in American history there was little vocational opportunity for women in the West. Arizona was still a frontier and whoring was the fate for many women in Deanna's situation. Caldera glanced around and noticed Benny's intense stare.

"What shall I do," Deanna said. It was a desperate plea tinged with a dark fear of an inevitable future.

Caldera felt the air, strength, and even hope flow from her body. He nodded over the batwings, indicating that Benny should join them. The temporarily deposed sheriff wasted no time.

Bull grinned and shook his head.

Prospect continued to stare at the table.

Benny pushed the batwing doors aside. "What's the trouble?"

Caldera said the words Benny had grown to hate. "Preacher's gone."

"What! We just—"

"We done crossed that territory. He don't want us following him this time. Deanna says so."

"It's his penance," Deanna said.

Benny spoke for both men. "I don't know what that means."

"It means the son of a bitch is finally gonna' get hisself killed," Caldera said.

"What the hell are we gonna do?" Benny's eyes were locked on Deanna.

The three lost souls stood there for a moment, no one knowing what to say or do. At last Caldera came to the only answer. He took Benny's hands and placed them around Deanna's. Their eyes met as Caldera took a cue from his father and spoke. "By the power vested in me by me, and by the town of Privy as deputy sheriff, and by the fact that I am damn tired of dealing with this crap, I hereby pronounce you two hitched. Now git!" He turned and stalked into the Armageddon, hacking his way through the smoke and foul air like a miner bushwhacking his way up a mountain after spotting a bit of color.

Stunned, secretly delighted and for the first time feeling a touch of hope in his heart, Benny refused to let go of Deanna's hands. "We should talk, Deanna."

She nodded. When she spoke, the fear had left her voice. "Let's go to the church. It is proper."

For the first time in years Benny and Deanna walked the streets of Privy without stealing furtive glances, arm in arm and their eyes locked on each other.

Inside the Armageddon Caldera related what Deanna had told him about Preacher. After that he had just enough time to down a shot of whiskey before Prospect stood up. He took Caldera by the arm. "We must go."

"Oh, Jesus," Bull said. Whelming frowned. "What's he talking about?"

"Pima horsehockey," Bull said. "Another drink or two or four wouldn't hurt you none, Prospect. You just fought a battle for Chrissakes."

Prospect shook his head. The man of two worlds was back in the land of the Indian. He spoke with formality. "We have killed an enemy. We have fought closely and breathed in his bad air. We must be purified."

Caldera suddenly realized what his Pima father meant. The whiskey would have to wait. "Sure, Prospect. I'll go with you."

With out further words the two walked out of the saloon, mounted up and headed south toward the Gila

Bull grumbled, "Horse... hockey!"

After a moment or so Whelming broke the silence. "What the hell are you folks going to do with Preacher, Bull?"

"Nothing. Preacher's cutting his own trail and there's not a damn thing you or me or anyone else can do to rein him in."

Whelming shook his head. "That Deanna's a fine woman. What's to become of her?"

Bull killed another shot of whiskey. "Ain't my affair." The table had become a somber place, which was not at all to Bull's liking. He poured himself and his engineer another shot of whiskey and beamed. Almost gleefully he said, "Did you know Caldera's an amigo with Geronimo?" The slightly stunned, confused look on Whelming's face caused Bull to break out into a booming laugh. "Hell, I got a story to tell you."

"This is a special place," Prospect said.

They made camp beneath a tall cottonwood near a dry creek on a broad expanse of desert just above the Gila. The view in all directions was unimpeded by town or village or road or any sign of humankind. Even their tracks coming in were soon erased by the gentle breeze blowing from the west.

"One of your holy places?"

"Not holy. Just special."

Once they were settled Prospect began removing his clothes. "Come. We must take a bath."

Respectful of Prospect and Pima tradition, but thinking about whiskey and cigars, Caldera stripped down. The men began the first of many ritual baths they would take during the next four days. They would also smoke tobacco and offer prayers. All their activities would be directed toward removing the foul breath and the touch of an enemy warrior. Without purification, evil spirits attached to the dead enemy would then attach themselves to the victors.

Although he had expected the days to drag on, Caldera found himself enjoying the experience. He and Prospect grew closer to each other than they had been in many, many years. It was as if the long years of vengeance were nothing more than a bad dream and the moment was just a continuation of those good, early days when a boy seeking a father and a man seeking a reason to live were united by the indifference of Bull Mckenzie. The peace, quiet, and eventually the purification rituals were a much-needed tonic for a confused and troubled soul. As with the man who had been known as Two Worlds, Caldera wondered where, if anywhere, he belonged.

Toward midday on their fourth and final day, Prospect thought he was having a vision. They had just finished a bath and a good smoke. Caldera closed his eyes and marveled at the sensations flowing through his mind. He really did feel purified. His thoughts were interrupted by Prospect's quiet exclamation.

"Lohgo... I must be crazy."

Caldera looked up and out across the desert. "I see it." The vision or hallucination appeared to be a small creature crawling through the scrub brush on the other side of the river. "What the hell is that?"

Prospect wiped his eyes. The creature was red in front and blue in back. As it emerged from the brush they realized the thing was no apparition. "That's a kid," Caldera said. Within seconds they were mounted and racing across the shallow waters. When they reached the child, apparently a boy, he had collapsed face down in the dirt. Caldera dismounted and rolled him over while Prospect popped the top of his canteen.

"I'll be damned!" Caldera said.

"Sikol." In Pima that meant "round."

"Yeah, it's one o' them little runts." He took the canteen from Prospect and allowed a little water to dribble into Round's mouth. The small man grabbed at the canteen and sucked at it. He coughed, spit and sucked some more. "Thank you," he rasped and then at last opened his eyes. "I know you." His voice was weak, but not too weak to register surprise.

"It's me, Caldera. This here's Prospect."

"Short's dead," Round said. He grabbed at the canteen and swallowed more water until he started coughing again.

"Better go easy on that. You're all right now."

Round suddenly sat up and grabbed Caldera's arm. "You gotta' get me to Mister Bull." His voice was filled with desperation.

"Sure, Round. We'll get you rested up and—"

"Now! We gotta' save her!"

"Save who?"

Prospect closed his eyes. His Indian sixth sense hit him like the leading edge of a flash flood racing through a narrow ravine. He took half a step back.

"Miss Belle!" Round said. "They're going to kill her!"

They mounted up and headed toward Privy. Caldera noticed dust blowing behind the trees from which Round had emerged. Mule deer? Wild burro? The racing of an Apache horse? Round threw up and began to shiver. Caldera gave the dust no more thought and kicked his horse into a fast trot.

Chapter Thirty-One

The only good doctor in Privy worked for Bull's mining interests taking care of the broken limbs, backs and bodies brought out of the rocky hills and mountains. His name was Marcy—Doctor Marcy, as he refused to allow anyone to use the term "Doc" in his presence. Marcy was a real doctor, too, not some alcoholic quack escaping a bad reputation or looking for someplace miserable enough to fund his dissolution. He was a legitimate physician with extensive experience in the recent war. Bull paid him well, knowing that men who healed would go back to work. Dead men dig no gold. They can't plant or harvest crops and they can't round up and brand stock. And the cost of funerals, even the cheapest ones, added up over time.

"Mr. Round, that is his name?"

"Yes, Doctor," Caldera said.

"He is in remarkable shape for the trial he has endured."

Caldera wasn't sure of the meaning of the expression on Marcy's face. It might have been surprise or disbelief.

They were under a cottonwood tree behind the Armageddon, for it was cooler in the shade than inside one of the buildings. Prospect watched Caldera. He was curious and afraid of the reaction at the young man's return to this tragic place. Belle had killed T'othern and the baby she was carrying at this very spot. It was here that she had placed the blame and the curse that had sent Caldera into madness and the vengeance trail.

"Pi-apekam," said Prospect.

"What's that," said Marcy.

"In Pima the word means evil, said Prospect."

Marcy stood up and closed his bag. "All he needs is a little rest and water and he'll be fine. As I said, really remarkable."

Benny arrived.

"I heard Shortround's back."

"Short's dead," Caldera said. His voice was flat and frighteningly calm. The old "dead" look was back in his eyes.

Round sat up when he saw Benny's badge. "You got to help Miss Belle! They got her!"

"Who's got her? Where? What kind of trouble is she in?"

"McCracken."

"Settle down. Are you sure?"

Round grabbed the sheriff's vest. "Please! We got to hurry!"

Benny shook him off. "Hurry where? And why? Spit it out."

Prospect noticed that Caldera's gaze locked on to the small man at the mention of the word "where."

Round stumbled through his story as if reciting a hastily learned play. "We was coming here, hoping for a grubstake. Mr. Bull might... you know."

Benny grunted, thinking *When pigs fly*. He nodded for Round to continue.

"They grabbed us crossing a wash west of town. Must be fifteen, twenty miles out. Took us to an old ranch house. I think they use it now and then."

"I know that place," Prospect said.

"Yeah," Caldera said.

Their eyes met. Prospect could find no humanity there.

"They had their way with Miss Belle. And when they was through they kicked—"His voice broke. "They kicked Short around like a ball. He's dead." Like an actor, he paused to allow the image to sink in for maximum dramatic effect. He was playing to a skeptical audience.

"So it was just you and Belle?" Benny asked.

"And Hephaestus. He ain't nothing but a slave. And Miss Belle, they just keep taking her and taking her and taking her."

"Well...." Benny let the sentence and the implication trail out.

Round sat up, angry. "A lady like that gets raped it's still rape! They won't stop! They just won't stop!" He sighed and sat back against the tree.

"How'd you get out?"

"You'd be surprised what little people can get in and out of. I slipped out at dark and followed the moon east. I knew I'd cross the road some time."

"How long?"

"I been moving three, four days. I don't know. I hid during the day and scrambled along best I could at night."

Prospect looked at Caldera. There eyes met and locked for an instant. "We should go," Prospect said.

"Is she worth it?" Benny was serious.

Caldera's voice was without emotion, almost lifeless. "Are any of us worth it?"

Prospect looked at Benny. "McCracken and his men are all in one place. This is your chance to end this problem."

"Yeah, we got no choice," Benny said. "Let's get as many men as we can and get moving."

"I'm going too." Round stood up. "I ain't leaving Miss Belle." His eyes showed a fierce with determination. "I can get in places none of you can. Might be an edge there." He paused. "They killed my brother. Miss Belle's all I got left."

Half an hour later the posse assembled in front of the Armageddon. They formed a small group as most of the able bodied men were in the mines or on the ranches. Prospect, Caldera, Benny, Round, Doctor Marcy and Lem Walker were willing to make the journey. Banker Chandler, who was now calling himself Colonel Chandler, joined in. As they mounted up, Bull and the area's most prolific writer rode up.

"I just heard about this little get-together. I'm in," Bull said.

"Such an adventure must be properly documented," said A. Noye. "It will be interesting to see the great she-bear humbled." It was a truthful statement. The purpose of the trip was to bring a violent end to the McCracken gang, but the focus of attention was on Belle.

Benny rode over to Caldera. "We'll get McCracken."

"Yes."

"We'll rescue Hephaestus."

"Yes.

"We'll rescue Belle."

"Yes."

"And she'll find her justice before a judge."

Caldera remained silent.

"I want your word, Caldera. Yours, too, Bull."

Their eyes met. Duty and logic faced pain and an anger beyond hate.

"She will receive justice, Caldera. I promise you that."

"You're calling the shots, Ben."

"Bull?"

"Hell, I'm just along to get a shot at McCracken."

Benny rode to the head of the group. He spoke quietly, forcefully and with command. "Like Prospect says, that old shack is about twenty yards from the well. If we can pin 'em down in there we can wait 'em out. Send back to Privy for food and water and we can starve 'em till they give up. That's the plan, at least." As he turned and led the small rescue party out of town, Prospect mumble something. Benny looked at Chandler. "What'd he say?"

Chandler grinned. "Something about plans and mice and men, I think."

Caldera rode to the right of the group, with them, but not among them, solitary once more.

"That's the old Arjeaux place. He went loco back in '68," Bull said.

Prospect nodded. "I found him... what was left of him."

They spoke in whispers as they surveyed the old adobe ruin and the harsh landscape surrounding it. The home had seen better days, but the rains had not yet melted it back into the dirt from which it had been constructed. A fairly new roof of ocotillo spines piled high with brush indicated new owners had moved in. The well, some twenty yards from the building, also showed signs of recent use. The surrounding land was flat for several hundred yards breaking into a series of rolling hills and washes further out. Achieving surprise would be a challenge.

Benny shifted on his horse. "See anything?"

Bull and Prospect shook their heads. The posse was strung out in the wash nearest the house. Caldera and Walker on each end of the line scouted the landscape in case some of McCracken's men should come riding in. They saw nothing.

Benny eased over next to Bull. "I think I hear somebody moving around."

"Yeah, but no voices. I think there's only one son of a bitch in there."

"One. No more," Prospect said.

"Whaddya think we should do," Benny said.

A slight clicking noise caught their attention. They looked to the end of the line where Caldera was checking the cylinder of his double action .45. He knew the condition of his weapon. He was making a statement.

"We can sit here and sweat, wait to see if they show up." Bull's voice betrayed his distaste for waiting.

Round scurried up the wash. "I can get in there and see."

"You ain't even armed," Bull said.

"I got this." He held up a little .32 caliber derringer. "Doctor Marcy gave it to me."

"Like I said, you ain't even armed."

Round pointed. "See them cactus patches behind the house? I can get to the other side and just about walk right up there. That cactus is a lot wider and taller than I am."

"Then what?" Benny said.

"There's a hole in the backside. There's a basket in there that covers it up. That's how I got out. I can get in the same way for a little look-see."

"Makes sense," Bull said. Prospect nodded his approval.

"Go ahead, but if you get caught you're on your own till we figure out what the hell to do."

"I won't let you down." Without hesitation Round began working his way down the wash toward the maze of cactus that would take him close to the old adobe.

"He's sure in a hurry to be a hero," Benny said.

Caldera spun the cylinder and clicked it into position. The fuse had been lit and there would be precious little time before something exploded. Several minutes passed before Round crawl out of the shallow end of the wash and walked toward the house. He didn't have to sneak or even bend over. The cactus patches towered over him like hedges in an English garden. Only when he reached the small clearing around the house did he run. The posse lost sight of him as he made it to the back side. Another minute passed.

"Well, whoever's in there ain't shot the little runt," Bull said.

"I wonder if they grabbed the little son of a—"

Round stepped out of the front door.

"What the hell?" Marcy said.

Round was jumping up and down and waving them in. He then ran back into the house.

"Let's go see what all the shouting's about." Benny started walking toward the shack.

"Somebody needs to stand watch in case McCracken comes back," Prospect said.

Chandler puffed out his chest. "That is the most dangerous task. I shall volunteer."

Benny rolled his eyes. "Okay, Colonel, ride down the road just a bit and keep a sharp eye out. You see so much as a dust devil you come running."

"Agreed."

Benny led the way, followed by Prospect, Walker and Marcy. Caldera rode drag. They dismounted, tied off their horses and entered the old house.

Marcy scratched his head. "As I said earlier, what the hell?"

The interior consisted of only one room, sparsely furnished with a couple of beds, a table and a few chairs. Shelves, pegged into the adobe walls, held canned goods, jars of food and spices, and a few other odds an ends. A pit in the center served as a winter heater and a year round stove. Hephaestus lay on one of the beds, covered from chin to toe with a cheap blanket. He appeared to be asleep. Belle stood stooped shouldered in the center of the room. Her right ankle was shackled to a long, thin chain spiked deep into a four-by-four wall post. Round was grunting and sweating, desperately pulling to break it free. Belle's hair was tied in the back with a string. She was barefoot and wore only undergarments. The look on her face reminded Marcy of a pet cat he'd once rescued after it had fallen into a bucket at the bottom of a well. She looked first at Bull and then at Caldera standing in the door.

"Christ, they got her chained like an animal," Walker said.

Even Bull felt a twinge of pity.

"You all right, Ma'am?" Marcy said.

"Yes." She sounded weak.

Round was making no progress at freeing the chain. He gave up with a whimper.

"Everybody stand down," Benny said. "Before we do anything I want to know what the hell is going on here. Lem, see if you can pry Belle loose while she tells us."

Walker found an iron bar and began working on splitting the chain from the spike.

Belle spoke with the voice of the defeated. Bull, Walker and Marcy had heard that voice often during the war. Prospect, Bull and Caldera noted defeat was absent from her eyes. She spoke with a slight breathless quality.

"It's McCracken. They caught us on our way back to Privy. Short is dead. They got that No Brains Monaghan and his Frenchman, too."

Bull winced ever so slightly.

She continued. "They brought us here. They been using me as a cook... and for their pleasure." If she felt shame, she did not betray the feeling. "Hephaestus ain't been nothing more than a slave and a punching bag."

Marcy looked at Belle. "Are you sick on injured, Ma'am?"

"I ain't ever been worse, but I ain't on my last legs either."

"Where's McCracken?" Bull said.

Belle looked to Benny. "They headed out three days ago. Left me chained to the wall to care for the place till they got back. Hephaestus took ill yesterday."

"You should've broken out and made a run for it," Walker said.

"They took our shoes and hid 'em in the desert. We wouldn't have made half a mile out there." She yanked violently at the chains. "I tried to break these,

Prospect glanced around the room and noted several articles that could easily be fashioned into temporary foot gear. *Miliga'n*, he thought. *How did white people ever conquer this land and its people?*

"Don't leave me here!" Belle said. Her voice was tinged with just a touch of fear.

"We'll all head back to Privy right away. You can ride double," Benny said.

Caldera stepped forward, walked between the line of men in the center of the room and faced Belle.

A slight sneer curled her upper lip.

"You say you been chained inside this old house four days?"

"That's right."

"Four days and four nights... inside."

"You can see the damn chain, can't you?"

"I got one question, Belle."

"What's that?"

"Where's your piss pot?"

Belle shrieked, jumped and began clawing at Caldera's face. Round pulled his derringer and fired upward at Lem Walker. Hephaestus sat up, pulled a single-barrel shotgun from beneath the mattress and fired a blast across the room.

Chapter Thirty-Two

The battle in the old adobe turned into a blood-soaked three ring circus. Lem Walker was thrown back by a shot to his right hip. As Round cocked the pistol for his second and final shot, Noye pulled his Colt and blew a hole through the little man's chest. He slammed against the wall and fell to the floor. Walker drew his pistol and looked for a target.

Hephaestus' blast took off Bull's right arm just above the elbow. As Marcy grabbed and struggled with the barrel, Bull reached for a pistol with his left hand. Walker, too occupied with survival to feel pain, tried to get a shot at the old black man, but the doctor was in the way. Marcy wrenched the weapon away and fell back to the floor. Within a heartbeat Noye, Walker and Bull Caldera put three bullets in Hephaestus. Two hit square in the chest and one hit him in the gut.

In the center ring Caldera had easily thrown Belle to the floor. More she-lion than human, she jumped again. Caldera's instincts were as sharp as when he'd ridden the vengeance trail. He easily side-stepped her move and knocked her unconscious with the barrel of his pistol as she flew by. He turned quickly to help his comrades, but the fighting was over. Marcy was already applying a tourniquet to Bull's arm. Noye had grabbed the doctor's bag and was rushing to help. Caldera walked quickly to the rear of the building.

"How bad is it, Lem?"

"You tell me. I'm afraid to look."

Caldera opened the man's pants and examined the wound.

"I didn't know you was that way, Caldera." He squeezed out the humor between grunts of pain.

"It ain't fatal, Lem. Looks like the bullet whanged off'n your hip bone and came on out. Miss Rachael's girls ain't lost their best customer, but you ain't likely to be running any leg races for a time." He grabbed a half-full bottle of whiskey from a shelf and poured it over both ends of the wound.

"Save some for the mouth."

Caldera grinned, handed the bottle over and then tore the ends of Walker's shirt to plug the holes. Walker drank deeply. "Almost worth getting shot for." He smiled, but Caldera saw that he was in terrible pain. Only then did he pause to assess the situation.

"Sons... a... bitches!" Belle was coming around. She was on all fours, still an animal. Her voice was slurred so that it was almost a growl. She was too incoherent to do much more than sway on the floor, but her head was still clear enough to hate.

Caldera grabbed the chain from the floor, sat her upright wrapped it around her wrists and tied it off. "I promised Ben not to kill you, but all I need is an excuse." *Where the hell is Benny?*

Caldera looked up. Benny was sitting up straight against one of the far walls. Prospect was wiping the man's forehead. A tiny stream of blood trickled from a small hole just above his right eyebrow. "Christ Almighty!" Caldera rushed over to his friend. Before he knelt down he knew Benny was dead, a single buckshot lodged somewhere inside his brain. Prospect looked up and shook his head. Quietly, as if talking to himself, he said, "Is the she-devil worth all this?"

Before he could wipe away the thin red stain a horse galloped up outside followed seconds later by the entrance of a breathless and terrified Colonel Chandler.

"McCracken! They got us surrounded!" He had barely slammed the door when shots from rifles and pistols, dug holes in the adobe walls, the shuttered windows, and the door. None of them came through.

"They just want our attention," Caldera said.

"They got it," Walker said.

The men were quiet for a moment, assessing the situation and their chances of getting out of the old adobe alive. Belle's eyes focused on Caldera. He hatred blazed across her face.

Outside, a voice shouted a gleeful hello. "Looks like we got ya' in a crossfire, Bull."

"Gayle McCracken." Bull spit the name, a curse.

More bullets slammed into each wall, emphasizing the point. The rounds were followed by shouts and laughter. Then there was nothing.

Caldera crawled next to the door. "They want us to sweat."

"Well, they got what they want. What next?" Walker checked his pistol to see how many rounds he had left.

"They wait. We wait," Caldera said.

"Ain't much of a plan," Marcy said.

"Ain't much else to do."

The men settled in as best they could. They were curious as to what might happen next, anxious as to the outcome. Prospect stretched Benny on the floor and covered him with a blanket. He looked at Caldera. "You will have to tell her."

Caldera nodded agreement. Bringing news of death to Deanna would be a challenge. Till then he faced the greater challenge of getting out of their trap alive. He glanced about the small room, looking for options, an idea, an edge.

Prospect crossed the room and checked Bull's dressing. He nodded in approval at Noye and Marcy. Bull was in pain, but he was alert. His stoic face and the cold look in his eyes showed that he was eager for a fight. "I should have killed that son of a bitch all them years ago." No one knew what he was talking about.

The men held positions scattered about the small room. They couldn't help hooking at the at the heavy wooden front door every minute or so. Would McCracken and his men be charging through, or would the trapped party be charging out? Either option seemed to end with the same deadly outcome.

"They're going to charge us," Walker said.

"Sooner or later," Marcy said.

"No. They'll wait us out. Starve us to death." Noye checked the cylinder on his Colt for the fourth or fifth time. He loaded a sixth round. He wasn't much of a shot. He figured he'd need every round possible if he was to stand a chance of hitting anyone.

"They'll wait till night and burn us out." Caldera's voice was emotionless, as if he were describing nothing more than the blowing dust. "They can't afford the time to starve us. Besides we'll make good targets backlit by the fire when we run."

"Not much time then. It's already dark thirty," Marcy said.

Belle remained silent, but she was scheming. She hadn't come up with a plan yet, but she would devise one, and very soon Caldera would be dead. Of that she was sure. She glanced at her bag stashed beneath the one table in the room. His death was certain, slow and painful.

Another series of shots slammed into the building. More laughter and taunts followed.

"They'll shoot us down like pigs," Noye said.

"Not all of us." Caldera looked across the room. Belle froze. "Why don't you tell 'em what this is all about, Belle?"

A low, animal grunt escaped her lips.

Caldera looked at Bull. "It's all about you."

Bull made the connection. He looked at Belle. The expression on his face showed a sudden realization that he really knew nothing about the woman who had shared so much of his life. "Why? I would have staked you."

"What the hell are they talking about?" Walker said.

"Ransom." It was the first time Prospect had spoken. He had realized the plot at the same time as Caldera.

"We were gonna' bleed you dry, you son of a bitch!" Belle stretched out the words, almost slurring them. "In more ways than one!"

"She's insane," Noye said.

"It makes sense. Bull's still the richest man in this part of the territory. What about the rest of us?" Marcy kicked up dust from the floor. He already knew the answer.

"How much are you worth?" Walker said.

Marcy looked at the floor. "'Bout as much as a .44 slug, I guess."

"Yeah."

"So they kill us and hold Bull till they siphon off... everything! Damn it!" Noye had just realized he'd never live to write the biggest story of his life.

Belle cackled. "We got you now."

Noye shook his head in amazement and agreement. His eyes almost glazed over as he evaluated the plan. "It could work. Bull goes off for months at a time. Money sent. Papers forged. Properties transferred. They could do it."

225

Bull pulled his pistol. "You really think I'll let that son of a bitch take me alive?" He stood up. He was shaky, but he was willing to lead a charge.

"So now it's come to it. Didn't waste much time, did we?" Walker's voice betrayed resignation, but was tinged with determination.

Prospect crossed the room and stood beside Bull. "You will need some help to stand."

"Shouldn't we wait till dark?" Marcy said.

"There won't be any dark once the fire gets going," Bull said.

"There's got to be another way. There must be at least a dozen men out there," Noye said.

Prospect appeared lost in thought. "But we in it shall be remembered: We few, we happy few…."

Noye managed a short laugh. "This is wonderful. I charge to Valhalla in a godforsaken desert following an Indian quoting Shakespeare."

Belle snarled again. "You can buy your way out of this, you bastard! McCracken'll trade blood for gold!"

"And then he'll kill us all just for the hell of it. That ain't gonna' happen, Belle." Bull staggered back, caught by Prospect.

Belle spit out a laugh.

"Ain't gonna' be much of a running fight," Marcy said.

Caldera spoke quietly. "There's another way."

Chapter Thirty-Three

While everyone's eyes were on Caldera, Belle glanced from the men to her bag and back again. If one outcome was certain that day, it would be Caldera's death. When no one was looking she twisted her wrists and arms, loosening the chain binding her.

"Round said he crawled out of here."

"He didn't have to. He was in on it," Noye said.

"Yeah, but he crawled in here from the back wall." Caldera walked to the rear of the shack and kicked a large basket placed against the wall. "There!" He pointed to a narrow hole under the adobe wall.

"If we had a small dog, we could send it out for help," Noye said. "He could bring back the burial party."

"Shut up," Bull said.

Caldera bent down on one knee to examine the hole. Prospect joined him. "We can dig this out in no time." Without another word the two men grabbed a couple of broken boards and began digging. A small haze of dust, like a low fog, soon filled much of the room.

"Let's go slow. McCracken's got to have this place surrounded," Caldera said.

"Most will be to the front and the sides."

"It's our only shot."

"It is a job for two men."

"You ain't leaving us are you?" Noye's voice was filled with genuine concern.

"We'll be back," Caldera said.

"There's no time to get help from Privy," Walker said.

"They ain't going to Privy." Bull winced in pain, but he was more than ready for the coming fight.

"Gayle!" Belle screamed at the top of her lungs. Before she could shout a warning, Marcy slapped his hand over her mouth. She bit like a wounded tigress, but he kept her from shouting any further. Noye rushed over and stuffed his handkerchief in her mouth. Marcy sucked blood from his hand and spit on the floor like he was sucking rattlesnake venom from a powerful strike. Noye tied a rag around her head and over the gag. She continued screaming, but no one outside could hear.

When the small tunnel was nearly through, the men stopped. "It won't take morn than a couple of seconds to punch through... when we're ready," Caldera said.

Bull walked over, his steps firmer. "I wish I could go with you."

"I wish I was in the Armageddon," Caldera said.

"McCracken figures he's got at least till late tomorrow before anyone in Privy gets curious and follows our trail. He's gonna' get his men fed and a little liquored up before he hits us. I figure sometime after midnight. You got time."

"This ain't my first round up," Caldera said.

Bull almost smiled. "Keep an eye on old Prospect here. I might have use for him someday."

Except for an occasional pot shot smacking against this wall or that, darkness came quietly and slowly. McCracken's men were confident—too confident. Some were getting drunk. All save a few were loud. The smell of roasting meat drifted under the door and through cracks in the windows.

"It's time," Bull whispered. "Get out there while they're stuffing their mouths. Find a spot and wait till they get sleepy."

"What if they start burning us out before Caldera and Prospect get 'em?" Noye said.

"Then we'll move a little faster." Caldera used his knife to slowly and quietly work out the rest of the hard-packed dirt. He finally made a hole into the darkness. He paused, listening carefully, and then began to enlarge the passage. When it was just big enough for a man to crawl through he stuck his head out. The desert was pitch black. With a slowness that was almost painful he crawled out. He could see no movement, hear no sound of man. He reached back into the passage and motioned Prospect to come. The two men crawled slowly into the desert. They were well beyond any point where McCracken's men were likely to be stationed before they got to their knees.

Caldera whispered, "How many, Prospect?"

"I have counted five voices. There are probably two or three more."

"That ain't too bad considering half of 'em are drunk. You want to work together or split up?"

"I am not so old that I cannot slit an enemy's throat in the darkness."

"If you have to start shooting just hunker down. I'll come at 'em from the other side."

"I do not think there will be a need for shooting." Prospect pulled his skinning knife. Caldera thought it glowed in the starlight. "I will go east."

"Meet you in front."

Eyes trained by desert hunting and warfare could see more by starlight than most men could see beneath a lantern. Caldera spotted three men within a minute. Foolishly, they were huddled together. One, a short and stubby fellow, tossed an empty bottle into the brush. "I'll git us some more burpwater. Be right back, boys." He skittered away, running low as if guns were trained on him all the way.

"Gotta' crap," said one of the men.

"Take it down wind."

The man stood up and farted. With a giggle he stepped into the desert.

Stupid. Caldera crawled slowly toward the remaining man, carefully pushing aside any twigs and debris that might snap and betray his presence. The man sneezed and in that instant of distraction Caldera jumped. Before McCracken's man could wipe snot on his sleeve, his throat was slit. He was dead by the time Caldera dragged his body under a nearby Palo Verde tree. He quickly put on the man's coat and hat and took his place. He kicked sand over the thin pool of blood and hunkered down.

Minutes later the dead man's compadre scrambled in. "Whooboy. I shouldn't have chowed down on so many of them hollypeenies last night." He sat down and looked at his silent companion. "You okay, boy? What's that?"

"That" was Caldera's blade, a gleaming silver streak in the darkness. A strong hand clamped down on his mouth as the blade sliced his throat just below his adam's apple.

He screamed in silence and died with his eyes wide open.

Caldera paused, looked around and listened. Silence. *Good.* No shots, no screams from the other side of the adobe meant Prospect was having similar luck. He began crawling toward the gathering of killers.

They were in high spirits, enjoying the first good meal they'd had in days—that and too much cheap whiskey. McKracken, the biggest and roughest looking of the bunch, glanced around, a disgusted look on his face. The men had been put to work collecting all the coal oil cans in the compound and stacking them at the edge of the adobe, but out of sight of the men inside. McCracken picked up a can, punched in two small holes, and tossed it on to the roof of the adobe. The oil flowed over the dried timber, ocotillo and brush roof. He repeated the process until all the cans were gone.

"Torch!"

The short, stubby man set down his new bottle of whiskey, grabbed a nearby torch and rushed to his leader. "Here y'go, Gayle."

"You want to throw it, Runt?"

"Can I?"

"Throw the damn thing, you idjit."

With a sickening giggle the man slung the torch toward the roof. It sailed completely over the house and landed in the arms of a creosote bush, which immediately started to blaze.

"Idjit!" McCracken kicked the stubby man in the groin. He stumbled back, tripped himself and landed in a pile of horse dung. Before he could get up a movement caught his eye. "Gayle! Injuns!"

Prospect, backlit by the flaming brush, tried to dash back into the darkness. Shots roared and he spun around and fell down. Several men ran to him.

"Don't kill him! Bring the son of a bitch over here!" McCracken said.

While his men dragged Prospect into the well-lit area in front of the adobe, McCracken grabbed another torch and easily tossed it onto the roof. He grinned as the roof sputtered and then glowed. He laughed as it burst into flame. He turned. "What we got here?" Two men shoved Prospect toward McCracken. Another followed closely, his hand on his pistol. All three men had knives stuck in their belts.

Prospect missed none of this. "I am called Prospect." The old Indian had been hit in the shoulder, but to Caldera, watching from the edge of the circle of light, the wound appeared to be a through and through. Prospect would still have a lot of fight in him. Caldera pulled both of his pistols and awaited the right moment. It would come. Prospect would see to that.

"Prospect, huh?

"I heared o'him, Gayle. He's that fancy talkin' Injun belongs to old Bull." He turned and walked toward the front of the adobe, keeping at an angle that prevented anyone within from blowing his head off. "Hey, Mister Big Time Bull McKenzie! We got your fancy pants Injun! You wanna' talk some trade, Boy!"

McCracken stepped over and gave the man another kick. "Shut up, Idjit!" He turned toward his men. "'Git ready to start shootin.' Kill 'em all 'cept Bull."

All eyes were on the leader and that's all the edge Prospect needed. With the speed of a rattler's strike the old Indian grabbed the knives of the two men nearest him. He slammed each blade into the stomach of its owner. In a single move he ripped the blades out horizontally and while the men were screaming he bent over. The third guard who was reaching for his pistol was slammed backwards as two blasts from Caldera's .44 slammed into his heart.

One of McCracken's men, a small, lithe figure, rushed toward Prospect. The old Indian flipped one of the knives in his hand and threw it directly into the charging man's stomach. He stopped running and fell to his knees, pulling the knife out with a shaky hand. He tried to throw it, but failed. He fell over and clawed at the dirt before dying.

A look of horror crossed Prospect's face. Their eyes locked just before the man died. "Circling Hawk."

The few remaining members of the gang were confused, torn between shooting at the obvious enemy in the light and the deadly killer firing from the darkness. Delay is a deadly force. Two men died before they could cock their pistols. A third took aim at the sure target. Prospect stood motionless before the dead Indian at his feet. Caldera fired with the gun in his left hand. The bullet struck the man's shoulder. He spun around, firing wildly. Another shot hit him square in the chest, and as he fell a final bullet ripped through his neck and jaw.

Prospect remained still as Gayle McCracken raced past him. The leader, now with no one left to lead, mounted a horse and ran for his life. Caldera ran into the compound and fired after the fleeing man, but his target was lost in the darkness. He looked around. Once satisfied that McCracken's men were all dead, he rushed to the door of the adobe and started kicking it down. "Get out o' there!"

"Stop shouting, boy." It was Bull. He and the others stepped around the edge of the building and moved toward the center of the compound. Belle was still trussed up.

Caldera brushed several burning embers from his face and joined them. Bull spoke. "I started shoving them out that rabbit hole the minute all the shooting."

"We'd'a been here to help you boys, but you two move too damn fast," Walker said.

"Jesus, the blood!" Noye said.

"You got 'em all?" Marcy glanced all around the compound.

"We're standing here aren't we, Dumbass?" Bull said. Then he pointed toward Prospect. "What's the matter with him?"

Caldera approached. "Prospect?"

The Indian turned his head. His eyes were glassy, vacant and appeared to be looking at something far, far away.

"Muhkig... mahsith... You are the death bringer." His voice was a monotone. "You make the land desolate and the people sick. Everywhere you bring... muhkig... death." He paused, looked around, and spoke again. "Hath no man's dagger here a point for me?" Failing to find the right words in his heart he had fallen back on his beloved Shakespeare. No one understood the words, but the meaning was clear.

Prospect's accusations ripped through Caldera's heart like a knife. He turned and marched toward his horse, wordlessly. He checked his pistols, mounted up and moved out toward the direction McCracken had run. Bull stepped forward, weak, yet determined.. Caldera reined-in the horse.

Bull's voice was as strong and as full of iron as ever. "Son, kill that bastard."

"He's already dead... Pop."

With a slight kick he was once again racing into the darkness.

Chapter Thirty-Four

Gayle McCracken knew the southern regions of the territory well, as he did northern Mexico, but suddenly he was a desperate man running in territory only vaguely familiar. He trotted his horse carefully through the washes, gullies and stands of cactus and Palo Verde, afraid of rushing headlong into a serious accident or death. He had to reach the main road so he could dash south. There he would find refuge and more men. Bull McKenzie'd had a few more days added to his life, but those days were still numbered. McCracken would return and certain death would ride with him.

Caldera knew the land so well he could have crossed it blindfolded. He also knew his quarry would head for the main road, the fastest route to Tucson. He moved quickly and made the road well before midnight. Lightning flashed several miles to the west. A storm was moving in quickly, a big one. *Damn! That's going to make tracking near impossible.* The thought didn't slow him down a bit. If he didn't catch McCracken on the road, he'd find him in Tucson or Sonora or wherever the hell he chose to hide. In the words of A. Noye, the goal was "mind accomplished." Gayle McCracken was already a dead man.

The few tracks on the road indicated riders traveling slow and easy. When he found hasty hoof prints headed west, he'd find McCracken. Lightning flashes illuminated his way as he trotted on.

When McCracken at last found the road, he halted, looked and listened. Nothing. He was surprised at the silence as he expected a posse from Bull Caldera's group would be on his trail. He glanced back. Still nothing. "Hell, we must've hurt 'em worse than I thought." More confident than ever, he moved onto the road and headed west at a fast trot. Soon the road would turn south and he'd be on his way to freedom.

He rode on, occasionally stopping to look and listen for someone, anyone on his back trail. He heard nothing.

Caldera plugged on too. His mind drifted every now and then to Prospect's harsh accusations. The old man's words stung. *Deathbringer*, he had said and he was right. What else had he brought to friend, foe and family? Death—his life had been given over to it. Like some faithful worshipper, he had brought sacrifices to the altar and now he was moving inevitably toward one more victim. He dreaded facing his Indian father when this was over.

The wind picked up and swirled dirt and dust around him like angry, stinging bees, but the wind soon died down. Lightning flashed, but still in the distance. He could see rain, but the storm was passing well to the north. At last he found the place where McCracken had entered the road. It was easy to spot. His tracks, easy to see in the bursts of light, were marked by a small prickly pear cactus trampled by his horse. McCracken was either getting lazy or overconfident. Caldera could track him anywhere. He was close, damn close.

"About time," McCracken said. The road had finally turned south and he was headed to the refuge of Tucson and then northern Mexico. He rode on at a trot for another hour, again stopping occasionally to rest his horse and watch his back trail. Once he thought he saw a rider hugging the side of the road. The figure, if it really was there, had been nothing more than a swift movement highlighted by a distant flash of lightning. He pulled his pistol and waited, but no one came along. He moved on.

Sometime, it must have been around three in the morning according to the stars, he felt confident enough to take a break. His horse was wearing thin and he was thirsty. A tall and distinctive peak just to the west meant he was near a well-known and reliable spring. He'd been there a few times during raids over the years. It was one of the few places north of Tucson he could find it with relative ease even in the dark.

He found the water hole. Unlike most men in the West, he drank first, only allowing his horse to drink after he'd had his fill. Recent rains had increased the size of the waterhole. It was now a long and narrow tank, looking something like a still creek into the darkness. *Time to move on.* Out of sheer spite, he pissed in the tank. As he buttoned up his trousers he thought he heard a faint splash in the distance, as if a fish had jumped in the water. But there were no fish in desert water holes.

"Hmmmf." No one in Apache country wanted to hear unexplained sounds in the night. He squatted down and drew his gun. When he pulled back the hammer the snap of it cocking sounded like a cannon blast in the dead night. There it was again, another splash, faint, but distinct. Someone or something was out there... and moving.

Interminable minutes passed. Sweat flowed into the edge of his left eye. He wiped it away with the palm of his left hand. "To hell with this," he whispered. He stood up slowly and moved into the darkness toward the sound. He crept at a slow pace, more used to sneaking the streets and back alleys of towns than the desert. He continually glanced far ahead and then down to his feet, making sure he didn't step on a twig, cactus or anything that would betray his presence.

Another splash, this one was closer. They had to be footsteps. Someone was walking through the shallow waters of the tank. The splashing was too loud and too slow to be an animal. Someone was stalking him. McCracken grinned. *I love a good ambush.* He settled on a clear spot next to the tank. A creosote bush provided some cover, sufficient in the darkness to prevent someone coming up the tank from seeing him until it was too late. He rested his pistol, still cocked, across his left arm and waited. Another splash. This was too good to be true. False dawn would arrive soon and would provide enough light to assure a successful kill.

Gayle McCracken grinned one last time just before he felt a sting on the side of his neck.

"That's what having your throat cut feels like, McCracken."

McCracken grabbed at his neck. Blood spurted hot through his fingers, tickled over his hands and arms. Shaking violently, he was already losing consciousness when he hit the ground. Caldera knelt down, took the pistol from the man's hand and waited. He didn't have to wait long.

The gray light crawled over the horizon to reveal Caldera's trap. He had tied a small melon-sized rock to a long leather thong which he tied to the limb of a small cottonwood tree hanging over the shallow water. A gentle tug dropped the rock into the water with a splash. Repeated tugs imitated the movement of someone sneaking through the shallow water. Silence. Splash. Silence. Splash. Silence. Slash.

Caldera took McCracken's gun belt and the personal items from his pockets. He might need them for identification to claim the reward. As the sun rose over the rugged mountains, he tied the body to the man's horse and moved at a slow, but steady pace back toward the adobe. And Prospect.

Chapter Thirty-Five

Caldera returned to a scene of bloody confusion. Members of the gang remained untouched, the blood from their bodies pooling and then soaking into the parched ground. Marcy tended to Bull's wounds. The big man was dazed from blood loss, but it appeared he'd survive to roar again. Belle sat on the ground, leaning against the adobe and clutching her bag. Her hands had been freed and her gag removed. Smoke billowed through the roof and occasionally through the windows and door. It swirled around her and, as if sickened, dissipated in the night breeze. She was framed in a backdrop of dark embers, still glowing red, appearing to all as a representative of the depths of Hell.

Prospect wasn't there and neither was the body of the Indian he had killed, the death that had caused old man to speak those harsh, hurtful words: *Muhkig... mahsith... You are the death bringer.* The look in his sometimes father's eyes when he said those words stung worse than any knife wound, more than any bullet he had ever taken.

"You got him! Well done." Noye was scratching out the story in his notebook.

"He earned it." Caldera paused. "Prospect?"

Marcy looked up. "After he made sure the wounded were in no further danger he took that Indian he killed and high-tailed it out of here. Don't know why."

"Circling Hawk." Bull's voice was weak, but steady. "Him n'Prospect were runnin' buddies back in the old days. Blood brothers or something like that."

"He didn't say anything. He just packed up and headed out." Marcy pointed to the east.

Caldera dropped his head for a second and then dismounted. He took a drink from a bucket on the edge of the well and looked out into the early morning sun, toward the Pima Villages and the death ceremony that was surely being performed. "Muhkig... Mahsith... I am the death bringer," he mumbled. He spat on the ground.

Marcy finished tending to Bull and stood up. "Good work, Caldera... damn good work. You've earned one hell of a reward tonight. MacCracken's worth more than his whole gang put together."

"Ain't interested."

"You're gonna' collect the reward aren't you?"

"Yeah, but it's going to Deanna. Anybody object?"

"Hell, man, if it weren't for you and Prospect, I'd be burnt meat about now. You do anything you want with that money."

"Yeah. Ben, he'd like that," Bull said.

"Do we take him back? He got burned up pretty bad in the fire," Marcy said.

"Bury him here. Deanna don't need to see nothin' like that," Caldera said.

"The dirt here ain't much different than that in Privy." Bull kicked at the sand. "Probably cleaner."

"What about the others?" Marcy said.

Caldera pointed to an old wagon at the edge of the compound. "We'll load 'em in that and take 'em back. We gonna' need proof if Deanna's to get her money."

Belle's eyes, full of hatred, stayed focused on Caldera as he and Marcy entered the cabin to retrieve Benny's body.

"Jesus!" Noye staggered back and retched.

"I seen worse." Caldera found a couple of singed blankets and a patchwork quilt that had survived the worst of the fire. They made for a colorful shroud as the two men wrapped up Benny and carried him outside.

Bull, weaving and wobbling a bit, had found a couple of shovels. "There's a shady spot out there near that Palo Verde. I think he'd appreciate the shade. Ben, he liked his comfort."

"We'll take it from here, Pop."

Bull plopped down and closed his eyes. His breathing was heavy and hard, but he was still breathing. His strength was draining away, like the blood seeping through his bandages, but he would not allow death in. *Not now... Not now... Not this time.*

After Benny had been buried they lined the plot with small rocks. Caldera placed a large, smooth stone at the head. "I'll come back here with a proper marker," Walker said.

"I wish Prospect was here. Somebody oughta' say some words," Caldera said.

"You knew him best, Caldera. You say something," Marcy said.

He paused, bowed his head for a moment, then looked up and cleared his throat. "This here is Backhand Benny, and he was my friend. Amen."

They stared at the grave. Marcy couldn't tell whether Caldera was too choked up to continue or whether he had just run out of words. A moment later they wordlessly walked to the wagon. It was in pitiful condition, but it would make the relatively short trip back to Privy. They piled on the bodies, Gayle MacCracken last. His eyes were wide open and full of horror and shock.

"If I remember right, this heap of flesh will fetch seven, eight thousand dollars. Hell, MacCracken's worth five thousand himself," Marcy said.

"It won't bring back Ben."

"Nossir. Nothing we can do about that. You're doing a good thing, Caldera."

"Let's get Bull up into the wagon. You handle the reins. I'll ride alongside."

"What about Belle?"

"Her call. She can squat back there with them sons of bitches or take a horse." He walked around the wagon and approached the woman. The growing light of the sun brought out the years of hard living, betrayal and death, and it brought out the lines and wrinkles in her face. Yet her eyes were filled with an ageless hatred. She reached into her bag as Caldera approached.

"We're heading back, Belle. You want a horse or the wagon?" He stopped to wipe the sweat from his eyes by running his forearm across his face. It was a deadly lapse of judgment. "'Course you could just stay—"

Belle stood up and dropped her bag. In her hand was a small glass jar full of a clear liquid. She smashed it against the adobe wall, still holding it in her hand. "You bastard!"

She screamed and bolted forward. As Caldera dropped his forearm she rammed the jagged glass into his gut and slashed across

239

his belly. Some of the clear liquid had remained in the jar and it flowed into the wound. She stepped back, her maniacal laughter shattering the sunrise. "Bastard! Bastard! Bastard!"

A gunshot later she was slammed back to the adobe wall a bleeding hole in her belly. She raised her head, slowly and feebly, the fire of hatred still in her eyes. "I... killed you... *all*...." Her bowels and bladder let go, and Isabella Delcour, Belle, Princess Dodu, and God knows who else, died in a pool of muck created by her own blood, waste and bodily fluids.

Bull holstered his .44 and leaned against the fence post at his back. "Had to happen some time," he mumbled.

Marcy ran to Caldera, who had pulled the small glass jar from his gut. The wound was not deep and there was surprisingly little blood. He sniffed the bottle and threw it at Belle's corpse, then looked at Bull. "Poison."

Caldera doubled over with a grunt that would have been a scream in most men. He fell to his knees. As Marcy joined him, another long, pain-filled grunt followed, and then another and another. Caldera tried to control himself, but the pain came on in ever increasing waves. "I'm... on... fire!"

He breathed in short gasps, each one more fire-filled than the one before. Sweat poured down his face. In the faint glow of the rising sun it looked like blood. "Fire...."

Marcy looked around in panic, not knowing what to do. He ran to one of the horses and grabbed a canteen, and he turned back to a terrible sight. Caldera lay on the ground, curled in a fetal position and suffering in unimaginable agony. He shuddered and then lay still. Marcy ran to him and found that he was still breathing. It was shallow, but the young man was still alive.

"We gotta' sweat it out of him!" Bull said.

"We'd better take him to Privy."

"No time, Marcy! Build a fire!"

Marcy did as he was told. Bull staggered around the compound, grabbing as many blankets as he could. While the doctor built a fire, Bull wrapped his son. "Get a blaze going, Marcy! He might be the only one of us worth saving."

"You got any medicine?" Noye asked.

"Only one kind." Bull staggered to his horse and pulled out a bottle of whiskey. "Don't know what else to do."

"Will that work?"

"Hell, I don't know! Might cure, might kill. It works on snakebite. We gotta' do something, and this is all we got to do it with, damnit!"

Bull began forcing small sips of the whiskey down Caldera's throat. Their eyes met and although he said nothing, Bull knew he agreed to the treatment. Between painful gasps he took the "medicine."

"Get mounted, Marcy."

"For God's sake why?"

"Ain't you got some potion or powder back in Privy?"

"Bull, there's no cure for what was in that bottle."

Bull cursed, kicked the dirt, and kept the fire and the whiskey going all morning. The rising sun added to the heat. He had no idea whether his treatment would work. He was just doing the best he could with what he had, guessing all the way. It was the way he'd lived his whole life, but for the first time someone else, someone he actually cared for, depended upon that judgment. It was a strange and uncomfortable feeling tinged with a fear he had never experienced.

Toward noon the bodies around him were just beginning to swell and the faint, sickly sweet smell of death was beginning to float on the air. Looking back and forth between MacCracken and his men and Caldera, he felt no sense of victory, not even a sense of accomplishment. He walked over to look at Belle. Her mouth was still frozen in a twisted smile of joy. In death she had still experienced victory.

"No, Belle. You ain't gonna' take him." He bent over and turned her smile into a frown.

He thought about piling up the bodies, even Belle's, and burning them out in the desert. There was plenty of wood around and enough coal oil to start a good blaze, but he remembered Caldera's plans. *Damn the smell. They, and the reward money they'll bring belong to Deanna.*

Caldera came around an hour or so later. He was as pale as the bleached sand beneath him. He bent over and retched. "I'm dying,"

"Can't say that for sure, Caldera."

"I can."

Bull looked away, not knowing what to do with the emotion he felt.

"Ride it out, Boy."

"Where's Prospect?"

"Burying that friend of his... somewhere."

"I never meant to—"

"He didn't blame you, Caldera."

His voice was a dry rasp. "You didn't see his eyes." He leaned over on one arm and dry heaved. "God, I'm burning up. Gimme another shot of that whiskey."

"You sure?"

"Afraid I'll turn drunk again?" He forced a weak smile, accepted the bottle, and with a struggle was able to take a sip on his own. He held it down, but not without a struggle. He handed the bottle to Bull and indicated that he should drink. Bull accepted and completed the little ceremony with several large swallows. He popped the cork back in the bottle.

Another hour or so passed without a word being said, and then Caldera struggled to sit up. He was a pale as ash from a dead fire pit. Weaving back and forth a little, he said, "I can't die here... not here."

"Die, hell. You're looking like you're gonna' pull through this thing."

"I done caught you in too many lies... Pop." He dry heaved again and again and again.

"Damnation, Boy."

Caldera struggled to his feet. "Help me onto one of them horses."

"You can't just ride out! Hell, Caldera, Marcy'll think of something!"

Marcy looked away.

"I got a right to pick my place of dying. It smells here." He winced. The fire of Belle's poison was still flowing through his veins. He looked at Bull. "You can't stop me." It wasn't a threat, just awareness.

Bull helped his son onto his horse. "Where you going?"

"I died out in the Superstitions once." He paused to choke back a dry heave. A confused look crossed Bull's face. Caldera looked east. "It's clean."

Bull handed him the reins. "I don't... I don't have the words, boy."

"You don't need 'em. Tell Prospect—" A massive cramp gripped his stomach. "Tell Prospect... I'll send him a message... if I can. Tell him... I'm sorry."

Bull nodded.

Caldera grunted painfully. "Nothin' left to say 'cept goodbye."

"Goodbye," Bull said.

Caldera, leaning forward, but steady in the saddle nudged his horse with his heels and rode east. Bull watched him and even followed the faint dust trail after he disappeared over a low ridge.

"Son."

Chapter Thirty-Six

Prospect sat perfectly erect and still despite the diabetes that was killing him. "Of course, I never got a message, Robert."

A small fire glowed in the center of his dirt floor. Ignoring the pleas of his sons, he had decided to spend his final days on the reservation and in his own home. Although I had only an outsider's perspective, I had to agree. A man who grew up under a shaman's care shouldn't have to go out surrounded by rubber hoses, needles, noisy machines and, worst of all, strangers in uniforms.

As he continued I was amazed by the strength in his voice. "Of course we looked. We looked for weeks, but we found nothing."

"Surely, and I mean this with all due respect, you would have seen vultures circling. You would have found some remains." I hoped my indelicacy hadn't offended the old man.

"We hoped for that, so he could receive a proper burial, but there was nothing. His trail was easy to follow until he entered the Slanting Mountains."

"Eh?" I was making notes in the semi-darkness.

"You call them the Superstitions."

"Did anyone ever find his horse or some sign?"

"No horse. No body. Nothing. After several weeks I was the only one searching. I looked for his message. I hoped for some writing in a saddle bag on the trail. A symbol scratched on a stone. Something"

Prospect had graciously permitted my wife to join us and I could feel her eyes boring into the side of my head.

I offered him another beer from the cooler I had brought. Even his sons no longer objected to his drinking. With the end so near what possible difference could it make? The old man enjoyed the slight sense of release it brought.

"I have settled all my old scores, Robert. I have made amends and said goodbye to friends and family. All my tasks are accomplished, save one."

"Caldera?"

"The words, the last words I said to him were more bitter than the bite of ko'oi, the rattlesnake. He took the meaning wrong, Robert."

"What do you mean?"

"I looked at him, my sometimes son, and I said 'muhkig... mahsith... you are the death bringer.'" Prospect choked up.

"Perhaps we should finish this later," my wife said.

Prospect smiled. "You are a most gracious lady, Mrs. Quiller, but I believe there will be no 'later.'" He paused for a second, collecting his thoughts or perhaps his emotions. "When I said 'you' I meant miliga'n, white people. I did not mean Caldera. He did not understand. It was a dagger in his heart. And I placed it there." He stopped speaking for a moment and I let him have that moment of peace and reflection.

My wife had other ideas. She punched me in the ribs with her elbow.

"Robert, it is the great sadness of my life that I could not make things right with Caldera. It is the one emptiness left in my universe. It is why I am now called Bitter." He looked up as if seeking something. "But I am bound upon a wheel of fire that mine own tears do scald like molten lead."

His mind was incredible. Even at his advanced age he could still quote Shakespeare like a professor. A slight sniffle told me a tear was running down my wife's cheek. To tell the truth, I had to clear my throat and fight back a tear of my own. I'd never seen such heartache in a man. I had to get back into reporter mode. "Why do you think he never came back, Prospect?"

"Why should he? Arizona was a place of anguish for him. Here he had lost his wife, his child and for a time his mind. He had killed many men and created many more enemies. He and Bull had come to something of an understanding, but Caldera would never have a family here. And I—"

And now everyone was fighting back tears.

"I hurt him beyond pain."

Once again I felt the elbow in my ribs. I took a deep breath and looked the old man right in the eyes. "Prospect, I have lied to you."

"You are miliga'n."

"Not maliciously. I... I... in a way, Caldera did send you a message."

"I do not understand."

"First, the lie. Robert Quiller is my name, but it is a pen name. I just use it for my columns in the newspapers and magazines. My real name is Robert Calder." The lids over those ancient eyes raised and suddenly I was staring at an honest to God Pima warrior, a man unsure of what he was facing, but alert and ready for anything.

"Why are you telling me this?"

I cleared my throat and took a sip of beer. "My mother was Cuban. She met her husband during the Spanish-American war. He was a scout, a tough old bird, following Colonel Roosevelt. He was one of the first Rough Riders. The way my mom told it, he was wounded behind enemy lines and was nursed back to health by this Cuban girl. What happened next was right out of the story books."

"Or Shakespeare, I suspect," he said.

I wasn't sure, but I think the old man had an inkling of where I was going. "They fell in love, got married and he brought her back to the states. She died a decade or so later, but not before they had a son. My dad was too much of a wanderer to raise a kid, so he left me with the family of an officer from the Rough Riders." I had to stop to prepare myself for what was to come next. "My name at that time was Caldera."

Only a slight pause in his breathing told me that Prospect fully understood what I was saying.

"Back in those days most people didn't have a lot of respect for Cubans... or any Hispanics really."

"That is the curse of the miliga'n."

"So, my step-parents changed my name to Calder and raised me in the Anglo tradition. They made up a lie about why I was left alone and never said much about my parents. At the time I was hurt, surely, but not bad and as the years wore on I gave the matter no thought at all. After they died I stumbled across a few letters, some newspaper clippings, and other bits and pieces of information about a Western bandit named Caldera. I'm a writer and I was hooked."

"You are his blood?"

"In a way, Prospect, I am Caldera's message. He lived! He lived a long, full life."

The small hut was as still as a church. I didn't realize it then, but I was holding my breath. Then Prospect started laughing. God, how he laughed! He laughed till tears rolled down his cheeks. It was as if the decades of heartbreak were being let loose to fly and disappear into the night air. Then he opened his arms. "My son."

"Grandfather."

Until that moment as an adult I'd never hugged a man. I'm not embarrassed to do that any more. We embraced, then looked at each other, and then we both started laughing. I hope I am lucky enough to feel such joy at least once more in my lifetime.

Later we settled down and began to sip more beer. Eventually my wife curled up on a blanket and drifted off into a gentle sleep. Doug and Tom nodded off, too.

And Prospect and I... well, we talked till the sun came up, spending the night in joy, confusion and wonder, speculating about the lost years of a mystery, of the man who had brought us together: the man called Caldera.

END

Prologue to the Next Book in the Caldera Series
Caldera – A Man of Blood

The witch stirred her bubbling vat of pinto beans with a walking stick. Nearby on a cracked slab of old planking flies circled a short stack of warm tortillas. Caldera tried to sit up, but he only had the strength to rest on his elbows to stare at the old hag. She looked more like a gnarled cottonwood worn gray by wind and water than a human being. He grunted in pain. Belle McKenzie's poison enflamed his arteries and veins and every breath seared his insides with agony. The gashes across his belly where she had raked him with the broken bottle of poison dripped blood onto the old woman's porch. She laughed – a coarse and sadistic sound.

He coughed as he spoke. "Where am I?"

"Hell."

He coughed again and wiped blood on his sleeve. A fleeting image from the past brought a memory. "The hell it is, old woman. This is your house in Privy."

"Same thing."

He struggle more, but could only find the strength to sit up, his back resting against a strong sapling cut down and used to support the flimsy roof over the witch's porch. The smell of pintos was strong. He was hungry and as he rubbed his belly he discovered that his gut wounds had healed.

"I'm dreaming, ain't I?"

"You're in the middle ground. Alone."

"Seems to be the way of things."

She stirred again. Whiffs of steam swirled from the pot and floated around the stringy gray hair hanging limp from her head. "Middle ground, Caldera. You must choose now your future pathway."

"A man ain't got no choice 'bout his future, old woman."

"You're not like other men. You choose. I help you." The wrinkled lines in her face squeezed into a horizontal position. No one other than the witch would have called that movement a smile.

The flames scouring Caldera's insides cooled down and floated away like a mist caught by the morning sun. The pain was gone. "I am dreaming. But I remember you. When me 'n Benny came to collect your taxes—"

"I made you a promise then, didn't I?"

"Yeah. I remember that, too."

"What did I promise you?"

"Pain."

"I deliver?"

"Yeah, you kept your damn promise."

"Then you know my words are true."

"Yeah."

"You believe?"

"Yeah."

"Say it!"

"Damn it, I believe."

"Good. Now I help with your future?"

"Just how the hell are you gonna do that, old woman?"

She stirred the pintos and raked the walking stick across the bottom of the vat to loosen some that had burned and stuck. She stuck her face down close, into the steam and breathed deeply. "I give you choice, young Caldera."

He rubbed his belly again and breathed in the rich, earthy smell. "I ain't so young."

"All the world is young to me. You make choice. Now."

"What choice, witch?"

"Famous choice. Caldera can live a long life, a good life, but nobody will ever know his name."

"Or? There's always an 'or.'"

"Or Caldera can be famous, maybe even a...what's the word...hero." Her face crinkled again. She apparently liked what was coming next. "But you die young, soon I think."

Caldera wasn't much of a thinker. He was brilliant at analyzing a situation and choosing the safest course to follow, but the concepts of organization, planning and strategy pretty much escaped him.

"I am dreaming."

"Choose your future, Caldera. What do you want!"

Caldera stood up, his strength fully returned, and walked over to the witch. He looked her straight in the eyes. "I want me a plate of beans."

About the Author

Dan Baldwin is the author, co-author or ghostwriter of more than 40 books on business, sales, real estate, motivation, and management. He is also a Western novelist – the author of Caldera, Caldera – A Man on Fire, and Trapp Canyon. He is the winner of numerous local, regional and national awards for writing and directing film and television commercials and projects. Baldwin is a resident of Phoenix-Mesa and has traveled extensively throughout Caldera's West.

Made in the USA
Charleston, SC
16 May 2013